Fate had placed Katrine in his hands.

Yet she was so young. So innocently beautiful. So gallant. How could he treat her as an enemy? Or allow her to wed a man the sound of whose very name brought gall to his throat? What had begun as a deliberate act to further his own purposes had now taken on the additional guise of protection.

'Maiden,' Raoul said at last, 'I will not return you as you wish, for I cannot believe the marriage arranged for you would be felicitous. I would not see you suffer more.'

Sarah Westleigh has enjoyed a varied life. Working as a local government officer in London, she qualified as a chartered quantity surveyor. She assisted her husband in his chartered accountancy practice, at the same time managing an employment agency. Moving to Devon, she finally found time to write, publishing short stories and articles, before discovering historical novels.

CHEVALIER'S PAWN

Sarah Westleigh

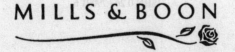

MILLS & BOON

*All the characters in this book have no existence outside the
imagination of the author, and have no relation whatsoever to anyone
bearing the same name or names. They are not even distantly inspired
by any individual known or unknown to the author, and all the
incidents are pure invention.*

*MILLS & BOON, the Rose Device and LEGACY OF LOVE
are trademarks of the publisher.
Harlequin Mills & Boon Limited,
Eton House, 18–24 Paradise Road, Richmond, Surrey TW9 1SR
This edition published by arrangement with
Harlequin Enterprises B.V.*

© Sarah Westleigh 1995

ISBN 0 263 79091 6

*Set in 10 on 12 pt Linotron Times
04-9507-78052*

*Typeset in Great Britain by CentraCet, Cambridge
Printed in Great Britain by
BPC Paperbacks Ltd*

CHAPTER ONE

KATRINE stood among the serving-women, heart thudding with suppressed excitement, savouring the giddy prospect of imminent deliverance.

Her saviour stood with his steel-shod feet planted firmly on the filthy rushes, his dark head thrown back arrogantly above his gorget, confident, vital, towering over the squat Rhun ab Brechfa, commanding the entire company with splendid mastery.

The brilliant tabard covering his cuirass, the only armour he wore apart from the gorget and the sollerets with golden spurs attached, seemed to vibrate with colour in the gloomy hall. Flanked by a slightly older knight and by his youthful squire carrying his shield and helm, backed by half a dozen men-at-arms, the young knight bowed gravely. He could well have walked into a trap, but he showed no sign of nervousness. Perhaps he sensed the air of defeat gripping the defenders. They knew that, were Rhun to try to hold him, his men without the walls would simply tighten their grip on the castle and storm it, using the siege towers and giant trebuchets they had been so industriously building over the last weeks.

Rhun returned the ceremonial greeting. The two men had met to parley before. The besieging knight, Raoul de Chalais, known to all as the Chevalier, spoke first.

'You agreed to a truce to discuss the terms for your

5

surrender, Rhun ab Brechfa.' The full-throated voice
rang around the hall, bouncing back off the bare stone
walls to assault the ears with a hollow echo which
exaggerated the foreign intonation and the mispron-
unciation of the Welsh name.

From a slit high up in the tower Katrine had
watched him oft over the last months of siege as he
rode impudently around the curtain walls just beyond
arrows' range, his panoply of heralds, banners and
escort set against a backdrop of the desolate Black
Mountains to the east and the Cambrian Mountains
more to the north. On those occasions the splendour
of his armour, the scarlet, blue and silver blaze of his
tabard and his horse's caparison had posed a teasing
challenge to those struggling to survive within the
defensive walls.

He had had to cross the River Tywi twice to encom-
pass the castle completely, since the near bank and
the ford the castle guarded were within arrows' range,
but this he never failed to do, crossing on a raft guided
and pulled by ropes spanning the river. He had men
posted on the opposite bank to prevent revictualling
or escape by this route under cover of darkness. Rhun
had cursed his foresight, for a convenient postern gave
access to the river.

'You leave me little choice, Chevalier,' responded
Rhun. 'I had not expected the castle I gained three
years ago to be invested without warning by so small
an English army, so deep as it is into Wales.' He
shrugged and spread his hands in a rueful gesture. 'I
had therefore not attempted to replenish my siege
stores. Given warning of another English invasion,
such as that led by the man you call Henry IV in the

second year of his reign, I would have made no attempt to hold my prize against superior forces but retreated to my stronghold among the forests and hills to the north, whence I operated before taking Dryslwyn.'

'You did not count on our pursuing you back from your unsuccessful raid on an English baggage train?' suggested the enterprising Chevalier, Raoul de Chalais, with a grin.

'No,' admitted Rhun. 'And you allowed me no time to evacuate but immediately demanded the surrender of the castle and all those within it.'

'Which you refused.'

'I miscalculated,' grunted Rhun, 'thinking that such an isolated detachment of the English army as yours would soon raise the siege and return to the safety of England, or at least withdraw to the security of Dinefwr Castle, which is still in English hands. And I must admit I hoped you would be driven off by my Welsh allies.'

None of these things had happened. Katrine knew that within the castle they were down to their last sack of flour, their last side of salt beef, their last tun of ale. The bailey no longer rang to the sound of clucking hens, quacking ducks or squealing pigs. A few starving dogs still barked as they hunted rats or whined pathetically beneath the trestles begging for scraps. The one thing the castle now had in plenty was water, which had run and dripped from every surface over the last week of incesssant rain, filling the cisterns and raising the level in the well.

Once the downpour had let up de Chalais had sent his heralds to demand again the castle's surrender. He

must not relish the idea of sitting before its gates
enduring a wet Welsh winter with the River Tywi
overflowing to flood the surrounding land. He had
already moved his lower camps to higher ground.

Supplies had posed no problem for him, for to the
east Dinefwr Castle, the ancient capital of the lords of
Deheubarth, set a few miles further up the river valley
on a high plateau, had, as Rhun said, remained in the
hands of its English constable, Jenkin Hanard, while
to the west lay the port of Carmarthen, now once
again in English hands and overflowing with imported
goods. But, however good the food and drink, pointed
silken pavilions could not provide much protection in
biting wind, while wet chilling rain reduced the camp-
fires to smouldering heaps and the ground to mire.

Katrine had prayed long and hard that the Holy
Mother would deliver the castle into the young
knight's hands. And now here he was, only feet away,
godlike in his radiance and power, discussing terms of
surrender with Rhun. He wasn't particularly handsome, she concluded judicially, yet he exuded a mag-
netism which rendered mere looks irrelevant. His face,
seen reasonably close to, fascinated her, dominated as
it was by intense, compelling eyes and a determined
cleft chin. His nose had been broken; it was both
twisted and flattened slightly. His full lips, stretched
now in a dangerous smile, excited her oddly. She
found it difficult to tear her eyes away or to concen-
trate on the words they were forming, had to force
herself to do both.

'King Henry decreed that the terms offered to those
who surrendered should be generous,' Raoul de
Chalais was saying, 'but that was at spring's end. You

failed to seize the opportunity, Rhun, unlike the rest of the southern leaders. You have kept me and my men encamped before your gates this several months. We therefore seek reward for our patience. We are,' he announced mildly, 'quite prepared to attack and, if our assault should fail—which I doubt—to sit the winter out. Whether you capitulate now or later, I shall hold the castle and its lands for King Henry, but its contents will be mine to dispose of as I will. My men will receive their share of the bounty. You will be delivered to the King to face a traitor's trial and death.'

'It is usual,' responded Rhun in an unaccustomed, placatory voice, 'to agree that if relief does not come by a certain date the castle will be surrendered. Say by the spring of next year? Most of your army may then return home for the winter. Should we not be otherwise relieved, the castle will submit without further siege or battle on the last day of March.'

Raoul de Chalais raised a sceptical brow. 'And where, then, will your loyalty lie?'

Rhun shrugged. 'In that eventuality I will swear allegiance to Henry and recognise his son as Prince of Wales. After some proof of my loyalty I would hope to regain the lands confiscated by him after the battle of Bryn Glas. My elder son died on that field near Pillath that day over four years ago, but I have another, and would regain that property which is his rightful inheritance.'

'Mayhap you should have thought of your sons ere you joined Owen Glendower in his revolt.'

To Katrine, the youthful voice sounded slightly

bitter, as though his words held some deeper meaning, some hidden pain.

'Henry's attempt to exact heavy communal payments from his Welsh subjects turned restlessness under King Richard into discontent and open rebellion,' replied Rhun heavily. 'This Welsh kingdom of Deheubarth is an ancient one, ruled independently by its princes from Dinefwr until the time of the Norman invasion. Owen Glendower can claim descent from them on his mother's side, which is why so many Welshmen are prepared to follow him in an attempt to end British rule. I cannot regret my stand, Chevalier.'

A decidedly derisive smile greeted this declaration. 'Yet you expect to escape the consequences of traitorous actions you do not repent.'

'You will, as you say, be entitled to the contents of this castle, poor as they are,' went on Rhun, ignoring de Chalais's remark. 'I fear that what little valuable plunder there was to be had in Wales has been severely depleted by years of fighting.'

'No doubt,' observed de Chalais cynically, 'that is why your French allies returned home so promptly. Mayhap Glendower would have been wise to look ahead before putting the Principality's towns to the torch.'

Rhun shrugged, his expression sour. 'They were peopled mainly by cursed English merchants. But, be that as it may, there remain here only a few pieces of plate, some armour and weapons, my fine Powys horse and my wife's palfrey.'

His narrowed eyes assessed his chances of winning some advantage over his enemy. As Katrine had cause to know, Rhun, honourable in most respects, could be tricky in his dealings. How many times had he broken his promise to apply to the Duchy of Lancaster, whose ward she was, for a ransom? She had pleaded with him to approach the family with whom negotiations for her betrothal to its heir had been in train. For some obscure reason it had not suited his purpose to facilitate her release, and he had done nothing for five long years.

He had found it easy to lull a child into obedience with false promises. But the opponent he faced today was more worthy. Raoul de Chalais had his gaze fixed on those calculating eyes. The dangerous smile reappeared on his lips.

'Your offer to surrender in the spring is tempting, Rhun ab Brechfa. However, I fear I must decline. You see, I do not quite trust you.'

'My dear Chevalier——'

A slender hand, raised from the glittering hilt of de Chalais's sword, cut Rhun's protest short. 'Your cause is lost. You cannot hope for relief. Glendower himself lost a battle in April, and Northumberland suffered a defeat at the hands of Charlton, the lord of Powys, in June. Owen Glendower is finished. He has lost control of these southern parts and retreated to his mountain fastnesses in the north. *He* cannot come to your aid.' He paused, noting the clenching of Rhun's jaw at this dispassionate assessment of his chances of obtaining relief. His own eyes narrowed. 'But I do not intend to take a chance. Having been granted respite, you may be tempted to change your mind. Or attempt to escape while my vigilance is diminished.'

'I assure you——'

Another wave of that slender hand. 'In the past I have often found assurances strangely lacking in substance. Be sensible, my lord, capitulate now. How much longer can you hold out without supplies? A month? Two?'

Rhun drew himself up to his full height, little more than Katrine's own five feet three inches. 'You underestimate our endurance, Chevalier.'

'Do I? We have watched you slaughter the sheep grazing on the grassy slopes of your mound. There is none left—no cattle for milk or coneys in your warrens. Even your stables are empty; you have slaughtered your mules and horses too. Although you claim to have a warhorse and palfrey yet alive.'

'They are alive,' Rhun insisted.

Raoul went on mercilessly. 'But have you enough fodder to keep them so? There is a little winter grass for grazing, true, but the fields of hay beyond your curtilage were not cut, the new growth not yet ready for the scythe, when we arrived, and the oats are little more than green shoots in the fields. And what hardships will you inflict upon yourself and your people in the meanwhile?' Receiving no reply, de Chalais spelt it out. 'Starvation and illness, mayhap death. Admit defeat *now* and submit yourself to the King's mercy.'

Rhun had not donned armour for the meeting, wishing, perhaps, to present the appearance of a pacific and reasonable man. Over a heraldic tunic in red and green he wore a flowing blue houppelande, encircled at the hips by a silver belt. The garment made him look as broad as he was tall and disguised the strong, muscular body of a fighting man. An ornate dagger hung in its silver sheath low on his thigh. Katrine could see the effort it cost him to retain his calm. Surrender went against his grain. His hand twitched and clenched but he was not foolish enough to touch the weapon. Instead he shifted his feet and prepared at last to come to the crux of his devious argument.

He inclined his head. 'I cannot fault your logic, Chevalier. However, one may always deny logic. As must you have done, since you, a Frenchman, fight for England rather than Wales.'

He was swiftly corrected. His head thrown back disdainfully, de Chalais asserted, 'I am a Gascon with some English ancestry. I am a true and loyal subject of King Henry, who rules Aquitaine as its Duke, and have no love for the French Charles.'

'I see.' Rhun's smile, though sceptical, acknowledged the difference. 'However, although I may have expressed hope, I have in fact little faith in the usurper's mercy after his execution of Archbishop Scrope. I feel I have little choice but to continue to resist you, with the consequences you have so obligingly detailed. I would rather die here than at Tyburn.'

In the short silence which followed these words Katrine's heart dropped to her scuffed shoes. Surely her hopes were not to be dashed, not now, when they had been so high? Should she try to call attention to herself? She had still not decided when de Chalais spoke.

'Then why did you agree to this parley?' The words were rapped out.

'I had hoped for better terms for my surrender. Mayhap, even yet. . . .' He paused a moment, timing his revelation for greatest effect, his eyes glittering in anticipation. 'I possess a jewel of great price which I am certain you will agree is more valuable than my poor life.'

'Indeed? Then pray produce it!'

'Kate! Here, wench!'

His sudden bark took Katrine by surprise. She jumped, then, as experience demanded, obeyed the odious Rhun. She stepped forward firmly, her chin held high. The splendid self-assured Chevalier must not think her cowed.

'Behold!' said Rhun triumphantly, grasping her thin arm to drag her further forward.

Katrine shook off his hold and rubbed the spot where another bruise would soon appear to mar her pale skin. She stared boldly into eyes which she saw on closer acquaintance were shining like chips of green ice. But as they swept over the shabby, unkempt figure their expression changed to one of merriment.

'Jewel?' enquired the Chevalier derisively. 'More a lump of worthless clay, I trow.'

Katrine glared at him, her dove-grey eyes sparking with furious anger at the insult. The expression in his changed to one of startled curiosity.

'You think her worthless clay?' Rhun enquired drily. 'But then you see only the serving-woman she is here, not the heiress of one of the leading noblemen of England. This wench,' he announced, 'is Lady Katrine Lawtye, daughter to the late Earl of Huntershold, a ward of Lancaster and prospective bride to the Earl of Wenstaple's heir.'

Katrine sucked in her breath, reminded all too vividly of the loss of her father and all that had followed it. Through an unwanted sheen of tears she saw the sudden flare of interest in the brilliant eyes still resting upon her, interest which changed in an instant to an icy, calculating stare.

'Lionel d'Evreux?' he murmured. 'You are betrothed to him?'

'Nay, Chevalier. She was on her way to Wenfrith to meet her prospective new family and to be betrothed when she fell into my hands.'

Rhun gave Katrine no chance to answer, even had she felt so inclined. A shiver ran down her spine at the menace she sensed in the Gascon's quiet voice.

'Daughter to an earl and a prospective d'Evreux bride,' he mused, and now indifference informed his whole manner. She must surely have imagined the menace. 'I have heard of the d'Evreux family, of course. The fortunate prospective bridegroom fought under Lord Talbot at Grossmont. And there is another branch, sprung from a bastard brother of the first Earl. The Marquess of Thame is, I believe, its most illustrious present member. He is in close attendance upon Prince Harry. But why should the presence here of this wench be considered of value to me? Neither her wardens nor her prospective spouse's family can believe her worth ransom, or she would have been returned long since.'

'That I did not demand, for she could be worth far more than a mere ransom. I intended that my son, Elwyn, should wed her.'

Katrine's gasp at this piece of information, the explanation of so much she had not properly understood, went unnoticed as Rhun ploughed on.

'When Elwyn was killed I determined to substitute my younger son, Dafydd. You see,' Rhun explained expansively, 'her inheritance is richer than any ransom I might reasonably demand. Her lands would augment my estates, and the lordship of Brechfa would be allied to those lordships held by Huntershold. Mayhap my son would have been granted the earldom.'

'An you lived to see the day!'

Rhun acknowledged the gibe with a shrug. 'I expected the rising to succeed. With the usurper Henry deposed, the entire Lancaster estate, including its wards, would become forfeit. The d'Evreux family would become enemies of Edmund, now the Earl of March but then the new king. The boy has a better claim to the throne than Henry Bolingbroke.'

'That is debatable,' put in de Chalais quickly. 'Henry is next in line of direct male descent.'

'But Edmund is descended from an elder son of Edward III, albeit by that son's daughter. His uncle, Edmund Mortimer, married Owain Glyn Dŵr's daughter——' he pronounced Glendower's name in the Welsh way '—and fights on our side, his purpose to rule England on behalf of his young nephew after Henry is deposed. Had that come about, I expected to be in a position to demand from Edmund what I pleased, and the marriage of my son to this wench would not have been denied.'

'*Mon Dieu*! A fanciful dream!'

''Twas not so fanciful but six months past. However, to my regret, circumstances have changed. I am now willing to trade the admittedly doubtful prospect of great wealth for our lives and a pardon.'

Raoul de Chalais merely laughed. His eyes had returned, now speculative, to rest on Katrine. 'You have nothing to bargain with, Rhun. When the castle falls the girl will be free without the need to spare your miserable life.'

'Oh, no,' said Rhun. 'When the castle falls, she will be dead.'

The room spun. Katrine swayed. Despite all she had suffered during her captivity she had never felt her life seriously threatened. It had been too valuable. Now, all in a moment, it seemed it was not, for the Gascon was laughing again.

'An empty threat, Rhun, for her death would seal the fate of every person left alive within the castle. Including that of your wife and son.'

He inclined his head towards an austere-looking woman, dressed in a grey surcoat over an elaborate green gown, who sat, listening intently, with the young Dafydd sitting at her feet. The child, only ten, looked more bewildered than afraid.

Katrine saw the lady Eiluned's lips tighten and her head jerk, making the heart-shaped head-dress and veil, a relic of better days, sway. That shrew would not yield an inch. She it was who, under Rhun's direction, had ordered Katrine's life over the past five years, and Katrine did not think she could ever forgive the woman her harsh treatment. Not once, so far as she could remember, had Rhun's wife offered their vulnerable young captive so much as a kindly word. As for Elwyn— But she preferred not to think of him, especially in the light of what she now knew. Dafydd was too young to have made much impact on her life as yet, except as a playfellow when so ordered. Had Rhun really expected such a mismatched pair to bed together? The idea was ludicrous!

Rhun seemed to have no real answer to the other's

challenge. He spread his hands deprecatingly. 'Their death would avail you nothing, Chevalier. But you would be denied the reward due to you for rescuing the wench.'

'Should I desire it,' commented de Chalais, throwing another glance in Katrine's direction. 'A poor, insignificant-looking creature to be possessed of so much wealth. If what you say is true.'

'It is the truth, lord,' burst out Katrine. He *had* to believe her worth saving!

She might as well not have spoken. 'I am sure I have no use for her,' mused the Chevalier, 'but I suppose there are those who could pay well for her return.' His eyes had not left her. Yet now, seeing her proud, defiant stance, he altered his expression yet again, and a slight smile relaxed his tight mouth. 'How old were you, maiden, when you fell into Rhun ab Brechfa's hands?'

Just in time, Katrine stopped herself from curtsying deferentially. She was of higher rank than the Gascon, however splendid he looked and imperious he sounded, and she must overcome the training of the last years and remember it. She lifted her chin a little higher.

'I was ten, lord, when he ambushed our train and killed my guardian and all his retainers before my eyes.'

De Chalais shot Rhun a grim look. The twist to his lips lacked humour. 'A fate I would not wish on my worst enemy,' he observed. Next instant, though, he was smiling, as if something had amused him. 'And you, Lady Katrine, how do you choose? Would you rather endure siege and predictable death at the hands of Rhun ab Brechfa, or cast yourself upon my mercy? I warn you, I have neither reputation nor time for softness. You will be in my power. But no harm will come to you an you obey me and do as you are bid.'

Katrine blinked. How very changeable he was! He sounded almost kind! Choice was not really an option, though. She had to trust him. He could be cold and forbidding when he wanted to be but she had glimpsed too much charm in him to believe him a cruel man. They were both on the King's side and her rescue would be worthy of reward if not ransom. Mayhap she could persuade him to send to the Earl of Wenstaple. Her future father-in-law would pay well, of that she was certain, and he would contact Lancaster's officials, perhaps even the king himself. She clasped her work-roughened hands together to prevent their trembling.

'My guardians and the d'Evreux family will rejoice to find me still alive,' she assured the Chevalier. 'I have little choice but to accept your protection but, I pray you, send to the Earl of Wenstaple. He will see you well-rewarded for my return.'

De Chalais pursed his lips, considering. ''Tis worth a thought,' he acknowledged, 'but—I may have other plans for you. Yes, I think I will keep you with me, for a time at least.'

'But why?' demanded Katrine desperately. 'Why will no one arrange my freedom?'

'You have heard Rhun's reasons,' returned de Chalais curtly. 'Mine are different but equally compelling. My lord,' he said, turning back to Rhun, 'I accept your terms. The immediate surrender of the castle, the wench and your oath of fealty to King Henry in return for the freedom of yourself, your retainers and

your family. You will leave this castle and return to
what manner of dwelling you may still possess. In the
spring I will support your suit for pardon and reinstate-
ment. Henry is eager to show clemency. An he
believes he may depend upon your loyalty henceforth,
I predict both will be forthcoming. Your hand on the
bargain.'

The Chevalier held out his strong, slender fingers.
Rhun placed his square hand within the firm clasp of
his adversary, his hesitation barely perceptible. His
choice, like hers, was one between certain death and
slight hope. No real choice at all.

'So we are agreed.' The Gascon's satisfaction was
plain to see. He issued his orders crisply. 'You will
prepare to leave Dryslwyn on the morrow, taking such
of your retainers and servants as wish to depart with
you. Those who remain must swear loyalty to me and
serve me as their liege-lord and, through me, King
Henry.'

'I have but five vassal knights and thirty fighting
men here. Most will doubtless wish to return to their
homes.'

De Chalais's eyebrows rose. An amused smile
curved his lips. 'You see, I was right, Louis! I win our
wager. The entire garrison was out on that raid! I
suspected there were few left inside but women and
servants, that there were not enough men-at-arms or
archers here to attempt a break-out.'

His lieutenant smiled, not at all disturbed to be on
the losing end of the wager. 'Or, methinks, to defend
it successfully had we been bold enough to attack.'

'But how much more agreeable it is to achieve our
objective without bloodshed!'

'There are those who would not think so, Chevalier.'

This was said with a smile. He was teasing his commander. Raoul de Chalais obviously knew it. He punched his friend on the arm.

'You know I am not afraid of a fight, *mon vieux*. And when I think one necessary my men follow me bravely, for they know I would never needlessly waste their lives. We have enjoyed our summer encamped before Dryslwyn's gates, but enough is enough. So— go back and tell them to strike camp after they have broken fast on the morrow. We will take up our quarters in the castle. 'Twill be crowded, for we number over a hundred men without camp-followers, but better that than spending winter in a field.'

The man called Louis looked reluctant to obey the order to leave. 'Will you return to the camp yourself?'

'I think not. I will spend the night here.'

'But——'

'I shall be quite safe,' de Chalais assured him softly, 'for if disaster should befall me you would lead my men and see to it that not a single member of Rhun ab Brechfa's family left this place alive, would you not? Just as Sir Hugh Layfield has been ordered so to do should our party be prevented from returning from this conclave, held under a flag of truce.'

'Indeed, Chevalier,' put in Rhun quickly as Louis assented, 'you have nothing to fear from me or my men. We have shaken hands on an agreement. I am a man of honour.'

Katrine doubted whether his idea of honour matched that of the Gascon and thought the Gascon did too, but despite his sceptical look he nodded. He

knew the Welshman's present position to be unten-
able. 'So be it. In any case, I shall be well-guarded.
Messire Louis Dubois here will leave, but my men-at-
arms will remain with me. Their sergeant——' he
indicated a man Katrine mentally likened to a chunk
of granite who stood behind him '—leads my
bodyguard.'

The sergeant bowed. 'You may rely on our vigilance, Chevalier.'

'This is but a small castle, your followers are many
and, as you anticipate, will find their quarters
cramped, Chevalier. As for tonight, the Lady Eiluned
and I will, of course, vacate the solar.'

'No need.' Raoul waved an airy hand, magnanimous
now that victory had been won. 'I will spread a pallet
in here tonight, with my men. Yours may be certain
they will rue the consequences of treachery. So go
you, Louis, and have my cook send in a side of roast
ox, bread, wine and other victuals. We will feast here
tonight. Rhun ab Brechfa and his household will leave
on the morrow with full bellies.'

Louis bowed, turned on his heel and strode from
the room.

Raoul de Chalais addressed Rhun again. 'Come, my
lord of Brechfa, it must be near time to sup.'

'I will order the trestles set up,' mutterd Rhun.

'And ask your lady to find this maid a better gown,'
added the Chevalier, eyeing Katrine anew. 'I cannot
comprehend why you should turn so *valuable*——' he
placed an ironic emphasis on the word '—a prize into
a mere serving-wench.'

'She had to earn her food and learn obedience,'

asserted Rhun defensively. 'These things every girl-child must learn before she is wed.'

'Even those born to noble houses,' agreed Raoul mildly. He caught Katrine's fulminating glare and merriment entered those green eyes, making them shimmer like the surface of a lake. 'However, I would see her looking the jewel you tell me she is.'

Rhun smiled, if thinly. 'By all means, Chevalier. Wife, see to it.'

Eiluned stirred. 'The girl has nothing else to wear,' she informed her husband frostily. 'As you well know, the garments she wore when you captured her have long been outworn and outgrown.'

'I feel certain you or one of the other ladies present will be able to find something suitable,' put in the Gascon before Rhun could answer.

'Indeed, wife. Is not the lady Myfanwy of about the same size?'

All eyes turned to regard a small woman standing behind Eiluned's stool, one of the ladies, wife to one of Rhun's knights who kept her company. She coloured slightly under the barrage of stares.

'Indeed, lord, I shall be glad to find the Lady Katrine something to wear. May hot water be sent to my chamber?'

'We cannot spare fuel to heat water, that you know full well——'

'Such economy is no longer necessary, my lord Rhun.' De Chalais's eyes roved over the sketchily cleansed hands and faces of those of Rhun's retainers present in the Great Hall, and a smile touched his lips. 'I would suggest that a large cauldron of hot water could be put to good use by many of your company.'

'No doubt it amuses you to mock us, Chevalier, but we have been conserving our store of fuel for cooking what food we had left. Hot water for washing makes a man soft.'

'I have always found hot water to be more pleasant to use and more effective at cleansing,' murmured the Chevalier mildly.

'You will be offered a bowl and towel as you approach the table, as is customary,' muttered Rhun.

'Come, Katrine,' said Myfanwy. 'You will order the hot water to be brought up, lord?'

Rhun nodded surly assent. Katrine followed Myfanwy from the hall. Passing through the screens towards the main door, the inner ward and finally the tower stairs, she paused to look back. Raoul de Chalais had already turned away. His clear tones could be heard issuing orders, disposing his men, his mind now fully occupied with the final surrender of Dryslwyn.

How good it felt to be bathed from head to foot in warm water! Herb-scented soap had been found and a faint perfume rose from Katrine's skin and pervaded the luxuriant mass of her hair, shining golden now the dirt had been washed from it. The lack of curl hardly showed once Myfanwy's woman had combed it and gathered it into frets.

Myfanwy had produced a clean linen smock and woollen stockings, which a tiring-woman had tied above Katrine's knees with blue ribbon. Myfanwy's green linen and wool mixture gown and the surcoat of saffron-coloured Welsh flannel proved to be only an inch or so too short. Katrine would have liked to present herself in silk and satin as befitted her station, for she wished to impress the splendid Chevalier, but at least the garments were more becoming than the dull brown candlewick kirtle Rhun had provided for her to wear. A pair of yellow brocade slippers a trifle too large for her feet poked out from under her skirts to complete her transformation. Some kind of unguent had been smoothed into her hands, which improved their feel, if not their looks.

'You'll do,' pronounced the Lady Myfanwy eventually. 'You look quite nice, child. See that you are polite to Sir Raoul de Chalais and I am sure he will treat you with the kindness and respect you deserve. He does not seem a vindictive man and he is not, after all, at enmity with the English, as is the Lord Rhun.'

Impulsively, Katrine held out her hands to the older woman. 'You have always shown me kindness, lady, and for that I thank you.'

Myfanwy took the offered hands and squeezed them. 'You have received scant consideration from my lady Eiluned, and it grieved me. Poor little soul, you did not deserve such harsh treatment.'

'I have often wondered why she seemed to hate me so. I had done nothing——'

'Except, my dear, to be English and a girl. I think she resented your intrusion into her family. Like her lord, she desired your dower, but did not wish to call you daughter. You could not take the place of the one she lost. She had two sons and now has only one, and had a daughter but now has none. It has made her bitter.'

'I am sorry. I did not know.'

'She does not speak of it. Come, child. We shall be late.'

Katrine entered the Great Hall feeling uncomfortably strange and conspicuous. Until today, during all her sojourn with Rhun ab Brechfa, at this point she would have been running backwards and forwards with trenchers, mazers, jugs of ale, bowls of fruit, platters of meat and fish and, once she had become strong enough, steaming cauldrons of pottage, stew and mayhap some vegetable. Lately, of course, the fare had been restricted. There had been fewer dishes to serve and no need to bring out the herb and spice boxes, for they were empty. The ornate salt-cellar was still set in its place on the board, but only as a symbol, for it too was empty. Or had been. There looked to be salt in it now.

Several of Raoul de Chalais's people had already arrived, bringing in supplies which must have included candles, for the hall was better lit than it had been for some time. The replenished fire burned brightly in the centre, its smoke mingling with the fumes from the candles to drift towards the rafters, there to escape through louvres built into the ridge. Even as she took a seat next to Myfanwy the heralds sounded a fanfare to announce the arrival of the Chevalier, Raoul de Chalais, the lord Rhun ab Brechfa and Eiluned, his wife.

A page knelt before them with a bowl of water. All three rinsed their fingers and dried them on the offered towel. They took their places.

Raoul de Chalais had discarded the last of his armour and changed into a brocaded tunic, sumptuously embroidered. He loked around. 'Where is the lady Katrine of Huntershold?' he demanded in a loud voice.

'Stand up,' hissed Myfanwy.

Katrine rose reluctantly to her feet, chagrin at the fact that he had not recognised her swamped by embarrassment. She had felt quite awkward enough sitting at the table above the salt, instead of taking her place at the far end of the boards among the servants once the meal was served, without being singled out for attention by the Chevalier.

'Ah!' His eyes pierced through her despite the flickering, uncertain light, the wafting smoke and the yards that separated them. 'So that is where you are hiding. Come here, maiden.'

Chin up, colour high, Katrine stepped elegantly round the end of the trestle to approach the dais. She mounted the step and moved towards the front of the table, where she would be facing Raoul de Chalais. Her heart beat so loudly that it seemed to her it must be audible to others in the silence which fell over the hall. Grace had not yet been said. The meal could not begin. Everyone was waiting. And watching.

He waved an impatient hand, beckoning her to his side. 'No, come here!'

She came to a standstill behind the padded bench on which those eating at the high table sat, and made a dignified curtsy. 'Lord. What is your pleasure?'

His gaze swept down the length of her body and up again. 'An improvement, I see. Yes, Rhun, I believe you did have a jewel in your possession. A rough stone, mayhap, in need of polishing. But the maid shows promise.'

Katrine clenched her fists. To be spoken of so, as though she were not there! 'Had Rhun ab Brechfa not killed my guardian and brought me here I would, by now, have been wife to the son of the Earl of Wenstaple! Mayhap then the jewel would have needed no further polishing.'

The Chevalier chuckled. 'Well-spoken, maiden. Lady Eiluned, I should be obliged if you would move along. Page, bring another trencher. The lady Katrine will sit by me.'

Katrine stared at him. He could not mean it! But she could see that he did.

She did not want to sit beside him. She found his magnificent presence too daunting. Nevertheless, she stepped gracefully over the cushioned bench and took the seat silently but mutinously vacated by the lady Eiluned.

CHAPTER TWO

ONCE Katrine was settled beside him and Grace had been said, in Latin, the volume of noise in the hall grew apace. The child de Chalais had instructed to fetch another trencher still stood before the table, as though rooted to the spot.

'Well, boy,' barked the Chevalier severely, 'why are you still standing there? How is the lady Katrine to eat?'

The lad, no more than eight years old, had his anguished gaze fixed upon the man's stern face. Katrine addressed him quietly in Welsh. Relief washed across the page's pinched features—the children, she thought, had suffered most from the recent deprivations—and he rushed off to fetch the required slab of specially baked bread.

'He did not understand you, lord,' explained Katrine quietly. 'Like many of the people here, he speaks little or no English, and your accent makes understanding the more difficult.'

'*Diable*!' The Chevalier looked comically disconcerted. 'You mean those who remain will not be able to understand my orders?'

'A few will, lord—the clerk, the steward, the cook and some of the grooms, many of whom will stay, for this is their home; they were here before Rhun came and learned English from the former constable.'

'Huh! And betrayed him!'

'Mayhap, lord. Remember, they are Welsh. This was originally a Welsh castle. Would you not do the same were Gascony invaded?'

'Invaded? Wales is part of the English kingdom!'

Before she could respond the page trotted back and placed the thick piece of bread before her. She murmured, '*Diolch*, Dai.'

'What did that mean?' demanded de Chalais.

'Thank you, Dai. Dai is the boy's name.'

He grinned ruefully. 'Mayhap I should learn to say—*diolch*, was it?'

Katrine smiled. 'You learn fast, lord.'

He addressed the page. '*Diolch*, Dai,' he repeated faithfully, then turned back to Katrine. 'Tell the child I am sorry I shouted at him.'

Katrine could scarcely believe her ears. A conquering knight, apologising? She translated, and the page responded with a beaming smile and a look of such adoring gratitude that Katrine realised the Chevalier had won at least one heart that evening.

Katrine suppressed her surprise and took up the conversation where the arrival of Dai had interrupted it. The Chevalier was an easy man to talk to. 'Wales is considered part of its kingdom by the English,' she pointed out. 'As Aquitaine is considered French by the French,' she added daringly. 'You must know Wales drove off many an invasion before the Normans brought Wales into subjugation. Even so, in Henry II's time it won back much of its independence.'

Before replying, de Chalais waited while his squire, a Gascon youth he called Hugues, served them both with some of the roast beef which had been carved and tasted by another of his men, who had also tasted

the baked fish, freshly caught from the river. The
Chevalier was taking no chances. She was, it seemed,
to share his mazer, which the squire filled with red
wine.

The Gascon brought out his knife and laid it on the
board ready for use, fingering its silver hilt as he
spoke. 'But subsequently,' he said, displaying more
knowledge of local history than she would have
expected, 'the first Edward took it back. Wales cannot
survive as a separate power, you know. It is not large
enough. Without England's arms behind it, Gascony
would have been conquered by the French long since.
The day must come.' He sounded grim but resigned.
'You argue well for the Welsh, maiden. Mayhap you
are on their side?'

'Nay, lord, how could I be? But I have come to
understand their point of view. Did not England itself
seethe under the iron fist of the Normans for
generations?'

'Aye.' He speared a piece of beef with the dagger
and raised it towards his mouth. 'No nation likes to be
conquered. But England has come to terms with the
situation. It would behove Wales well to do the same.'
Two rows of strong white teeth gleamed as he slid the
meat between them.

'It had done so before Henry Bolingbroke came to
the throne,' pointed out Katrine. 'They consider him
a usurper, and he treated Owen Glendower shamefully, although Owen had served in his household and
was his friend.'

'So much strife and bloodshed brought about by a
quarrel over a small piece of land,' remarked de
Chalais ruefully.

'You are a knight, lord, yet you decry fighting and bloodshed. This seems strange to me.'

'It does? Not all fighting men are bloodthirsty, lady. Certain things must be fought for or defended, that is true. You are surprised that I decry war, but come now, think. Who suffers most when great lords engage in battle?' His eyes met hers intently, a clear, sparkling green, as he answered his own question. 'The people of the land over which they fight. The ordinary people are left homeless and destitute, their towns and fields burnt, their women violated. War is sometimes necessary, but always best avoided. And,' he added on a lighter note, 'fighting in and conquest of a strange land always presents a language difficulty.'

So saying, he lifted his brows in a quizzical smile which Katrine found it impossible not to return.

'In the present case you would do well to exercise patience, lord, and wait for your commands to be translated.'

'I have found that few in the villages understand English or French,' he acknowledged. 'I should have realised. But someone could surely have told the lad . . .'

'They were all busy about their own duties, lord, except your squire, who, I think, does not speak Welsh. Even I was otherwise occupied.'

'In trying to think of an excuse not to sit by me,' chuckled the Chevalier, making her blush.

'"Twas an honour I had not expected, lord.'

'Nonsense! You knew full well 'twas your due.'

Having briskly dismissed her words for the prevarication they were, the Chevalier lifted the brimming cup his squire had set between them and handed it to her. 'See if the wine is to your liking, lady. It comes from Gascony and was but recently landed at Carmarthen.'

Katrine sipped, tasting the fruity wine with its rough edge experimentally. 'I am unused to drinking wine, lord, but it seems acceptable enough.'

He threw back his head and laughed. 'The best Bordeaux wine, acceptable? Maiden, you must acquire the taste.'

'As you have done for our ale, lord?' enquired Katrine innocently. She had seen him turn away the offer of the rather sour remnants of the castle's cellar and could not resist the gibe.

'Nay, lady! I shall never accustom myself to the disgusting taste of your small ale! An you require a less intoxicating beverage, I will have some wine watered for you.'

'My thanks, Chevalier, but I shall not drink much.' She took another cautious sip before handing back the wooden vessel. 'I believe I do approve its taste. Not all Englishmen drink only ale. Both my father and my guardian were used to drink such wine.'

'We export enough to English shores. Eat your meat.'

So saying, the Chevalier used his knife to spear another piece of the roast flesh and lift it to his own mouth. Katrine longed for the fish, but did not like to reject the beef. Obediently, she picked up the slice on her trencher and took a bite.

'When did your father die, maiden?'

The question came sharply, without preamble. Katrine swallowed. The meat went down in a hard lump. But another kind of lump remained in her throat as the tears sprang to her eyes. Head lowered, she stared blindly at the damask cloth.

'Both my parents died when I was eight, lord, struck down by the same fever.' Her voice quivered and she cleared her throat. 'My father's will left me a ward of the Duke of Lancaster, but John of Gaunt had just died and King Richard had confiscated his estates.'

She paused, not wishing to recall the troubled months when she had been in the care of servants, awaiting the pleasure of the King. A betraying tear escaped the corner of her eye. She scrubbed it away with her finger.

Raoul could not explain the feelings she inspired in him. She was almost betrothed to a man with whose family he had long considered himself at enmity. He should despise her, yet 'twas not the wench's fault; she had not chosen the alliance herself. Instead of indifference or disdain he found himself filled with concern for her. Even tenderness. She showed such spirit in adversity. Since his own mother's death he had become unused to experiencing such gentle emotions and they took him by surprise.

'So what happened?' His voice came out more brusque than he'd intended in his attempt to mask his feelings.

Katrine's head jerked up. Her tears had dried. She spoke fiercely. 'Richard left my disposal to the duchy's chancellor. He dispatched me to live under the guardianship of Lord Frinton, who administered the Brecon March on the duchy's behalf.'

'Frinton was not kind?' asked Raoul more gently.

'Kind? He saw that I was fed and educated. I had a woman to see to my needs.'

'I see.' All her courage could not disguise from him the desolation she had felt at being torn from her roots and forced to survive among strangers. 'Is that when you began to learn Welsh?'

Katrine's hands relaxed their grip on each other. She almost smiled. 'A few words only. But enough to get by when I was taken to Rhun's hall in the forest.' The incipient smile broke out, impish and challenging. 'Listen, lord. Can you hear one word spoken by those belonging to the castle that is not in Welsh?'

Now was not the time to enquire about the where-abouts of Rhun's hideout. Raoul lifted his brows and tuned his ears to the babble of conversation filling the hall. He grinned. 'It is difficult to tell, but I can certainly hear many using the Welsh language among the English and French of my own people. You speak Welsh fluently now?'

'Well enough. I have had five years in which to learn,' she reminded him briskly, and took another bite of meat.

Raoul had been eating steadily. He took a drink of wine, wiped his mouth and regarded her keenly. Fate had placed her in his hand, an instrument he could use in achieving his ends. Yet she was so young. So innocently beautiful. So gallant. How could he treat her as an enemy? Or allow her to wed a man the sound of whose very name brought gall to his throat? What had begun as a deliberate act to further his own purposes had now taken on the additional guise of protection.

'Maiden,' he said at last, 'I will not return you as you wish, for I cannot believe the marriage arranged for you would be felicitous. I would not see you suffer more.'

She looked at him in astonishment, her gaze wide under arching golden brows which matched her glorious hair but not her sweeping lashes, which were comparatively dark and threw her dove-grey eyes into enchanting relief.

'Suffer, lord? Why should marriage to Lionel d'Evreux bring me suffering? The family is honoured throughout the land.'

'I cannot explain.' He became aware of Rhun, straining to hear what was being said. He doubted the Welshman could, given the level of noise in the chamber. Nevertheless, he lowered his voice a little when he answered her. 'Of course, thinking you dead, the family may have arranged another match for him, in which case. . . But I will see you happily settled before the next year is out. My word on it.'

Beyond Katrine, the lady Eiluned looked to be absorbed in her own disagreeable thoughts. She had drawn as far away as she could from the child. She was not attempting to listen. Though why being overheard should concern him he did not know. Mayhap it was simply that he preferred to keep his softer side hidden from his enemies. And Rhun was an enemy. He could make no mistake over that.

The impact of most of what he said skated over the surface of Katrine's mind. Only the last part caught her immediate attention, for what he had said earlier had made an impression. 'An I am obedient to your wishes,' she muttered.

Raoul offered a wry smile. 'Was I so harsh, maiden? I would value your co-operation, however. I shall need an interpreter. May I rely on you for that service?'

Katrine almost melted under this new onslaught of charm. But she had learned to be wary. Charm could hide much devious intent. His refusal to treat with the Earl of Wenstaple or with the officers of the Duchy of Lancaster could not be so easily explained away. She was still completely in his power. A trickle of perverse excitement brought a small shiver to make her spine tingle. Confinement under his authority would not be so harsh as under Rhun's; that had already been demonstrated. If he wanted her help he would not treat her ill. She might actually enjoy her new duties.

'I shall hold myself ready to be of service, Chevalier,' she assured him demurely.

He smiled, nodded approval, but merely said, 'You are not eating. Hugues, serve the lady with more meat.'

Katrine plucked up her courage. 'I would prefer to try the fish, lord. It is normally very good and it is a long time since I last tasted it fresh. We have not been able to reach the river.'

'So I should hope!' Raoul addressed his squire again. 'Serve the lady Katrine with whatever she wishes.'

Katrine broke off a piece of fine white bread such as she had not seen for weeks. 'At least today we shall not be reduced to consuming our trenchers,' she remarked as she slipped the bread into her mouth and prepared to attack the portion of pike that Hugues had placed before her. 'Do you not like fish, lord?'

'Well enough, but I prefer fowl,' said Raoul, cutting a leg from a chicken placed before him. He held the

drumstick and bit into the flesh. 'This has more substance. Have you really been starving?'

Again, the words were rapped out. He had a habit
of firing unexpected questions, taking her by surprise.
Rhun leaned forward and she saw his anxious
expression. He could not hear what was being said
and it bothered him. Mayhap it bothered him to see
her being treated with the respect due to a woman of
her rank. But Rhun's frown no longer held any terror
for her and she would not tell lies or even half-truths
to accommodate him.

'Not starving, lord,' she answered truthfully,
'although we have been on short rations. The store-
room is almost empty. We would have been starving
within a month.'

'As I thought,' said Raoul with satisfaction, and
turned to the man on his other side. 'I still fail to
understand why you held out so long, my lord Rhun.
You must have known that every other leader in the
area had given up. Carreg Cennen surrendered
months ago.'

Carreg Cennen was another outpost of Dinefwr
Castle, though it was to the south of the River Tywi.
Between them, the three castles formed a kind of
triangle. From Dryslwyn's tower the others could be
seen outlined against the eastern sky.

Katrine did not strain to hear Rhun's reply. Rhun
was a stubborn man and did not like bowing to the
inevitable, but his deeper motives in all he did had
always remained a mystery. Perhaps he did not really
know himself what they were. It no longer mattered.
It threatened to be another year before she was
restored to those who had legal charge of her, but

meanwhile she would be under the protection of the Chevalier Raoul de Chalais. That could scarcely be a change for the worse.

At first, Rhun had left her to sleep in the hall among the other serving-women and the children. Then, when she'd become nubile, Myfanwy had taken her to sleep among Eiluned's ladies. Even in that chamber men intruded—some husbands, some lovers. She had slept with a kitchen knife beneath her pallet, but a look and a sharp word, the threat of Rhun's displeasure, had been enough to deter any attempt to deflower her, though she had never felt entirely safe. Seduction was rife and rape not unknown.

With Eiluned and her ladies gone, what would become of her? Did the Chevalier have women in his camp? All armies had followers and she was certain his was no exception. The followers would include women, as necessary as farriers, fletchers and merchants. Some would be wives, others whores.

Did de Chalais have a woman? A wife, even? A small knot of anxiety formed in her stomach, though she did not know why. Because she hoped he was not wed, or because she feared that if he was not there would be no lady to protect her?

She studied de Chalais out of the corner of her eye as she took another drink of wine. The mazer had been emptied and filled several times already, though she had drunk little. He looked relaxed, mellow, not speaking much now, enjoying his victory and the entertainment provided by a group of travelling minstrels who had attached themselves to his train. They were not at all like the Welsh bards Rhun had welcomed, who sang songs of past glories and repeated old prophesies of deliverance.

Knights like Raoul de Chalais tended to remain bachelors unless they were the eldest son of a noble house, when a suitable wife would be found for them at an early age to secure the line, as she had been found for Lionel d'Evreux. He had been barely seventeen at the time, the heir because an older brother had died without issue. He'd be twenty-one now. Had he waited? Or had the family presumed her dead and found him another bride? That possibility had not occurred to her before the Chevalier had mentioned it, and even then she had not absorbed its implications at once. She had been so certain that the d'Evreux family would be prepared to pay for her return! But it scarcely mattered. She had never even met Lionel. The men who controlled her destiny would soon find another suitor for her hand.

She knew nothing of the Gascon. His face gave nothing away.

'Lord.'

She drew his attention a trifle nervously. But if he could ask questions, so could she. He turned to her with a courteous smile. When he raised his dark brows like that a multitude of furrows erupted on his forehead. They did not detract from his looks. She rather liked them.

'Aye, maiden?'

'Are there ladies in your train?'

The brows disappeared beneath his hair. 'Women, aye. Ladies? I doubt you would call them that.'

His tone of voice mocked. Katrine compressed her lips and lifted her chin. 'Then I shall lack a chaperon,' she retorted with all the dignity she could muster, though being a mere three inches over five feet tall, and in any case sitting down, it seemed woefully inadequate. But the smile disappeared from the Chevalier's mouth and his eyes took on that assessing look she was coming to recognise. She had surprised him again.

'Forgive my thoughtlessness, lady. The situation must be remedied.' He paused a moment, eyes narrowed. 'The lady Myfanwy seemed willing to help you. You like her?'

'She has been kind to me in the past. Yes, I like her.'

'Then I will ask her to remain with you.'

Doubt brought a frown to Katrine's brow. 'She may not wish to, lord. Her husband is a vassal of the lord Rhun. When he leaves, she will go with him.'

'Is there anyone else?'

Katrine thought of the other ladies with whom she shared a chamber and shook her head. 'They too are wed. And have never shown me the same kindness.'

'Then Myfanwy it must be. I will speak with her. Her husband may stay too, an he will swear loyalty to me and the crown. You will need a tiring-woman too. Who would you have serve you?'

'Dorcas Jones, lord,' said Katrine without hesitation. Dorcas, a young village woman who had served under the English constable, had taken her under her wing and saved her from the worst of the spite and rough treatment meted out by the other servitors until they had tired of the sport and learned to accept, even respect her. 'She is quite young, though several years older than I, and I have always been on good terms with her. She is inexperienced in the personal duties required but I would not mind that. She will learn quickly.'

The Chevalier, with characteristic speed, made up his mind. 'Send Dai to bring her before me.'

Dai, hearing his name, rose from the rushes where he had been sitting cross-legged. Despite his tattered motley hose and worn tunic he possessed a dignity derived from his breeding. Dai was Eiluned's nephew, serving as a page in Rhun's household while being instructed in the ways of a Welsh gentleman and knight. The clerk—who was in minor holy orders—was supposed to teach him his lessons while his uncle educated him in the skill of arms. He had joined them mere months before the siege began.

It would have been more useful had the clerk taught him English rather than Latin, thought Katrine as she passed on de Chalais's order. But by the time he joined Rhun the rising had been under way for several years, and to teach the boy English would have seemed to the Welsh like a betrayal.

Dorcas came from the far end of the trestles, where she had been sitting. A tall, rather thin young woman, she was dressed much as Katrine had been. Raoul's narrowed eyes came to rest on her as she approached. He noted that she moved well and had a clean, intelligent face. A strand of brown hair had escaped her cap and as he watched she thrust it back with a large, capable hand. She did not mount the dais but made obeisance from the floor below.

Raoul de Chalais wasted no words on pleasantries. 'You belong to Dryslwyn, I believe. Are you willing to remain here with the castle in my hands in order to serve the lady Katrine as her tiring-woman?'

Dorcas's brown eyes widened. Her English was not perfect, but good enough. 'Her tiring-woman? But, lord, it's not trained I am.'

'The lady Katrine has asked for your services. Is that not enough?'

Incredulous, Dorcas sought to meet Katrine's eyes. 'Katrine—my lady——'

'You will soon learn, Dorcas. I want no other to serve me.'

'I take it you will stay?'

'Willingly, lord.'

'Then that is settled. You may begin your duties immediately.'

'I will call you when I wish to retire,' Katrine told her.

'And now send Dai to fetch the Lady Myfanwy.'

Myfanwy mounted the dais to stand before the Chevalier and he explained the situation. 'Will you remain to keep the lady Katrine company? Your knight may stay here with you an you both desire it.'

'You wish me to stay, Katrine?' demanded Myfanwy.

'Indeed, lady, I ask it as a favour. You have shown me kindness in the past. Will you not keep me company while I must remain here?'

Myfanwy hesitated only a moment. She addressed the Chevalier.

'I am willing, lord. But I must speak with the lord my husband on the matter.'

'Very well. Bring him to me.'

From the moment Dorcas had stood before him de

Chalais had had to raise his voice. Rhun was now openly listening to the conversation with Myfanwy. He forbore to comment, but Katrine saw his eyes take on a thoughtful gleam.

'Lord.' She touched the Chevalier's arm to draw his attention, for she spoke low, so that Rhun should not hear. The contact brought a resurgence of all the feelings she had experienced upon being told to sit by him. She removed her hand as though she had been bitten. But the touch had done its work. The Chevalier had turned to her. 'Lord,' she repeated, fighting down an uncomfortable blush, 'I would not trust Sir Gruffydd any more than I would trust Rhun.'

Those brows flew up again. 'You think I do?'

'I do not know, lord.'

'He will swear an oath of loyalty.'

'Which he will not hesitate to break.'

'Should I give him the opportunity,' murmured de Chalais. 'Think you I have survived this long without encountering and combating treachery?'

'I only thought to warn you, lord.'

Her dignified reply disguised a wealth of hurt feelings. She was trying to help the man!

Raoul sensed this. He should not have reacted in so hostile a manner. But he did not like being taught his business by a mere child, and a girl-child at that.

He looked at her again, and somehow his gaze became entangled with hers. Those dove-grey eyes had become pools of reproach. But there was something else in them, too. A lingering awareness of that touch, which had made her shy away and brought the blood to her cheeks. It had shocked him too, but he had dismissed it. He did not dally with children. He had laughed at her for not wishing to sit by him, thinking her reluctance born of adolescent fancy.

Yet she was old enough to be wed. Had the face and figure to tempt any man.

'May I present my lord and husband Sir Gruffydd Gethin, Chevalier?'

The interruption came as a welcome diversion from thoughts he would rather not entertain. He had no room in his life for entanglement with any woman at the moment. Particularly not with one so closely associated with the d'Evreux family.

'Sir Gruffydd.' He acknowledged the other man's bow. 'Your wife has told you of my request?'

'Aye, lord.'

'And your response?'

Katrine caught the the slight nod of Rhun's head, giving permission for Gruffydd to stay. She wondered whether the Gascon had noticed it. His gaze was fixed on Gruffydd, whose glance had not wavered, though he must have seen the movement of his lord's head.

'My wife has a soft heart and wishes to stay. I will remain with her since it seems our cause is lost and Owain Glyn Dŵr no longer has need of my sword.'

'You will take the oath of loyalty?'

'Whenever you wish, lord.'

'Good. Do any of your fellow knights stay?'

'I think not, Chevalier.'

'Then you must learn to mix with mine. We will meet on the morrow, after the Lord Rhun——' he turned to acknowledge the man at his side '—and his train have left. All those remaining here will need to take the oath.'

'I believe most of the local people who were here

before the castle fell into Welsh hands will remain,' said Rhun. 'They are used to serving English masters.' He made it sound like a matter for scorn.

'Dai!' Eiluned spoke for the first time that evening, her voice sharp. 'You will come with us tomorrow. Go to your pallet and prepare.'

'Have I the lord's permission?' Dai was not looking at Rhun, but at Raoul.

'What do they say?' the latter demanded of Katrine.

'The lady Eiluned has instructed the boy to retire to his pallet in preparation for his departure on the morrow. He seeks your permission, Chevalier.'

'He has it.'

As Katrine translated, Raoul gave the lad a kindly smile. Dai grinned back, all anxiety banished from his expressive urchin face. Katrine watched as the page descended from the dais and made his way to a dark corner of the hall. This was where he slept, with several other pages, all scions of leading Welsh families, attached to Rhun for their education as he was.

'He seems a likeable lad. And bright. He should learn to speak the English tongue. He will need it as he grows older.'

'Mayhap, when the rising is finally subdued, the Lord Rhun and his clerk will countenance such a move. But at the moment English is anathema to them.'

'They would deny the lad a decent future?'

'No,' said Rhun heavily. The minstrels had paused and he had caught Raoul's words. 'His future lies in Wales.'

'Yours did not,' Raoul pointed out. He knew, as did Katrine, that, like his leader Glendower, Rhun ab

Brechfa had served in the households of English lords and fought with them during the Scottish risings of Richard's reign. It was there that he had learned his military skills. 'Would you deny the boy the advantages you yourself enjoyed?'

'He will learn to cherish Welsh independence above worldly advantage.'

''Tis a dream, Rhun, and will never be achieved by force of arms.'

'A dream, yes, but one which will not die.'

'But you will keep your word, my lord, and swear fealty before you leave on the morrow?'

'I will swear.'

The minstrels struck up again, but Raoul made a sign and they stopped. 'It is time we all retired,' he announced, his voice raised to a commanding shout which brought instant silence. 'We all have a busy day ahead of us on the morrow. I will wish you all God's blessing this night.'

So saying, he rose. Servants rushed to clear the boards and remove the trestles. His bodyguard moved to take up positions behind him. He turned to Katrine and bowed.

'Sleep well, maiden.'

Katrine returned his polite gesture. 'God be with you, lord.'

'I look forward to the morrow.'

Katrine grinned. Rhun and Eiluned had already moved away. 'As do I, lord. I may not be free, but I am a lady again, and for that I thank you.'

'You were never anything else,' Raoul assured her.

CHAPTER THREE

THE castle was early astir next morning as Rhun and
his party broke their fast and prepared to depart.
Katrine wished she were leaving too, but not to go
with Rhun. She longed with aching intensity to travel
in the opposite direction, to England and home.

Home? Her true home was barred to her, being in
the hands of the Lancaster officials until she wed or
came of age. Or had some other claimant already been
installed? The thought sprang into her head, bringing
with it a chill of dread. Like the possibility of Lionel
marrying someone else, this circumstance had not
occurred to her before. She might have lost everything.

'Twould involve her guardians in a long and bitter
legal battle to recover what was hers. If they ever did.
But, since Lancaster was now King, mayhap that
difficulty would be slight. On the other hand kings
were capricious creatures. He might have presented a
favourite with her inheritance as reward for loyal
service. What would they do with her then? No one of
worth would wed her and even a nunnery would be
loath to accept her without a dowry.

She felt ready to sink into despair until she remembered that Rhun had been certain that her fortune
would come to Elwyn or Dafydd were she to marry
one of them. He had assured the Chevalier that it was
still hers. His promise to de Chalais might be considered a trick were it not for the fact that he'd been

keeping her for Dafydd to wed. He must know it was not lost. Mayhap he had allowed rumours of her survival to reach England. Mayhap he had even been involved in secret negotiations. If so they had come to nothing, thank God.

The worst of her sudden panic subsided. But the fact remained that at the moment she had nowhere to call home. Wenfrith, the main seat of the d'Evreux family, might become so should they still agree to a match between herself and Lionel. And as her husband he, of course, would reclaim and take over her estates, which would mean she could return to Huntershold. But for the moment Dryslwyn was as much home to her as anywhere else, although it was in Wales and not England. With everything so uncertain mayhap being forced to remain was not so great a hardship. The Gascon had promised to see her settled. And against all the odds she trusted him to keep his word.

Rhun, on the other hand, had proved devious. She watched suspiciously as he took his oath of fealty. In his heart of hearts he could not mean the words he was saying. Yet he placed his hands between those of the Chevalier and recited them as though he did.

'The mounts are ready saddled,' Raoul informed him after the short ceremony. 'I trust those which were yours will be strong enough to bear you and your lady home. Good food will soon put flesh back on their bones and bring strength to their muscle. They are both fine animals and I trust you to return them to me in good health, my lord, together with my pack animals and the hacks I have provided to carry the other ladies of your party.'

Raoul had not felt able to insist on some of his men accompanying Rhun to bring back the horses, for he could scarcely spare enough of his force to be certain of winning should Rhun turn upon them. Besides, since the Welshman intended to return to his hide-out in the mountains, he had categorically declined an escort, declaring himself ready to walk if need be. It would have been unwise to inflict such an added indignity. A new bargain had needed to be struck. Rhun had offered to return the mounts and Raoul had acquiesced, albeit reluctantly. Were Rhun ab Brechfa to break his word the loss would be slight. Better that than to reinforce the potentially dangerous enmity already simmering between them. His own position had improved since moving into the castle, but was still vulnerable. No one knew when a new uprising might inflame the area.

'Our thanks for allowing us to take them.' Rhun spoke stiffly, as though the words hurt him. 'They will be treated with every care.'

'I shall look for Gruffydd Gethin to return with them within the month,' Raoul returned, reminding the other man of the terms of the agreement.

'You have my word, Chevalier,' said Rhun sullenly.

Eiluned, who had been standing silently by, suddenly demanded, 'Where is my nephew, Dai?'

'Dai?' Rhun looked round. 'Is he not here?'

'He is not.'

'Then we must search for him. With your permission, Chevalier?'

'Of course.' A frown settled on Raoul's brow. This was awkward. He had taken a liking to the boy and did not wish to see him beaten for disobedience, which would surely be his fate should Rhun discover him hiding. Everyone else destined to leave the castle was gathered in the hall. Dai could not have missed the summons. Even most of those who had chosen to remain had taken their oath of fealty to de Chalais and the King and were present for the leavetaking. Lesser members of Rhun's meinie had been free to choose, but not Dai, for Rhun would never grant his wife's nephew permission to stay. The lad was in his charge, entrusted to his care by his brother-in-law. His loss would impinge heavily on Rhun's personal reputation.

Raoul became aware that the maid Katrine's eyes were fixed upon him, wide and apparently innocent. Did the wench know something? Tempted to ask, he desisted. Rhun must be familiar with the castle by now. Let him organise the search. If the boy was ingenious enough to avoid discovery, let him stay. He returned her stare with equal blandness. If she had been a party to Dai's disappearance she would have him to answer to later. For he could see trouble ahead, greater than had Rhun been forced to walk from the castle. But he would not interfere. A new challenge would not be unwelcome. He had mayhap been too weak over the horses. The question of the page was more important, however, involving as it did the lad's entire future. A spice of extra danger would keep both himself and those under him on their toes.

Louis was already back and standing at his side. 'Keep an eye on the search,' murmured Raoul. 'I would not have the child hurt.'

Katrine kept her gaze fixed on the Gascon. His eyes had not met hers for long but she had seen the flare of

suspicion, quickly masked. Did he think she had
helped Dai to hide? Worse, had he sent Messire Louis
Duval to assist in finding him? Louis had spoken to
some of the English men-at-arms and they had scattered, following Rhun's searchers. But in the hall, at
least, they merely stood watching as trestles were
moved, the space behind the stacked boards investigated, every nook and cranny explored.

She could guess where Dai had chosen to hide. He
should not be discovered.

The search went on for a full half-hour. Pitchforks
thrust into the small mound of remaining hay in the
stable loft failed to unearth anything but rats. Rhun's
retainers looked down the well and into the cisterns,
searched among the remaining stores. Dai was
nowhere to be found.

'Mayhap he managed to leave the castle during the
hours of darkness?' suggested de Chalais. 'No doubt
my men's vigilance was somewhat reduced last night.
In the circumstances, a wily child might easily have
escaped detection.'

'Mayhap.' Rhun did not sound convinced.

'He must be found!' Eiluned, that austere, heartless
woman, whose only soft spot seemed reserved for her
son, sounded almost distraught. Katrine did not
believe it was concern for the lad which made her so,
but fear of her brother's wrath.

Dafydd, who had shared lessons with his cousin,
grinned fleetingly behind his parents' backs. Katrine
hoped he did not know anything, for if he did they
would soon get it out of him. Dafydd, like herself, had
learned discretion when it came to defying his father.
He was small for his age and had been thoroughly

cowed, his spirit crushed. Even for Dai he would not risk a beating, whereas she would.

Dafydd's glee, transient as it had been, was noticed by Gruffydd, standing near his old master ready to accompany him from the castle but sworn to return to his wife, bringing the Gascon's horses with him.

'Ask your son,' he grunted, loud enough for Rhun to hear, but in Welsh.

'Dafydd?' Rhun turned on the boy. 'What do you know?'

'Nothing, lord,' cried Dafydd. His voice did not tremble. Katrine knew the effort that must have cost him. He was terrified of his sire.

The stock of Eiluned's riding-whip cracked down on her son's head. Her softness for Dafydd did not extend to the repudiation of chastisement. 'Tell the truth, boy, or worse will befall you!'

'I did,' sobbed Dafydd, cringing.

That blow must have made his head ring, thought Katrine, and sprang to the lad's defence. 'Why should he know, lady? Dai would have told no one, lest you questioned them!'

'Keep silent, wench, or 'twill be the worse for you!'

'Your threats no longer have any power over me, my lord Rhun!'

The Gascon intervened. 'What is the problem?'

Katrine, in her new role as interpreter, hastened to explain, her indignation spilling over into words. 'They will beat him for naught!' she ended.

'The boy must learn to tell the truth,' asserted Rhun forcefully.

'An the child knows aught, I am sure he will tell us

and save everyone a deal of trouble. What do you know, boy?'

The Gascon spoke with clipped authority. His hard face had set into grim lines. The child could not know that his anger was directed at his parents rather than at him, but Katrine had seen the way the Chevalier's hand had clenched convulsively as Eiluned's blow had struck home.

'The Chevalier asks if you know where Dai is,' translated Katrine quickly, although it was hardly necessary, since Dafydd knew some English, learned from his parents. She hoped her intervention and reassuring smile would give him courage. 'He demands the truth.'

Dafydd gulped. 'I don't know anything.'

'Then why did he smile?' demanded Gruffydd loudly.

Katrine had gone to stand by the Chevalier. She translated swiftly.

'Because I was glad he'd got away,' sobbed Dafydd, with as much defiance as he could muster. 'He wanted to stay here.'

'For that insolence, my son, you will be sent away to a household where you will not have your mother's skirts to hide behind!' blustered Rhun, administering a hearty slap to aggravate his wife's blow. 'But for the war you would have gone to another household for training long before this. But your mother pleaded . . .'

He allowed the sentence to trail off, its implication quite at odds with Eiluned's recent behaviour. But it was probably the truth. As she translated for the Gascon's benefit Katrine noticed a gleam of hopeful interest enter Dafydd's watery eyes. The incident could work out in Dafydd's favour. But the problem of Dai's whereabouts had still to be resolved.

'The page is nowhere to be found and I am convinced your son knows nothing of the matter,' summed up de Chalais briskly. 'There is naught you can do but depart without him. Your men have searched every inch of a castle they know well. He cannot be here.'

Eiluned tried to protest. Rhun breathed fire and threats against anyone discovered sheltering the boy. But they left without him.

Katrine stood beside the conqueror of Dryslwyn at the top of the steps leading from the Great Hall, watching the party pass through the gatehouse, trail across the bailey, cross the drawbridge spanning the ditch beyond the curtain wall, emerge from the barbican and carry on down the undulating slope which would take them to the bottom of the mound on the far side from the river. This was the direction from which any invading force must come. On the three sides nearest the river the slope was almost precipitous, a natural defence which, augmented by the high curtain wall, made attack from those quarters almost impossible.

The steps offered an extensive view, since the ground fell away in all directions. They watched the straggling party reach the level ground, pass through the huddle of huts at the foot of the hill and set off along the valley, travelling at the pace of the slowest pedestrian.

''Twill take them days,' Katrine remarked at last.

Before the Gascon could reply four sturdy

Englishmen presented themselves at the foot of the steps, mounted and leading a laden packhorse.

The Chevalier descended to speak with them. 'Keep well out of sight,' he told them. 'Should Rhun see you your lives will be worthless.'

'We know, Chevalier. You forget, we come from Keswick, where the terrain is very similar.'

'I do not forget. But have a care. These Welshmen are dangerous.'

'No more so than the Scots,' grinned the leader of the group. 'Do not fear for us, Chevalier. We volunteered for the task because we have succeeded in similar missions before.'

'An you succeed this time, my gratitude will be boundless. God go with you.'

As they rode off and de Chalais rejoined her Katrine asked, 'They are following Rhun ab Brechfa, lord?'

'Aye.'

'To what end?'

'You are inquisitive, maid. But there can be no harm in your knowing. They are to keep an eye on my horses, and to discover where Rhun's stronghold lies.'

'I spent many months there. 'Tis a hall within a stockade.'

'So I guessed. But could you find it again? And would you, an you could?'

'I would, lord, but no, I doubt I could find it again. It lies deep in the Cambrian Mountains, in a wooded valley. But once the Tywi is left behind the way is tortuous and indistinct. Your men will need endurance and wit.'

'I believe they have both. But now, maiden, tell me, where is the page?'

'Dai, lord?'

'Who else?' demanded Raoul sardonically.

'How should I know, lord?'

A slight flush had risen to her cheeks but she met his eyes fearlessly. 'How, indeed?' he drawled. 'Unless, mayhap, you helped him to conceal himself?'

'I would not do that, lord.'

'Why not?'

'It would not do. What I do not know I cannot reveal.'

'Like Dafydd. But you guessed he would attempt to remain behind?'

'Not until he was discovered to be missing. Then I guessed. You treated him kindly, lord. His allegiance was transferred then.'

'Very well. Could you find him? He may be afraid to come out.'

Anxiety entered her eyes. 'You will not send him back to the Lord Rhun?'

Raoul smiled. 'Nay. He has earned his freedom from that lord's clutches.'

'Then I believe I do know where he may be.'

'Show me.'

Katrine nodded, prepared to lead the way to the small chapel situated in what was known as the household tower, since it held the chambers occupied by privileged guests and members of the household. The solar lay between it and the Great Hall and could be approached from both directions, since a doorway opened into it from the hall. But those who slept in one of the tower rooms dared not approach the hall by passing through the solar without permission. They must descend to the courtyard, brave the weather, and enter by the outside steps.

So Katrine did not turn back into the hall but led de Chalais down the steps and through the ward to the outside entrance to the tower. The buildings formed a defensive square with the gatehouse tower in the opposite corner, behind them as they walked. The guard occupied that. The off-duty knights, squires, men-at-arms and archers, together with the servants, slept where they could, mainly in the Great Hall. Stables, the armoury, the forge, various stores and a garde-robe tower all opened into the courtyard on their left with other offices, including the wine-store and the dairy, located in the undercroft to the Great Hall, on their right.

The chapel, being small, was used mainly for private prayers, meditation and confessions. Since the clerk held only minor orders, visiting priests celebrated mass there before a select few and administered the sacrament to the remainder of the household in the hall.

An altar some six feet wide and half as deep took up much of the space in the little chamber, its cloths still reflecting the glories of past, more gracious occupation. Where it had been disturbed and rumpled by the searching men-at-arms the gold thread used in the embroidery of the frontal caught the pale light from the slit window, drawing attention to the snowy linen covering the top. Keeping the chapel clean and tidy had been part of Katrine's duties and she knew the time and effort which had gone into scrubbing the linen with lye soap, starching, drying and ironing it to the crisp, gleaming whiteness on which stood a carved

wooden crucifix and four silver candle-holders, innocent now of the fat candles which, in better times, had
been kept burning in them.

De Chalais looked about the bare chamber which,
besides the altar, contained only a faded tapestry hung
on the wall behind it, two prie-dieus facing it and
another prayer-stall set against a side wall beneath a
statue of the Virgin Mary.

'In here?' he demanded. 'They must have searched
beneath the altar and there is nowhere else to hide.'

'Wait, lord.' Katrine stepped forward and lifted the
ornate frontal to reveal the solid blocks of stone fitted
together to serve as the altar. She spoke again, fairly
loudly, in Welsh. 'All is well, Dai. The lord Rhun has
gone. It is safe to come out now.'

There being no immediate response, she leant forward and pressed a small irregularity in the surface of
the stone. The central section of the front swivelled
almost noiselessly to reveal the hollow interior of the
altar.

'Come, Dai,' said Katrine, 'The Chevalier will not
send you back to the Lord Rhun.'

Still no response. Katrine shot an anxious look at
the Chevalier and bent forward to search the secret
compartment intended to hide holy artefacts against
pillage, a compartment she had discovered quite acci-
dentally one day when she and Dai had been alone in
the chapel. Eager inspection had shown it to be quite
empty and they had agreed to tell no one of their find.
Even such a small thing as a shared secret had enli-
vened the drudgery of serving under Rhun and
Eiluned ab Brechfa.

'Dai!' Her anxious tone told Raoul that something

was amiss. He watched, frowning, as the maid sank to her knees and crawled halfway into the small cavity, leaving only her rounded posterior protruding.

'Is he there?' His voice came out harsh, for mixed emotions had a grip of him. Curiosity, anxiety, impatience and, yes, a stirring of carnal desire roused by that part of her anatomy presented so temptingly to his view. What the devil was he doing, wasting time looking for a disobedient page in the company of a hostage who promised to become a temptation and an embarrassment were he not careful?

Next moment, every emotion had gone except concern. Katrine emerged from beneath the altar, dragging the inert figure of the missing Dai.

'I think he's dead,' she gasped, close to tears.

Raoul bent down and shifted the child to a better position on the floor before feeling for the pulse in his neck.

'He's alive,' he announcd, 'but only just. He was on the point of suffocation. I believe there was no air in that chamber.'

'Can you——?'

'I know something of what to do. I have seen men resuscitated before.'

He was on his knees beside the boy, untying the neck of his tunic. Then he bent forward as though to kiss him. Katrine clenched her fists. What good could kissing do? And it seemed wrong. . . .

But the Gascon was not kissing Dai, he was holding his mouth open and puffing his own breath into the lad. He did this several times before lifting his head.

'Hand me one of the candlesticks,' he commanded.

Wondering at this strange order, Katrine nevertheless jumped to her feet and brought him the polished silver stick. De Chalais took it without even a nod of thanks, all his attention centred on the page, and held it before Dai's mouth.

'Ah!' His exclamation exuded satisfaction. 'He breathes!'

He handed Katrine the misted silver, giving her a brilliant smile. Next instant he was bending over the boy again, repeating his treatment. And then Dai's chest suddenly heaved. He gave a great sigh and opened his eyes.

Raoul sat back on his heels, his green eyes shining. Katrine had not imagined he could look so tender. She stood, clutching the candlestick, which she had forgotten to replace, tears of relief streaking her cheeks.

'Oh, Dai,' she cried, 'what a fright you gave us!'

He was, understandably, bemused, especially as Katrine had instinctively spoken in English.

'The lord Rhun!' Dai whispered. 'I must hide!'

'He is gone,' Katrine assured him, this time answering him in his own language. 'You are safe. Messire de Chalais has promised me that you will not be returned to Rhun ab Brechfa.'

A beatific smile spread over Dai's face, which was rapidly regaining its natural colour. Weakly, he gripped the Chevalier's hand. 'Thank you, lord. Thank you,' he murmured.

Katrine, finding the candlestick still in her hand, replaced it upon the altar and went to close the secret compartment.

'Wait!' De Chalais left Dai's side to inspect the interior of the chamber. Not that anyone but a small child could get more than head and shoulders inside. He drew back, holding the stub-end of a candle. 'Does this open and close from the inside?' he demanded, indicating the slab.

'Yes, lord. When Dai and I discovered it, while I was replacing the cloths after cleaning them, we tried it out. Dai took a candle in and found the knob. He swung the door closed and then pushed the knob and it opened again. So of course he thought it would be safe enough to hide in there.'

'It was. But he forgot he needed air to breathe.'

Dai had struggled to sit up. 'The candle went out,' he told Katrine plaintively. 'I would have opened the door but I could hear men searching the chapel. I had to wait. And then I don't remember. . .'

When Katrine told the Chevalier what Dai had said, he looked down at the candle in his hand and gave a grim smile. 'Candles do go out when they lack air. Dai is lucky to be alive.'

'They must have searched the chapel last and we came here almost straight away,' said Katrine. 'I am so glad I trusted you!'

Raoul raised his dark brows. 'Do I appear so unworthy of trust?'

'N-no, lord,' stammered Katrine, confused. 'But I do not truly know you, and Rhun ab Brechfa. . .' She trailed to a miserable halt.

'Has killed your trust in human nature, I perceive. But I am not Rhun; my word is my bond. Tell me, maiden, was the chamber empty when you found it?'

'Yes, lord. The lord Rhun,' she said unnecessarily, 'did not know of its existence. I suppose no one did, except the true owners of the castle. And they have long been gone.'

'Taking their valuables with them, no doubt. Well, it has served a useful if almost disastrous purpose, but you must both promise me never to use it as a hiding-place again.'

'I do, lord, and I am certain Dai will too.'

When asked, Dai nodded vigorously. He would never enter that tiny sealed chamber again, even to save his life.

'He had better rest awhile,' said de Chalais. 'Where does he sleep?'

'In the hall.'

Raoul frowned. 'He will find little peace there.'

'He could use my pallet, in the chamber above. I am certain the Lady Myfanwy would not object.'

'Take him there, then. I must return to my duties.'

'The other doorway on this landing leads directly to the solar,' offered Katrine shyly. ''Twould be the quickest way back to the hall.'

'My thanks. I shall expect you to join me immediately Dai is settled. You may,' he added with a slight smile, 'use the short route to the hall on this occasion. Dai should be recovered in time to serve me at supper, if not at dinner. He may assist my squire, be my personal page. Do not keep me waiting long, my lady.'

Katrine helped Dai up the stairs to her chamber, where she found Myfanwy's tiring-woman, Olwen Ellis, fussing about with her mistress's clothes.

'What are you doing here, Dai Prys?' she demanded sharply. 'You should be gone with your uncle and aunt. They spent nearly an hour searching the castle for you, you wicked boy.'

'I take no reprimand from you, Olwen Ellis,' said Dai with sudden spirit. 'I am son to Hywel Prys while you are nothing but a serving-woman.'

'You are a page, no more, whoever's son you are!'

'Peace!' cried Katrine. 'Dai is to remain at Dryslwyn. I have brought him here on the orders of Messire Raoul de Chalais, whom he is to serve,' she went on firmly. 'Dai almost died attempting to escape the cruel clutches of the lord and lady of Brechfa and is to rest on my pallet.' She bent to spread the blanket more evenly. 'At least until dinner. Leave him be, Olwen, or the Chevalier shall hear of it.'

Olwen snorted. 'The Chevalier! Who is he to come here lording it over us folks who have been here all our lives? I care nothing for Messire Raoul de Chalais.'

'Then you should have departed with Rhun ab Brechfa. You have sworn fealty, Olwen; you cannot break your oath.'

Katrine did not know where she found the strength to chastise a woman who, until the previous day, had been able to order her about. Some of the Gascon's authority must have rubbed off on her, she supposed. His treating her as a lady, recognising her rank, had resurrected her own pride in who she was.

'I care naught for him, either,' muttered Olwen. 'My true allegiance is to Owain Glyn Dŵr and Wales. But I have sworn, and I will serve King Henry since I must, for it seems that in the end none of us Welsh will have any choice.'

'Wales is part of his kingdom, Olwen Ellis; he will

guard it well. An you did not rebel, he would have no cause to treat you harshly.'

'You English!' Olwen spat. 'You will never understand!'

'Mayhap not. But let us not quarrel, Olwen. Keep your oath and we will have no cause.' Dai had already slumped on the pallet Katrine had prepared. She addressed him with a smile. 'Rest well, Dai. I will come to you again before dinner.' She turned to the older woman. 'Do not tease him, Olwen. He has been badly frightened and needs to recover.'

'Frightened? Why, what happened?'

'He hid in a chamber and could not get out.'

'And the soldiers did not find him?' asked Olwen, incredulous.

Katrine shrugged, affecting indifference. She had no intention of telling Olwen of the secret hiding-place; such knowledge belonged to no one except the Lord of Dryslwyn or he who stood in his stead. 'They were careless.'

'Wait until the lord Rhun learns of his nephew's whereabouts! He is the boy's guardian.'

'He will not know, at least not for a while. The Chevalier will deal with the lord Rhun.'

Katrine spoke with the utmost confidence. Her admiration for the young knight had grown apace during the morning.

When she re-entered the hall, descending the wooden staircase from the gallery, she revised her opinion somewhat. His imperious bark of, 'There you are! Come here, maiden!' raised her hackles again. If only he were always as gentle and considerate as he had been in the chapel!

But Raoul de Chalais, she was beginning to discover, possessed a many-faceted character. Of course, he must be stern and decisive with this men. The trouble was, he sometimes seemed unable to soften his approach when dealing with her. Yet at other times. . .

But this was not one of his more gentle moments. She approached him, eyes flashing indignantly, memories of more congenial moments swamped by his present attitude.

'I am here, lord,' she announced tightly. 'Would you have had me leave Dai to Olwen Ellis's mercy without spending a moment to explain?'

He stared at her haughtily. 'Olwen Ellis?'

'The lady Myfanwy's tiring-maid. She was in the chamber, about her duties. Dai's presence required explanation.'

He looked about to question her further but then, remembering that others were listening, desisted. 'I have need of you to tell me what this oaf is saying,' he declared instead, indicating one of the local servants with an impatient swing of his hand. The man stood before him in his brown homespun, looking like an idiot, but Katrine knew him to be an efficient keeper of the household stores. ''Tis devilish inconvenient that they speak no English.'

'Or that you do not speak Welsh,' retorted Katrine tartly. 'What do you wish to ask him?'

Raoul knew that venting his ill-temper upon the maid had been wrong. A commander should never berate his troops unfairly. He admired her the more for standing up to him. Not that she could be allowed to see that.

However, he modified his tone to explain his difficulty and Katrine relaxed enough to translate efficiently.

'Messire Raoul de Chalais requires a full list of all remaining stores,' she explained to the man.

'Tell him to give it to you so that you can present it in a language I can understand,' snapped Raoul, who was finding his attempts to communicate with his new churls frustrating. He had appointed Katrine of Huntershold his interpreter, but it irked him to be so dependent upon the maid's ability to speak Welsh.

'There are others here who speak both languages,' she pointed out when they had done. 'The lady Myfanwy for one.'

'But none was present in the hall. Where is the lady Myfanwy?'

'In the kitchen, I imagine. Now that the lady Eiluned has gone she will expect to take control of the household.'

'Ah, yes.' Raoul looked at her sharply. 'I had not thought of that. I certainly need a chatelaine, but she is of lesser rank than you, my lady of Huntershold. I believe you have the right to that honour.'

'Me, lord?' Katrine's astonishment seemed to cause him amusement, for she caught a gleam of merriment in those green eyes. 'I am but a chattel—a hostage—of no account in this household.'

'Mayhap you were treated as of no account, maiden, but Rhun guarded you well for your fortune. As for me, I consider you to be a valuable asset which I desire to enhance rather than denigrate. Do you consider yourself able to take over the duties of chatelaine?'

'I was trained from an early age for such a responsibility, lord. And, having served here among the other serving-women, I believe I have practical knowledge of their problems. I can view the running of the household from both sides. But the lady Myfanwy——'

'Will do as she is bid, which will be to assist you in every way.' He gave a lopsided grin. 'My cook may not take kindly to obeying your orders.'

'Then mayhap you should instruct him so to do. Dinner should be served within the hour. Would my lord wish me to ensure that all is well?'

Raoul suddenly grinned. 'Your lord would most certainly wish that. Your lord will accompany you on an inspection of the domestic quarters. Come, my lady chatelaine. I would see my dinner in preparation.'

They heard the ructions before they had progressed beyond the draught screens protecting the hall from the entrance lobby. The noise grew louder as they trod the passage between the wardrobes. Heat from the great fires hit them almost like a wall as they entered the kitchen. It was months since the hearths had blazed so brightly. More recently there had been virtually no fuel.

The tempting aroma of roast ox came from a spit turned by a dog in a wheel. Cauldrons hung from hooks bubbled over the flames and someone was pounding away at something in the huge stone mortar. Ragged scullions were everywhere, cleansing and chopping, mixing and kneading. But these things faded into the background at the sight of Myfanwy, standing by helplessly while Raoul's brawny, volatile Gascon cook waved a knife and shouted at the Welsh cook in fractured English. The Welshman, seeking to keep control of his kitchen, screamed back, partly in English, partly in Welsh, when the unfamiliar language deserted him.

'Silence!'

Raoul's imperious bark brought the shouting match to an abrupt end. Then both men began to make their protest to him, speaking together.

'Silence!' roared Raoul again. 'Yves, you may speak first. Be patient, your turn will come,' he told Morgan, the Welsh cook.

It seemed that both men were determined to prepare only food of the kind normally enjoyed by those for whom they cooked. Raoul sighed. He could put neither man in complete charge; that would not be fair. Yet he could not tolerate constant discord.

'Yves,' he instructed at last, 'you will provide the food for my men; you know their likes and dislikes. Morgan, you will continue to prepare food for those of the former occupants who remain. Samples of all the dishes will be presented at the high table for my consumption. Is that clear?'

Both men were used to obeying orders. They could do nothing else but acquiesce in their leader's solution.

Katrine began to wonder whether the Chevalier possessed the wisdom of Solomon.

CHAPTER FOUR

OVER the next few weeks life in Dryslwyn settled into its new routine. Myfanwy, having discovered the impossibility of keeping order in the kitchen without the authority of the Chevalier behind her, relinquished her self-imposed responsibility without apparent bitterness.

'It is the lady Katrine's right, of course,' she acknowledged. 'I was merely attempting to ensure that dinner was served on time.'

The Chevalier, with irresistible Gallic charm, offered his appreciation. 'My thanks for that, lady; 'twas something I had overlooked. I trust that I may rely upon your continued goodwill and assistance?'

No woman would be proof against that smile, thought Katrine ruefully, except mayhap Eiluned, had she still been there. She was not, therefore, surprised to see a faint blush appear on Myfanwy's cheeks as she assured the Gascon of her co-operation.

Both cooks, told that Katrine's word was law on household matters, reluctantly bowed to her authority. So did the remainder of the staff. To her astonishment Katrine found little resentment from the serving-women, among whose number she had so recently been counted. Even the steward bowed to her warrant, under that of the Chevalier, and such other men as were left from the old order soon fell into the way of doing her bidding.

'People feel they have a friend at court,' explained Myfanwy with a smile. 'Many of us have long admired your spirit, my lady, and benefited from your compassion. You are young, but not without natural authority.'

'But I am forced to spend so much time at the Chevalier's side,' grumbled Katrine. 'My duties as interpreter hold me there when I should be supervising other things. How should I manage without you to assist me?'

'How, indeed,' agreed Myfanwy complacently. 'The Chevalier knew your rank took precedence and awarded you the position. He also knew that I was able and willing to carry out the duties of chatelaine. What better solution than to appoint me your deputy? He is a clever young man, Messire Raoul de Chalais.'

'Yes, he is, and wise beyond his years. He manipulates people,' said Katrine rather bitterly.

Watching him placate the two cooks, she had thought him wise. He was, of course. But she had come to realise that, when he applied his talent to matters that concerned her, wisdom was not the word she wanted to apply.

However, she found the time spent translating for the Chevalier interesting rather than boring and his company pleasant and stimulating. He wanted to know every detail of the management of the castle — where it had previously obtained its supplies, who worked the fields, who tended the animals, who brewed the beer and mead, how long it took to winch up a bucket of water from the deep well which penetrated the centre of the mound to the depth of the river's water table, and which of the villagers, with whom he had

wisely ordered his men to remain on good terms while
encamped near by, owed service to the lord of
Dryslwyn. He was, she could tell, determined that the
life of the castle should return to normal with all
speed. Memories of the bitter siege must be buried
under his reign of strict but fair discipline.

Of course, when he was with his own knights, men-
at-arms and archers she was not needed. From time to
time while carrying out her other duties she saw them
practising archery in the butts, drilling in the bailey,
or engaging in mock sword-fights both mounted and
on foot. A quintain had been erected, at which others
practised their knightly skills.

New milk-cows had been acquired and, passing one
day from dairy to hall, Katrine's curiosity got the
better of her and she strayed through the gatehouse to
watch. She could not help laughing in delight as one
after another of the knights and squires charging the
quintain's wooden dummy was knocked from his horse
by the swinging sandbag.

Noticing her merriment, Raoul trotted over to speak
with her.

'They will be more accurate and speedy next time,'
he grinned, leaning from his saddle to speak. Beneath
his basinet his forehead was beaded with sweat. The
odour of hot metal and steaming horse was almost
overwhelming, despite the overcast day. ''Tis a salu-
tary lesson to be unhorsed by a sandbag fixed to the
end of a wooden beam.'

Katrine eyed the lance held upright in his right
hand. 'You have yet to try your skill, lord?'

Her dove-grey eyes held speculation as well as
challenge. Raoul met them with supreme confidence.

'Aye, maiden, I shall make three courses. I too must keep in practice. 'Tis not easy to hit the target fair and square so that it does not swing, or to escape quickly enough if it does. Besides, I would not ask my men to do that which I disdain.'

'You have already fought long and arduously with the sword and mace, sir knight, both on horseback and on foot,' Katrine pointed out provocatively. She had been watching him on and off all morning as she'd gone about her duties. The hall steps afforded an excellent view, and many of the windows overlooked that part of the bailey. This was not, of course, the first time she had watched his apparently tireless performance. He was already shaking his head in dismissal of her words but she pursued her thought. 'Do you not fear that fatigue will make you careless?'

'If it does, then I am not fit to fight a battle, which can often last the length of a day. If I am unhorsed, my lady, then I must train the more. But——' he gave her a confident grin '—I vow I shall not lose my seat.'

Of course he was using his fighting saddle, which supported him front and back, freed his hands for his weapons and protected the lower part of his body. An elaborate affair, it was constructed of hard leather and wood, padded and covered in velvet, decorated with braid and metal. Even for this practice his animal was armoured and caparisoned in scarlet, blue and silver.

He wore the minimum of armour himself, for the weapons were all guarded, but he had donned his weighty cuirass, which had a bracket bolted to it to take the butt of the lance when it was lowered, a basinet with dependent chain-mail to protect his head and throat, and thick leather gloves to protect his hands. Apart from any consideration of safety, his horse must be fit enough to perform under a heavy load.

His shield, half blue, half red per pale, was charged with two silver bars. Her father's charge had been a golden falcon, belled and jessed, on a plain black ground. As his heiress she was entitled to use it in a lozenge until she wed, when——

Katrine cut the thought off short and answered him instead. 'I shall view your prowess with interest,' she assured him with a mischievous smile. 'An you remain in your saddle, my admiration will be unbounded.'

He threw back his head and laughed. 'That, *ma chérie*, will be something I shall consider a treasure beyond price.'

Katrine's cheeks flamed. Her untutored attempt at teasing coquetry had been neatly turned back on her.

'I doubt that, lord,' she returned stiffly. 'I will not waste my time further.'

She turned, prepared to walk off in a dignified huff. His humorous, apologetic tones called her back.

'Nay, maiden, do not leave. I did but tease you as you teased me. Watch, and mayhap I shall afford you amusement yet. Although,' he added wryly, controlling his increasingly restive destrier with easy expertise, 'knowing I have you for audience will put me on my mettle. So mayhap my confidence wil not prove misplaced.' He gave her a self-deprecatory smile. 'I have been known to fail. But,' he added softly, 'not often. In anything I undertake.'

'That, lord, I can believe. Very well, I will remain to witness your joust with the quintain. It will afford me amusement whether you remain in the saddle or no.'

Katrine let him know by the tone of her voice that he was only partly forgiven. Yet the smile he threw at her as he gathered his horse ready to move off brought a responsive gleam to her eyes and a small curve to her lips. It really was impossible to dislike the Chevalier for long.

He wheeled his horse and set off towards the far end of the tilt-yard. His watching men gave a cheer as he couched his lance across the great horse's withers, its butt in its bracket on his right, its point at the left of the horse's neck, and the destrier thundered towards the quintain. And then a laughing groan went up. The Chevalier had missed his mark and been clouted to the ground. He sprang to his feet on the instant, caught the obedient charger, retrieved his lance and leapt into the saddle again. Grinning widely, he made his way back to the start. As he passed he gave Katrine a cheery wave.

She was not laughing. Seeing the proud Chevalier knocked from his perch had failed to give her the amusement or satisfaction she had anticipated. Besides, she was not entirely certain he hadn't done it on purpose. He had been so sure of himself, and the cries of his men on seeing him fall had held more surprise than anything else. He was treating her as a child, to be indulged and diverted. All the same, she remained to see him make another pass at the dummy. This time his attack was faultless and the cheers of his followers echoed back from the wall behind her, making Katrine's heart squeeze. They loved him for his modesty and good humour as well as his courage and pride. And when he made his third charge, escaping the swinging sandbag despite a slightly off-target blow, the cheers became deafening.

As he dismounted, and his men gathered round him, Katrine slipped away to the kitchen and her duties. By dinnertime, she told herself firmly, she would be able to face him again without feeling shamed.

Supplies continued to arrive by river from Carmarthen, though now, of course, they were brought straight into the castle. A couple of laden boats and their escort were due to arrive on the morrow, despite the swollen state of the Tywi. Another spell of rain would cause it to flood, and when it did its course would become difficult to distinguish in places.

After supper Myfanwy sang to the accompaniment of a harp. She had a sweet voice, and when some of the local men present joined in a chorus the rafters vibrated with that special harmony only the Welsh seemed able to produce.

'Would you like to visit Carmarthen?' Raoul asked Katrine during a moment when he could make himself heard. 'We could return with one of the vessels; 'twould be less arduous than travelling by road. Methinks you need new gowns, maiden—a cloak for the winter, some fairings, mayhap. There are merchants aplenty in that town, despite the havoc wrought by Owen Glendower and his men. We could lie a night or two at the castle. Would that please you, my lady?'

'Oh, yes!' Katrine had quickly recovered from the embarrassment of the morning. Neither of them had mentioned it since. 'But can you leave Dryslwyn, Chevalier? Suppose it is attacked?'

'The possibility seems remote, and Louis Dubois is well able to order its defence. I feel the need to visit a town myself after so many months spent in this barbaric wilderness. But there is one condition to your going, my lady. You will tell no one that you are Lady Katrine Lawtye, heiress to the late Earl of Huntershold. You will be merely Demoiselle Kate, a child under my protection. Leave any explanation of your presence to me.'

'Why, lord?' choked Katrine, her first excitement dimmed by his unaccountable determination to continue to hold her, to ensure that no word of her whereabouts reached those who could ransom her. Not that she had felt in much need of help recently. In truth she found the prospect of leaving Dryslwyn and the Chevalier's protection somewhat depressing. She felt safe with him, and who could tell what awaited her back in England? But the knowledge that she was not free to do as she liked rankled. 'And I am no longer a child!' she declared with spirit. 'I am a woman grown!' His referring to her so had been hurtful. Did he truly look upon her as a child? She did not wish to think so, though why what he thought should make any difference to her remained obscure in her mind.

'My reasons are my own, and no, unfortunately you are no longer a child,' growled Raoul, fighting his growing desire to treat her very much as a woman. 'But for this trip at least I shall regard you as such. And I require your word that you will not seek to escape me, to send messages or in any other way abuse the freedom I allow. Do I have it?'

Katrine nodded mutely.

'Your word,' he insisted. 'Your parole. Do you swear?'

'I swear, lord,' whispered Katrine.

Raoul nodded. 'Very well. Be ready to leave soon after dawn on the morrow of the morrow.'

'I must have a woman to travel with me,' Katrine pointed out, determined not to be intimidated. 'May Myfanwy accompany me?'

A frown corrugated Raoul's brow. 'Myfanwy would undoubtedly wish to take her serving-woman. I shall need my squire, Hugues. We cannot take Dai, for fear he is recognised by friends or relations visiting Carmarthen, so I must choose another page to run our errands. With our guards that will make a large party.'

'Too large, lord?' asked Katrine anxiously. Having been promised escape from the castle, if only for a day or two, she did not want to lose the opportunity. 'Mayhap Dorcas would be sufficient chaperon?' she ventured.

Raoul nodded. 'On this occasion I think she may. The lady Myfanwy will mayhap be disappointed not to accompany us, but in any case she will be needed here.'

Myfanwy did suffer some disappointment at not being included in the party but the prospect of having sole charge of the household in Katrine's absence did much to assuage it. Louis took his exclusion philosophically. He knew that as second-in-command he must remain to defend Dryslwyn. All the same, in the privacy of the solar he teased his friend, speaking in Gascon French, as they always did when alone together.

'You indulge the little one,' he accused him, accompanying his words with a mischievous grin. 'I shall begin to think you harbour tender feelings for her, Raoul, my old friend. Beware, or the maid will creep into your affections and your bed.'

'You know full well that she is under my protection, Louis. She is the only woman in the castle in honour forbidden my bed! Not,' Raoul added quickly, fully aware that he lied, 'that I have any inclination to seduce such a young, immature virgin. What sport could there be in that?'

The two men had enjoyed many a bawdy night together. Louis knew that Raoul's tastes ran to well-endowed, experienced women who could lay no claim to his hand. When he wed it would be to someone worthy to be the wife of the seigneur of the recovered de Chalais estates. The little Katrine was worthy, too worthy in truth, being daughter to the equivalent of a *comte* in their own land. But his friend had been much in her company of late and he had seen the way she could soften the Chevalier with a glance from her dove-grey eyes.

'None, my friend, none!' he asserted with a chuckle. 'But, nevertheless, you are growing fond of her—as are we all, I vow!'

'She is a taking child,' agreed Raoul, 'and has suffered sadly at the hands of Rhun ab Brechfa. She deserves some consideration, even from her captor.'

'Who vowed he had neither the reputation nor time for softness,' Louis reminded him wryly.

'I wish to see her dressed in a lady's finery,' said Raoul softly. 'Rhun was stupid. She will fetch a larger ransom an she looks worthy to be a d'Evreux bride.'

'Ah,' responded Louis. 'I see. 'Tis that which interests you, my friend. But she has been captive for five years. Mayhap Lionel d'Evreux has found himself another wife.'

'Then he and his family will discover what they have lost. And will undoubtedly feel in honour bound to empty their coffers to obtain her freedom.'

'But the King is her guardian——'

'And they his favoured nobles. They will exert every muscle, pay any price, to retain his favour.'

'You have it all worked out,' said Louis thoughtfully. 'I pray you are not misled, not blinded by your hatred——'

Had Katrine seen the Chevalier's face then she would have shuddered. As it was, even Louis felt a chill infect his spine.

'Nay, Louis,' said Raoul, the green ice of his eyes reflected in his voice. 'You have no call to fear that. They will pay. In one way or another, they will be made to pay.'

Despite the autumnal chill Katrine enjoyed the leisurely journey along the placid, looping Tywi. Powered by several oars driven by strong arms, the vessels floated through a gentle, cultivated landscape, passing between green water-meadows and lush pastureland backed by wooded hills. The valley was wide at this point, the high, barren hills left far behind. A few farms and hamlets lined the river, and a scattering of sheep and cattle grazed, those few still left to their owners by successive foraging armies. But of human beings she saw scarcely any.

It was dusk by the time the small flotilla eased under

the bridge to land its passengers on the quay before
the castle gates.

Katrine gazed up at the huge stone edifice standing
forbiddingly upon its man-made motte, built in the
first Edward's time to guard the bridge and prevent
enemy penetration further inland by river. The river
widened appreciably as it headed south towards the
sea. Ships lined quays laden with barrels, baskets and
bales while ant-like figures toiled to unload a huge
variety of supplies and fill the ships' holds again with
wool, cloth, dried and salted fish, and anything else
the merchants had to sell.

During the journey Raoul had remained with his
squire and the sergeant of the small personal escort he
had brought with him. Katrine wished Dai could have
accompanied them; he would have enjoyed the trip
down the river. No doubt he would have sat at the
Chevalier's feet in the bilge-water and got thoroughly
wet. She could just imagine it as she sat in a following
boat with Dorcas and some of the returning
Carmarthen escort, watching the Gascon at ease with
his men.

The Chevalier needed no one to translate for him
that day, so why did she feel discarded because he had
chosen to travel in a different barge? Two evenings
ago he had been friendly, even warm, when he had
invited her to accompany him. Since then he had
withdrawn, become almost hostile. It didn't matter a
bit, but all the same she missed his company, missed
his laugh. Missed his kindness and concern. She could
not think what had caused the change in his attitude.
She could remember nothing she had done to displease him. Mayhap it had nothing to do with her.

Mayhap he had something on his mind. Not that it looked like it as he laughed and joked with his escort, she thought as his rich laugh rang out over the peaceful countryside.

Mayhap he regretted his invitation. She had not asked who would pay for her new clothes, thinking the money would come from the King's purse, like all de Chalais's supplies and the pay for his men. In due course the King could reimburse himself from her inheritance if he so chose. If he had not already sequestered it or given it away.

Dorcas, excited by the unexpected treat, had chattered away happily all day. She too would benefit from a new gown, one more befitting her position as Katrine's tiring-woman. She could sew well and spent the day planning all the things she would make her mistress.

'You must buy chaisel for smocks, lady, as well as flurt silk, samite and sarsenet. Then there is satin and saye, not to mention sendal and velvet. And for the winter you must have flannel and frieze——'

'Stop!' cried Katrine, laughing. 'Where did you learn of all these clothes?'

'From the English ladies, before Rhun ab Brechfa took the castle.' Dorcas sighed. 'They were great days. I listened and learned, although I was still young.'

'And their women taught you how to sew; I remember you saying so. Well, it seems your skill may come in useful at last. Between us, we should be able to make some passable clothes to wear.'

'Oh, yes, my lady——'

Katrine cut Dorcas short. 'You must remember to

call me mistress,' she reminded the girl. 'Otherwise the Chevalier will be most displeased.'

'Aye, mistress, I'll not forget. I wouldn't want to anger him; he's a deal better to serve than Rhun ab Brechfa, although he's a Frenchman.'

'Not quite a Frenchman,' Katrine pointed out. 'He's Gascon, and Gascony is ruled by the English King.'

'Whatever he is, he isn't Welsh, but there, it doesn't bother me who rules as long as I've clothes on my back and enough food to eat. What good does rebellion do, I'd like to know? It just makes beggars of us all.'

Katrine thought of the denuded pastures through which they had passed and the way so many towns had been sacked and put to the torch, and silently agreed. But all she said was, 'Be sure you remember.'

Life was, she thought, bound to be difficult over the next couple of days. Dorcas, or even one of the Chevalier's men, could forget and address her by her title at some time. But that was Raoul de Chalais's problem. He had laid down the rules. She would abide by them but could not answer for others' indiscretions.

Raoul introduced her simply as Demoiselle Kate. The constable appeared incurious. His garrison included few women other than servants and Raoul kept her at his side most of the evening so that Katrine had little opportunity to speak with anyone without him being within earshot. Once she retired for the night she and Dorcas were left alone in the tiny chamber allocated to them, apart from visits by a groom of the fires, who saw to the candles and the brazier, and a groom of the bedchambers, who brought hot water, soap and towels. Tomorrow, Raoul had promised, they would seek out the merchants. Dorcas, although excited by the events of the day and the prospects for the morrow, was soon breathing deeply and steadily on her truckle-bed. Katrine, enjoying the unaccustomed privacy of a closely curtained bed and the luxury of a feather mattress, lay wakeful.

The Chevalier had been courtesy itself since their arrival at Carmarthen, and the saints knew what bribe he had used to secure the use of this chamber for her. But for the first time she had felt him to be her gaoler, watching her every move, ready to pounce should she say a word out of place.

Did he not trust her parole? Or did he merely think her stupid? Whatever the reason for his attitude, it rankled.

The town of Carmarthen, snug within its ancient walls, had quickly recovered from the depredations of conquest and reconquest. Damaged buildings had been rebuilt and supplies quickly replenished by the many ships busy plying the tidal waters of the Tywi. Having herself been sequestered from such an early age, Katrine had no memory of merchant houses with such extensive selections of goods on display. Her guardian had kept her within the bounds of his hold in Brecon until they had started out on that fateful journey to Wenfrith, so she had little with which to compare the wares on offer in Carmarthen. She had never seen the like of the shimmering silks and satins, of the serviceable broadcloth and fustian, the fine chaisel and lawn. Neither had she imagined such a choice of trimmings, of furs and tippets, cauls and headdresses. She had been with ladies wearing gowns made from such materials, of course, had even worn small imitations of them herself at Huntershold in the distant past, but the cascades of colour, the mixture of textures displayed through the open windows of the mercers' establishments made her cry out in delight.

Seeing her pleasure, Raoul indulged her.

'The fabrics please you, maiden? Make your choice. You will require warmth for the winter—silk beneath a thicker surcoat, mayhap? Do not consider the cost. Since you are under my protection 'twill be put down to the King's account,' he said, confirming her surmise.

With Dorcas, Raoul and the merchants' wives to help, Katrine chose blue sendal, green sarsenet and brown fustian for kirtles, then scarlet ingrain, more sober grey cendryn and a beautiful saffron velvet for cote-hardies and sideless surcoats.

'This Welsh flannel would do for your mantle,' suggested Raoul.

Katrine considered the attractive brown mixture and nodded. 'And this blue, mayhap, for a cope? I shall need a hood to protect my head against wind and rain.'

'Aye.' Seeing Katrine's interest caught by the display of trimmings, he added, 'The sempstress will know which of those to use.'

'They are so beautiful,' sighed Katrine, eyeing richly coloured braids, golden tassels and strips of fur longingly.

'Dorcas shall have a gown of this brown kersey and a cope of flannel. And Dai shall have new tunic and hose in red and blue motley, with my silver fox's head emblem on his breast.'

'He will be delighted!' cried Katrine.

'Dressed as he is at the moment, he is a disgrace to my retinue,' grinned Raoul. 'As for you, Hugues,' he said, turning to his young squire, 'mayhap a new tunic and hose would not come amiss either. I am certain you would wish to melt the hearts of the ladies.'

Hugues blushed. His fresh countenance was prone to such infusions of blood, and this embarrassed him the more. But he was a sturdy lad and not uncomely. Katrine thought he would grow into a stalwart man.

'Thank you, lord,' he managed.

'And for myself. . .'

The Chevalier's voice tailed off as he began to examine broadcloths and brocades for surcoat and pourpoint. The latter, Katrine had already discovered, since he often wore one, was popular in France, a short, padded, close-fitting tunic fastened down the front, which emphasised the Chevalier's already broad chest and shoulders and narrow waist and hips. Beneath, his hose clung lovingly to muscular thighs and calves. For his new garment he chose a scarlet brocade. He often wore vivid colours, which matched his personality. Not that he had need of brilliant hues, for whatever he wore he would stand out in a crowd; his height and presence guaranteed that.

He had mentioned a sempstress, so perhaps she would not be required to make the garments herself. Katrine's eyes began to sparkle anew. Although willing, she had not relished the prospect of days of tedious sewing, however much she desired new clothes. As for Dorcas, since the promise of a new

kirtle and cope her eyes had been fixed on the Gascon
as though he were a god. Judging by the threadbare
state of her present garments, she had worn them for
many years. Katrine herself had not received new
kirtles from Rhun, merely another hand-me-down as
she'd grown out of the one she had been wearing.
Decidedly, the Chevalier's protection was more agreeable than being held hostage by Rhun.

After leaving the mercers' they visited the sempstress and tailor, who took their measurements and
orders, promising that the finished garments would be
sent on to Dryslwyn within the week.

There was still a little time before they needed to
return for dinner, and so Raoul led Katrine on a tour
of the narrow streets. They investigated the premises
of silversmith and goldsmith, skirted round the mal-
odorous shambles where animals were killed, mounds
of entrails festered and meat was sold, and passed
quickly by the smelly fishmongers' stalls. The fish was
fresh enough, but the watery slime covering the
ground stank. Escaping this unpleasant street, seduced
by pungent, heady aromas, they lingered awhile to
watch a woman weighing out spices and herbs before
passing on to stop to examine a display of gloves and
purses. The appetising smell of freshly baked bread
and hot pies filled one narrow street, from which they
emerged to discover a Franciscan friary, no doubt the
source of the bells tolling the canonical hours which
had marked the passage of Katrine's sleepless night.

The town was busy with people, and pack-animals
passed back and forth. A group of sick and ragged
beggars crouched before the gates of the friary, which
opened to allow a man to come through into the

street. Not a friar in a grey habit, but well-dressed in flowing houppelande and velvet cap, he tossed a few coins to the beggars as he passed.

Katrine gave a small gasp and lowered her head, pulling her veil forward to hide her face.

'What is it?' demanded Raoul.

'That man,' whispered Katrine. 'He must not see me an you wish my presence here to remain unknown.'

The man looked about to make for the street they were in, and this seemed likely since it led to the commercial quarter of the town. Raoul reacted swiftly.

'Turn back,' he muttered, shepherding both women before him. 'This way.'

A few steps away a narrow alley ran off to the left, leading through to another street. Raoul urged them into it and then, with Katrine hidden behind him, turned to watch the man pass by. He had not noticed their curious manoeuvre, or if he had he chose to ignore it.

'It is safe for us to proceed now,' said Raoul, urging them through to the other street. 'Who was he?'

'The steward of Lord Frinton's household at Brecon. His son took the cowl. He must be here to visit him and to obtain supplies.'

'You did well to recognise him, and I am grateful to you for your discretion, demoiselle. However, you were a child of ten when last he saw you. He will not be much changed, but you have grown and matured. Such evasion may not have been necessary.'

'I did not wish to risk discovery since it is against your wishes, lord.'

'For that you deserve more than merely my thanks,

lady. Come! I believe this will lead us back to the
castle, and if I remember correctly there is a stall
here. . . Ah, yes! Allow me to purchase some of this
golden cord for you to use to prink your hair. A trifle,
no more, but,' he declared, paying the woman behind
the stall from his own purse, 'a token of my thanks—
and trust.'

Katrine accepted the gift, her cheeks flaming. Her
first gift from a man! And from such a man! But, she
told herself sternly, it meant nothing. Had he not said
it was a thank-you offering? And a token of trust.

That, perhaps, was the most important thing. If the
incident had served no other purpose, it had won her
the Chevalier's confidence. Which pleased her. But
she could not help pondering on the reason why she
had instinctively avoided the steward, had felt panic
at the sight of him rather than an urge to break her
word and seek his help. And the answer came, breathtaking in its simplicity. In truth she had no desire to
escape the Chevalier's hold.

CHAPTER FIVE

THEY did not eat at the high table, the constable reserving the places on the dais for those he considered more important. This suited Raoul, who had no wish to draw attention to Katrine. He insisted that her place was by his side and the steward, beguiled by his frank manner, accepted without question that her rank entitled her to be there.

Katrine had watched the charade last evening, her amusement laced with a growing resentment at his obvious mistrust. Now, however, her mood more sanguine, she took her place with pleasure rather than rancour. But, having sat down beside him on the bench and looked around the company, she gave a small gasp of consternation and gripped her escort's arm.

'What is it?' demanded Raoul, disturbed in several different ways to find her little hand grasping his arm as though for dear life. Katrine was not given to gratuitous touching.

'He is here,' she whispered urgently. 'The Brecon steward. He sits there, just below the salt. He must have sought hospitality in the castle.'

Raoul replied in an equally low voice. The noise level in the hall was enough to render their conversation private. 'No doubt he lies here whenever he visits Carmarthen. He was probably at supper last even, although you did not see him. Take no notice,

Kate. If he thinks he recognises you, deny knowing him. He cannot be certain. But if you keep out of his way I do not think you have much to fear.'

'I do not fear, lord,' asserted Katrine. 'My concern is to keep my word.'

'I know. You do not understand, but, believe me, your remaining incognito is necessary to my plans. But those plans do not include inflicting harm on you, little one. Trust me; be patient. All will be resolved within the year.'

Katrine nodded and relaxed. She did trust him. And if he did not fear her being recognised, then neither would she. She kept as quiet and behaved as unobtrusively as possible during the meal and afterwards sat quietly with Dorcas in a corner of the hall working on a new smock, which Dorcas had cut out from lawn delivered before they themselves had returned from the morning's expedition. She would have sought more light for her sewing but, fearful of recognition, strained her eyes to tack and sew the seams. Dorcas, aware of the difficulty, made only token protest.

'We could retire to your chamber, mistress,' she suggested.

'There is little room there, Dorcas, and merely an arrow-slit to give light. I prefer to remain here.'

Here, the Chevalier could keep her within his sight. Not only mistrust had kept him near her but also concern for her safety. Knowing he trusted her, she no longer resented his surveillance. A garrison of rough soldiery inhabited the castle and, although she was well used to taking care of herself when in the company of those she knew well, here, among strangers, the Chevalier's protective presence was welcome. He himself slept in the hall, but had set one of his trusted bodyguards to lie across her door. It would be all too easy for her to be ravished in the bustling confusion of the castle, where privacy was at a premium and some men considered all women potential whores.

A short distance away the Brecon steward had engaged in conversation with his Carmarthen equivalent. The Brecon man was eyeing her with interest. Her stitches became large and uneven as she held her breath and tried to watch the man from behind the veil of her lashes. He laughed, said something obviously bawdy to his companion and turned his attention to the Chevalier, whom he eyed with mild amusement. She was being cast as the Gascon's woman, she supposed, but the man's curiosity seemed not to extend beyond this prurient interest. As his attention wandered away she began to breathe again, and proceeded to unpick the terrible stitches she had just made. Her hands still trembled, and she wondered a little that possible discovery should affect her so when indeed it might be to her advantage to be recognised. And wondered too that being cast in the role of the Chevalier's woman amused rather than distressed her.

Before long the Brecon steward rose and left the hall, but not before stopping by the Chevalier, bowing obsequiously, making himself known and offering his congratulations on the ousting of the Welsh rebels from Dryslwyn. 'The King's administrator in Brecon will be thankful to hear the news. Is the Prince of Wales aware of your triumph, Chevalier, or may I ensure that the news is conveyed to him?'

'I thank you, Sir Steward, but I dispatched my own messenger to inform Prince Henry that Dryslwyn is now held for the King. But tell me, sir, I have heard that the previous administrator, Lord Frinton, I believe, was ambushed by Welsh rebels and killed—is this true? Were you serving at Brecon then?'

Katrine held her breath again and stabbed her finger with her needle. The Chevalier was altogether too audacious for her comfort. She sucked the blood from the prick and bent her head assiduously over her work, her ears straining to follow the conversation. The noise in the hall was less now than at meals and neither Raoul nor the steward had troubled to lower his voice.

'So you know of that terrible massacre.' The steward put on a sombre face. 'Aye, lord, I was steward then, and as such not, I give thanks for the mercy, one of the party travelling to Wenfrith with the maid. We lost our lord and many good men that day and the little Lady Katrine disappeared. Her body was never found.'

Raoul looked equally sombre. 'Dead?' he asked.

'It must be assumed so. No ransom was ever demanded for her return or I would have heard.'

'She was heiress to the Earl of Huntershold, was she not?'

'Aye.'

'What became of her inheritance?'

Raoul's attitude was careless, as though the answer to his question were of little interest. He lounged on the bench, his long legs stretched before him, his hand toying with a horn of ale. But Katrine, who knew him by now, recognised a thread of steel beneath the casual tone of his voice.

The steward shrugged. 'I have no knowledge of that, Chevalier. It is still administered by the Lancastrian officials, I imagine.'

'I would have thought the King might have taken it to himself, or awarded it to some loyal follower as reward.'

'Mayhap he has, but, if so, word of it has not reached my ears and I meet many of the duchy officials in the course of my duties. The King is not anxious to sequester estates, even of sworn enemies. He remembers too vividly the consequences of King Richard's action in confiscating his Lancastrian inheritance when his father, old John of Gaunt, died.'

'Which led to Richard's own downfall at his hands. Aye, I can see he might be cautious. But no doubt he will do something with it one day.'

'When this pestilential uprising has been quelled, and there is no possibility of the maid's return, no doubt he will, Chevalier. However, I must not linger but make haste to begin my journey if I am to arrive in Brecon on the morrow.' The fellow made another obeisance. 'God go with you, lord.'

'And with you, Sir Steward.'

Raoul nodded, not rising to bid farewell to an inferior. Still bowing, the man made off. Katrine wondered why he had bothered to stop, but then remembered his initial enquiry. Having learnt of the Chevalier's exploits from others, he must have decided to speak with him to angle for the important task of relaying news of Dryslwyn's fall to those in high authority. In that quest he had been disappointed, but in his eagerness to please he had been free with his information, suspecting the Chevalier of nothing more than idle curiosity.

As for Raoul, his general expression was thoughtful but the suggestion of a smile lifted the corners of his appealing mouth. The fullness of his lips seemed slightly to overflow the lines nature had originally drawn and, as usual, the glint of his strong teeth could be glimpsed between them. He had adroitly turned the man's pushiness to his own advantage and now had good cause to believe that her fortune remained intact and that a substantial ransom could be exacted for her return.

In due course.

Katrine bent her head to her work again. Her worst fears for the future had been assuaged, the steward had gone and she could relax and enjoy the remainder of their visit. It would be short enough. They were to return on the morrow an the weather held. If not, and heavy rain fell overnight, they might be forced to travel by road.

No downpour prevented their using the river, although a morning mist hung over the water, shrouding its course in mystery. But the banks could be clearly seen, in some places the flow a mere inch or two below their top. Above Carmarthen the river soon ceased to be tidal, the rise and drop in its level barely discernible, but for the first few miles it did look as though, in places, the high tide had caused neighbouring meadows to be flooded. By the time they reached Dryslwyn the mist had cleared, the mountains were visible, apart from the peaks veiled in low-lying cloud, the sun was out, though dying, and here the river still remained confined within its banks.

From beneath the red cross of St George fluttering from the tower a horn had rung out to warn those in the castle of their approach. As soon as they had climbed the hill Raoul's own standard would be broken out to join it. Katrine anticipated entering the castle again with surprising eagerness. Now that its atmosphere was no longer infected by the presence of Rhun, Eiluned and their following, Dryslwyn seemed to extend welcoming arms.

She gave a little sigh of satisfaction as she prepared to mount a saddled mule. A string of pack-animals had been led down to the water's edge but no horses, although Raoul had ridden down at the head of his marching bodyguard. How was he to return?

'They have forgotten your destrier, lord,' she said as he helped her into the saddle.

'Nay, they but obey my orders. 'Tis not far and I am always glad to stretch my legs after such a trip. Come, I will lead your animal. Or,' he suggested with a teasing smile, 'do you consider yourself able to manage a difficult mule?'

Katrine gathered the reins before giving him an indignant look. 'You know I am not! I learnt to ride a pony once, but——'

'That was long ago,' he finished for her. 'When the palfrey is returned you shall ride that.'

'May I?' Katrine's face glowed. 'How I should enjoy the exercise! Thank you, lord.'

Raoul led the mule around the foot of the outcrop and up the track leading up to the castle. A couple of his men went before them and the remainder brought up the rear, guarding the pack-mules, now loaded with supplies, which Raoul himself had acquired. Katrine noted kegs of brandy and several casks of wine being carted up. The cellars were far from empty now but this delivery was special, she guessed, and meant for the Chevalier's own consumption.

They passed through the barbican, crossed the drawbridge and emerged into the bailey. As his standard was raised on the watch-tower two men-at-arms stepped forward to salute their leader.

Raoul released the halter of her mule and strode off to meet them.

'You are safely back!' he exclaimed. 'Well done! You were successful?'

As the sergeant took his place at her mule's head and led it towards the courtyard Katrine realised that the men speaking so animatedly with Raoul must be some of those he had sent after Rhun. By the satisfied looks on their faces they had managed to discover the whereabouts of his hide-out among the Cambrian Mountains. She wondered what use the Chevalier intended to make of the information.

Over a meal served to them in the solar, since supper had been over for some time, Katrine, despite feeling unaccountably awkward and subdued, asked him. Louis was present, enjoying a cup of wine though not eating, but both Hugues and Dai had been dismissed once the food had been placed before them.

Louis exclaimed, 'I have been wondering that myself!'

Raoul gave that expressive shrug which spoke so much more eloquently than a mere English lifting of the shoulders. 'Nothing, my friends. Knowledge is power. Naturally, I have arranged for a discreet watch to be kept on his stronghold so that he cannot make any move without my knowledge. Two of the men remained on watch and others will be sent to relieve them. The tours of duty involved will keep my company on its toes during the winter. Come, Katrine,' he said, lifting his cup and changing the subject, 'do you not like this wine?'

'Indeed, lord, but it is strong and I cannot add water since we share a cup.'

''Twill do you no harm and you will be retiring anon. Here——' he thrust the brimming cup into her reluctant hand '—drink up!'

Apprehensive, Katrine eyed the deep ruby liquid in the silver vessel. 'Do you wish to see me intoxicated, lord?' she demanded.

Raoul thrust his thumbs into his jewelled knightly belt, threw back his head and laughed. 'Indeed, maid, that eventuality would indeed divert me! I wonder how you would behave? 'Twould be an interesting experiment.' He gave a deep chuckle then, seeing Katrine's agonised expression, sobered. 'Come, Katrine, I do but tease! You are grave this evening, lady. I merely wish to bring a smile to your lips, to see roses on your cheeks, a sparkle in your eye, to be assured that the journey was not too much for you and that, despite the alarms and excursions met with in Carmarthen, you enjoyed the outing. I would not wish to cause my sweet hostage distress,' he assured her earnestly.

'I am sure you do not, lord. If I seem grave now it is because I am overwhelmed by your kindness.' To her distress her voice began to quiver. 'To replenish my wardrobe, to allow me to eat in the solar——'

'My dear child! Have you no notion that it is I who should be honoured to eat in your presence?'

Raoul ignored Louis's startled expression and quelled his own astonishment that he should voice such a sentiment. He who considered himself the equal of any man—and certainly more than the equal of any woman! But her rank did outweigh his, even were he to regain his lost lands in Gascony, and he could not ignore that fact indefinitely. In different circumstances he would be considered subservient to her, however much he might resent it. Only her isolation, her helplessness, gave him dominion over her. And chivalry demanded that he did not abuse his power.

Meanwhile, it could do no harm to humour the child. He prepared to exert his considerable charm to bring her out of her sombre mood. 'Come, Katrine, you may be a hostage under my protection, obliged to abide by my wishes, but that does not diminish your rank! I see the abominable Rhun's treatment has deprived you of your sense of self-worth. I am shocked. I had thought you to possess more spirit.'

Katrine's chin jerked up. 'Indeed, lord,' she replied with dignity, 'I have never forgotten who I am, and I executed the menial duties imposed upon me by Rhun and his lady with dignity and pride. I merely wonder, lord, what ulterior motive you have for treating me so well.'

'Ulterior motive?' exploded Raoul, springing to his feet. 'What do you mean, maid? What do you imply?'

Katrine's face was scarlet but she spoke firmly

enough, for answering anger had come to her rescue. 'That mayhap you thought to make me so grateful that I could deny you nothing, lord. So I would prefer to remain sober and not, in future, be invited to share the intimacy of your solar.'

With its intrusive curtained bed, which took up much of the floor space, she might have added.

Raoul stood over her, his anger hitting her like a physical blow. But she refused to flinch.

'You insult me, wench,' he grated. 'Do you imagine I could ever be interested in an inexperienced maid? Or capable of forcing my attentions on her even if by some remote possibility I were?' He took a deep breath and delivered his *coup de grâce*. 'I can assure you, Lady Katrine, that I have returned from Carmarthen well-satisfied by women capable of fully meeting a man's needs. You may leave us.'

Shaking like a leaf with shock and mortification, Katrine rose to her feet. 'Gladly, lord.' She dipped a small curtsy, which included the speculating, faintly amused Louis Dubois, and stumbled to the door, wondering what on earth had possessed her to make such a scene, and why the knowledge that Raoul de Chalais had lain with some woman—or, worse still, women—while in Carmarthen should cause her so much pain.

Katrine spent the night trying to work out what had made her so edgy, so stupid. The root cause, she decided, was that she did not understand Raoul de Chalais, did not know what to expect from him. One moment he was her chilly captor, the next a charming companion, one moment open and friendly, the next cold and withdrawn. He had distanced himself on the journey to Carmarthen, behaved like a gaoler, and then indulged her with clothes and fairings. Between times he had acted as her protector. Then, back at Dryslwyn again, he had suddenly invited her into the solar with its intimidating bed. He and Messire Louis Dubois, friends and companions of long standing, had behaved as such men did, talking, laughing, enjoying a joke, though they had been mindful of her almost silent presence. Then Hugues and Dai had been sent away, leaving the three of them to enjoy a greater intimacy.

It was at that point her unease had become acute. To be alone with two young virile men. . .and to be told to drink deeply—she was not so naïve as that. One or other or both. . .

After her experiences with Elwyn and other men she had, quite simply, feared the worst. She was in their power. They could, in truth, do with her what they liked. Of course, spoiled goods would not command such a high ransom, but mayhap they did not care, or thought the sport worth the price——

But it was not Louis Dubois she feared. Although always meticulously courteous, he largely ignored her. On the other hand the Chevalier. . .

She always felt a little awkward in his presence, and if he touched her strange sensations ripped through her body. It was the Gascon she mistrusted. Or mayhap herself?

That unwelcome thought gave her pause. Did she actually want him to make love to her? No one ever had, though the awful Elwyn had tried, but if anyone did she would wish it to be him—a foolish whim, for in all probability Lionel d'Evreux awaited her. If not he then some other man of her guardian's choosing. She must not, could not, indulge in daydreams involving Raoul de Chalais. He would never be considered as a suitable husband for the heiress to the Huntershold estates.

Husband? She must be mad! After Elwyn, surely she hated the thought of belonging to a man, of being forced to endure his unwelcome attentions. But she had to admit that it had been her own inclinations, not the Chevalier's, that had made her so wary that evening. No wonder he had been incensed.

She blushed in shame as heat suffused her body. And she had, she admitted to herself, actually been jealous of those unknown women who had lain with Raoul de Chalais. Which of the women had it been? Or had he not slept in the hall at all, but spent the night somewhere else? She would never know.

But he had made his position abundantly clear. Tears pricked her lids, foolish tears of frustration. She need not have worried; he had no interest in the likes of her, an inexperienced maid.

How could she face either man on the morrow? Yet she must. The only way to restore the old relationships would be to apologise.

Whatever it cost her, she must make the effort.

She made it at the earliest possible moment. Raoul accepted her apology with kindly indulgence. She seethed.

But later, when she asked herself what other attitude he could have taken, she saw that kindly indulgence, as to a child who had misbehaved and was sorry, had probably been the right one. It had relegated the entire episode to the realms of inconsequence and allowed them to resume their previous, easy relationship without loss of face on either side.

Well, she had lost face, she supposed, but since the matter had been treated with such indifference it scarcely showed. She was still chatelaine of the castle, and still spent much of her time at the Chevalier's side acting as interpreter. Soon, she thought, that duty would no longer be necessary. An apt pupil, he was quickly picking up spoken Welsh just as he had English. He understood and spoke the latter almost like a native, but she doubted his ability to write it. His retinue included an English priest, Sir Graham, to do any necessary correspondence and keep meticulous account of the Chevalier's military expenditure. He acted as chaplain to the company, which was just as well, since Rhun's cleric had departed the castle with his master. Not that the Chevalier could not write. He often scrawled notes in French, in a spidery foreign hand.

Katrine knew her letters, could read a little, write her name, make a simple list and attempt a note, but her formal education had abruptly ended when she had fallen into Rhun ab Brechfa's hands. However, native wit and intelligence got her by, and she scarcely noticed the lack as she struggled to run the household. Some ladies who ran much larger establishment than Dryslwyn could not read or write a single word apart from their name. Nevertheless, she made a friend of Sir Graham, an older man, stocky and greying, who had been a warrior priest ever since taking holy orders, and in her spare moments practised what he had been persuaded to teach her.

Raoul caught her at it one day as she sat in a corner of the hall, fingers stiff with cold, tongue caught between her small white teeth, copying out, on a scrap of old parchment, the words the clerk had given her.

'What do you, maid?' he demanded, bending over her to see.

Katrine jumped. Her breath caught in her lungs and a tide of heat suffused her body. She struggled to answer him but it was several moments before her breath escaped its prison and she was able to speak.

'Nothing, lord.'

'Nothing? Methinks you speak a lie!'

She knew by the tone of his voice that he was teasing. She tried to pull herself together, but how could she with him bending over her, trying to read what she had written?

'I meant, nothing important. Sir Graham is teaching Dai and the other pages and has kindly agreed to help me. He gave me these words to copy out. I wish to improve my reading and writing. I have done none since I was ten.'

'A worthy endeavour,' murmured Raoul, 'but scarcely necessary.'

'You can read and write in your own language, sir, and I wish to be able to do the same in mine!'

'Aye, I received a good education until my father was dispossessed nine years ago, when I was fourteen. The lord I was serving as squire turned me out and I had to find another lord willing to accept my loyalty to him and to the King.'

'Dispossessed?' queried Katrine. 'I had heard you had lost your family estates, but not how or why.'

'There is scant reason why you should not know, though I seldom speak of it. 'Twas because my foolish father rebelled against the former English King. 'Tis why I now serve Henry. I would show my loyalty and regain my father's lands in Aquitaine, be entitled to call myself the Seigneur Raoul de Chalais, not merely messire, as I am now.'

Katrine smiled up at him, her composure fast returning. 'I shall address you as seigneur, lord. It seems we both need to regain a lost inheritance.'

'Yours, I believe, is still secure.'

'I was sitting near enough to overhear your conversation with the Brecon steward and was so afraid he would think you unduly inquisitive! But I was reassured. I thank you, seigneur, for asking.'

A faint pink flush stained the Chevalier's cheek-bones and he straightened, releasing her from his overpowering proximity. Although he did not exactly look uncomfortable, Katrine suspected he was. Which meant he had made the enquiries for his own benefit, not hers. He had wanted to make sure she was still worth a substantial ransom. There was no reason to feel depressed. What else had she expected?

'I was curious,' he said, shrugging. 'I will leave you to your studies, Lady Katrine.'

With a small bow he turned and strode off, calling for one of his men.

A stir ran throughout the castle the day Sir Gruffydd and his squire returned with the horses and mules. Myfanwy looked pleased to see him, although Katrine suspected that she had not missed her husband much. He was a rather overbearing person, who often indulged in aggrieved silences.

Raoul greeted him coolly. 'We had become concerned for you, Sir Gruffydd. You are some days overdue.'

'The weather, lord, has been atrocious. The Tywi has already overflowed its banks, the roads are thick with mud. I am surprised that the journey did not take longer.'

Raoul nodded, accepting the excuse, at least outwardly. 'Your return is welcome, sir. We have need of the animals ourselves now the river is unnavigable. Dai, fetch Sir Gruffydd a horn of ale.'

Dai, who had been hovering nervously behind Raoul, scuttled away. By now Raoul could have given that order in Welsh himself, but Dai was fast learning English and the Chevalier liked to give the lad a chance to exercise his new understanding. Katrine felt superfluous.

Sir Gruffydd reacted violently when he saw the boy. 'Dai!' he bawled. 'What do you here?'

Dai stopped, looking scared but defiant. Before he could respond the Chevalier waved him about his business and addressed the Welsh knight.

'He was discovered long after you had left, Sir Gruffydd. He begged to remain and I could see no reason to refuse his plea. I had no wish to dispatch an escort to return him to Rhun ab Brechfa, knowing the reception he would receive, even had I known where to send him. He will do well enough here until he can be returned to his parents.'

'Who placed him in the care of the lord Rhun!'

'Who abused his power over the lad. I will not argue
further. The boy remains here as my page. You will
treat him kindly.'

'I had not thought you soft, Chevalier,' sneered Sir
Gruffydd.

'Neither should you now, my friend,' responded
Raoul quietly, a dangerous glint in his eye. 'But there
is a difference between softness and pity, as every
knight should know. Wrongs should be righted. Rhun
treated the lad ill. I choose to right that wrong. You,
Sir Knight, are at liberty to break your oath and rejoin
your old master. But an you remain here you will
acknowledge my authority. I shall hold you to your
word.'

'Husband.' Myfanwy had glided forward, her skirts
barely disturbing the rushes on the floor. 'Dai is happy
now. The Chevalier is a just master. Be at peace.'

Gruffydd appeared to relax. He shrugged and
laughed. 'I apologise, Chevalier. 'Twas the shock of
seeing the lad. The lady Eiluned was most concerned
for him. But if my wife is happy with his continued
presence, then so am I. I abide by my oath of loyalty.'

Raoul nodded. His green eyes studied the man
before him, assessing the worth of his declaration. He
gave a faint smile.

'Very well, Sir Gruffydd. Welcome back.'

CHAPTER SIX

As CHRISTMAS approached, Katrine turned her attention to organising the necessary feast. It could not be
as sumptuous as she would like because of the circumstances, but some kind of effort was required and
almost anything would be an improvement on the
celebrations she had known during her time with
Rhun. The Welsh, English and Gascons had their own
traditions, but they could all share the mass, which
the Chevalier's priest would celebrate, and the feast
which would follow.

In an effort to ensure that the food met with
everyone's approval she consulted with Myfanwy and
the two cooks, who were now working together almost
amicably. All were agreed on one thing. They must
have at least two oxen to roast.

'And sucking-pigs,' said Yves the Gascon.

'We cannot spare them,' said Katrine decisively.
'The new sows' litters must be allowed to grow to full
size to feed us later.'

Yves looked about to sulk while Morgan, the Welsh
cook, smirked.

'You will have to make do with Welsh lamb,' he
crowed.

'The lambs the Chevalier acquired must be allowed
to mature too,' decreed Katrine, and, seeing the
sudden scowl on Morgan's face, explained, 'When
food is abundant such luxuries are in order, but in

present circumstances, with the countryside denuded of livestock, we must be sensible and allow the rams to grow and the ewes to breed.'

Myfanwy nodded. 'The lady Katrine speaks good sense.'

'Then what would you suggest, my lady?' enquired Yves, still truculent. 'All the animals brought in, except the breeding livestock and the young, were killed last month for lack of fodder.'

'And the meat has been smoked or salted. If necessary we must make do with that. But several rams were left alive. One must be retained for breeding but you may slaughter the rest,' decided Katrine.

'They will provide little enough meat to go round, look you,' grumbled Morgan.

'I know. I will speak to the Chevalier. Mayhap he can organise a hunt.'

'There'll be precious little game left running wild,' grunted the Welsh cook.

Katrine knew that well enough. The entire countryside had been scoured almost clean of food. 'Then we shall have to make do with other dishes. Use your ingenuity—make potages, bake pies and flans, both sweet and savoury. We have butter and cheese in plenty, milk and cream, fish and flour. Even poultry and eggs since the new flock was imported. The Chevalier has obtained plentiful supplies of sugar, dried fruit, herbs and spices. Surely enough to provide us all with a feast worthy to celebrate the birth of Christ!'

'I have my book of receipts,' offered Myfanwy. 'That, with your knowledge, should suffice.'

Both men bowed. 'Ladies,' murmured Yves, his bad

temper dissolved, the light of challenge in his eyes, 'you put us on our mettle.'

'Indeed, so you do. We will produce a feast fit for the King himself!'

Katrine smiled at Morgan's words, left Myfanwy still conferring with the cooks, and went off to find the Chevalier.

Raoul and his men were gathered in the Great Hall servicing their equipment, since the weather outside was atrocious. Constant wind and rain had prevented all but the most hardy from straying far beyond the confines of the inner ward. Katrine remembered the men of the lance keeping watch in the Cambrian mountains and shivered. The duty was not popular and after being relieved the men returned suffering from exposure but, with the resilience of seasoned campaigners, they soon recovered in the shelter and warmth of the castle, even if some of them did continue to wheeze and cough for weeks afterwards and complain of painful joints.

The Tywi was in full flood, the roads almost impassable, but somehow supplies had got through from Carmarthen. The pack-animals and their drovers had arrived sodden, covered in mud up to their hocks and thighs, but, like the soldiers, they were used to such hardship and by the next day had recovered enough to begin the return journey. Unless snow fell to make the road impassable they would be back in ten days. The castle, housing so many, needed a constant supply of victuals and other goods. Which, Katrine noted, included such things as bows, arrows, pikes, halberds and other weapons for the armoury, horseshoes and metal plate for the smith and armourer, leather for the saddler. When spring came the Chevalier did not intend to be caught unprepared.

He came quickly to her summons, leaving Hugues busy polishing rust from his master's breastplate.

'Something troubles you, lady?'

Briefly, Katrine enunciated the problem.

'Dinefwr has both oxen and deer roaming within its domain,' Raoul mused. 'If this weather would only clear we could ride out to ask the constable to spare us some festive cheer. Mayhap I should send a messenger.'

'Nay, lord! The rain cannot last much longer; it is bound to clear soon. I have so enjoyed riding the palfrey since Sir Gruffydd's return. I would rejoice in such a visit. We could wait another week, at least, before deciding to send a messenger.'

'You think to keep me company when I go?' drawled Raoul.

'You did say we, lord.'

'But we need not necessarily include you, my dove. I should, naturally, take a troop of men-at-arms with me and possibly Louis, an he can be spared from his duties here.'

Katrine's discomfort had been rising, but now it reached gigantic proportions. Because he had been indulgent towards her recently she had presumed too much. And the way he called her his dove! 'Twas almost insulting. Her face turned scarlet, only to blanch, for he had rammed home the message that she was subject to his whim.

'You choose to toy with me, seigneur,' she protested hotly, 'to play with words. You earlier promised me the treat——'

That lazy smile which wrought such havoc with her senses broke out. 'And you shall have it, maiden,' he assured her softly. 'But methinks I am entitled to recompense for such indulgence. . .'

'Recompense?' spluttered Katrine, her anger fuelled by his teasing, for there was only one kind of reward she could envisage and to imply that he intended to claim it was beyond a jest.

'Why so incensed, my dove?' murmured Raoul. 'Would you not enjoy a kiss?'

Before she could collect herself to make a reply he had leaned forward and touched her mouth with his.

It was scarcely a kiss at all but it ravished her. She gasped and staggered back deeper into the recess where they stood, needing the support of the wall, wildy hoping that no one had noticed the Chevalier's action. Although the hall was full most men were occupied, and they stood in shadow. He would not have dared to steal a kiss otherwise.

'How dare you?' she stormed, echoing her thought, channelling her overwrought reaction into indignation.

He stood, relaxed, amused, refusing to take her protest seriously. 'You seek to impugn my honour once more, Katrine?' he said softly, but that dangerous edge was in his voice. 'You still think I have designs on your maidenhead?' Katrine gasped in shock and his smile widened. 'You should be more discreet, my dove. I have accepted your apology once. You have no guarantee that I shall do so again. What a deal of pother over one small, brotherly kiss.'

It had not been brotherly. She knew it; he knew it. She would not apologise. She lifted her head and spoke with all the new authority at her disposal. 'If you will excuse me, seigneur, I am needed elsewhere.'

His smile taunted. 'Are you? How very convenient. Do not try my temper too far, my dove. I may be tempted to return you to the state in which I found you, or even to send you back into Rhun ab Brechfa's care.'

The internal gymnastics of Katrine's heart and stomach brought on sharp nausea. But she would not give in to it, show her terror or plead with him. 'I would rather that than be ravished by you, seigneur,' she returned with dignity. 'He did at least intend to unite me in honourable marriage with one of his sons.'

'Why, so he did,' Raoul's voice drawled again. Mockery shone from those brilliant eyes. Mesmerising eyes. Katrine could not look away. 'Dafydd might suit you well as a husband, maiden, since he would be incapable of bedding you at all.'

Tears, all unbidden, sprang to Katrine's eyes. 'You are unkind,' she choked. 'You mock and tease me and there is naught I can do to prevent it.'

''Tis well you realise it, my dove. But remember it is teasing. An I do anything truly to offend you, then my apology will be abject.'

Arrested, she stared into his eyes. He had sounded curt, almost derisive, yet she did not doubt he meant what he said.

Equally curtly she retorted, 'I trust you will give me no chance to demand it.'

'An you do not try my patience, maiden. Now, let us call it quits and forget this ridiculous quarrel.'

He held out his hand, his eyes commanding her to take it.

It was a gesture of reconciliation, the kind he would offer a comrade, and she reacted to it automatically.

She should have known better. The pain on contact ran up her arm and pierced her chest. A pain she could well endure, a pain to relish. But she snatched her fingers away and made her escape, completely confused by both the man and the emotions he roused in her. Something inside her seemed to be unfurling; strange new feelings held her body in thrall. She had protested herself a woman grown, but she was not—not yet. He had been right to infer that she knew nothing of the emotions which should exist between a man and a woman. But now—now she understood what was happening to her. Raoul was teaching her that there was more to achieving womanhood than mere puberty. Womanhood came awkwardly, painfully, bringing with it strange feelings, curious longings, unspecified desires.

Raoul stood watching her departure, cursing himself. What had possessed him to kiss the wench, to succumb to a long-standing temptation justified by his telling himself that he intended it as a slight reprimand, a token of his mastery over her, that was all? It had devastated her; she was too naïve to hide her reaction. He knew full well how women responded to his advances, had made enough capital out of it in the past. As a knight sworn to defend the honour of such as Katrine he should have been more careful of her.

As for himself—never for a moment had he expected his action to rebound, to release surprising emotions he would rather not acknowledge. His response had been astonishingly powerful but he had an advantage—he was practised in hiding his feelings, covering them with mockery. The last thing he wanted was to become emotionally involved with the wench. Now he had to feel guilty as well as—well, protective, and, he must admit it, tempted. He'd been battling attraction ever since he'd first truly noticed her, when she'd shown such pride and spirit in the face of Rhun's cruelty and his own scathing dismissal of her as worthless. But all along she had been merely a pawn in his game of retribution. Once he had levelled the score with the d'Evreux family he would have no further use for Katrine Lawtye, admirable as she was in every way. A young, innocent virgin had no part to play in his personal plans for the future. He had long ago decided that when he wed, as he must one day, a youngish, wealthy widow would suit his purposes best, bringing with her as she would not only riches to restore his estates but experience to warm his bed.

He must, he acknowledged, tread warily where Katrine was concerned. Her presence was troublesome, and in other circumstances he would have lost no time in dispatching her back to England for the substantial reward certain to be forthcoming. But no ordinary maiden had fallen into his hands, rather a gift from God, so it had seemed, and he needed her both as introduction to his enemies and as the instrument of his revenge.

No, he could not send her away, but he must resist the temptation to toy with her, to succumb to the challenge of her pride, her courage and her beauty. She was, after all, under his protection. A fact that for a few moments he had forgotten, or chosen to disregard.

Raoul, he told himself irritably, Louis was right.

You are becoming soft, or careless. You can afford to be neither.

A flurry of rain came in from a damaged shutter, sprinkling droplets on his head and shoulders. With a muttered oath he shifted away, striding back to join his squire.

It is this cursed waiting, he thought, being cooped up here for the winter, forced to curb my impatience for action. But once Christmas is over spring will soon come, the campaign will begin and we shall leave this bleak fortress to rejoin Prince Henry for a final push against the remnants of Glendower's rebellion. Before summer's end I shall have exacted vengeance and be rid of the wench. Meanwhile, I suppose I shall have to take her to Dinefwr, since I cannot break my word.

The rain ceased, the sun broke through, bringing deceptive brilliance and sparkle to the water, for its rays were too weak to thaw ground hardened by a sudden, heavy frost.

The horses, skittish after long days spent in their stables, at most being exercised round the bailey by dripping, miserable grooms, were as delighted as their riders to be out in the crisp air as the sun rose, picking their way over furrowed, treacherous ground where one false step on the iron-hard mud could result in a fall, a broken leg, disaster.

Myfanwy rode beside Katrine. Since they would be returning before nightfall both she and Louis had been allowed to join the party, Raoul considering that those left behind could manage perfectly well on their own for one day. Sir Gruffydd rode behind the ladies, leading their mounted escort, with the men's singing echoing cheerfully across the valley. Raoul and Louis rode ahead, followed by Hugues and Dai, the boy astride a small Welsh pony.

Raoul had scarcely spoken to her since that kiss, distancing himself from her. She had sat stiffly beside him at meals, acutely aware of him, wishing she could absent herself from his proximity, which she found increasingly painful. He seemed not one whit disturbed by her presence, behaved with the necessary courtesy but otherwise ignored her most of the time. While she—to her shame—she longed for him to repeat that kiss, properly. She wanted to discover the full secrets of womanhood, to have *him* show her.

But that was impossible. She would lose her reputation, her prospects of a good marriage, her future. And for what? Who was Raoul de Chalais? A Gascon knight, no more, despite his promotion to banneret and seigneurial claims. She had already decided she would never be allowed to wed him. Even if she wished to. Which, she stoutly protested to herself, she most certainly did not.

What, she wondered, had brought on this sudden preoccupation with marriage? Until Raoul de Chalais had entered her life she had thought no further than the fact, the ceremony during which she would be united with some shadowy male figure whose household she would be expected to run. Well, she was running a large household now, and small thanks she received for it! But efficiency in that direction had nothing to do with the intimate side of marriage, about which she had been too young to speculate when she had set out on that fateful journey to her prospective bridegroom's home.

Her new, disturbing awareness was all the Chevalier's fault. She glowered at his straight back, clad in padded jupon under a blue, fur-lined, velvet cloak. Chain-mail protected his head and throat—just in case. He rode easily, master of himself and all about him, even Louis, no mean figure of a man himself. But he lacked the Chevalier's panache.

Katrine had worked in the castle long enough to pick up some ripe Welsh oaths. Silently, she used them all, cursing him for his cool indifference to her and her feelings. Beneath the fur-trimmed hood of her heavy cope her face was set in mutinous lines, her dove-grey eyes brooding, intent on the man ahead.

Her palfrey's hoof slipped on the frozen ground, bringing her thoughts abruptly back to the task in hand. Myfanwy, beside her, guided her own mount, a castle hack, round a large pothole.

'The way ahead could be dangerous,' she remarked. 'Take care, my lady.'

Katrine glanced sharply at her companion. Did her words hold a double meaning? No, probably not. Myfanwy appeared quite guileless, although her gaze had lifted to rest on the Chevalier's broad back.

'It is so cold,' Katrine said, wishing to divert Myfanwy's attention. 'My fingers are frozen to the reins!'

'And my foot to its stirrup,' laughed Myfanwy in return, shifting her gaze to glance down at the toe of her riding-boot. 'But what a splendid morning to be out!'

They continued to chat in a desultory manner about the household at Dryslwyn, and to speculate about Dinefwr. Myfanwy had never been there before.

'But I am told it is larger than Dryslwyn,' she said.

'That,' grinned Katrine, 'would not be difficult!'

'There is an excellent view of the castle from here!' exclaimed Myfanwy a few minutes later as they forded a tributary of the Tywi. 'See?'

'Oh, yes! What a splendid sight!'

Set high on a natural outcrop, just like Dryslwyn, Dinefwr stood out against the sun, solid as the rock upon which it was built. A huge round tower rose at one end while several smaller square ones broke the skyline above the rectangular keep.

The approach was tortuous and steep. First they had to climb up to the plain from which the outcrop sprang, then wind their way round its base and on up to the castle itself, from where the flooded Tywi and its valley lay spread before their gaze, as magnificent as it was from Dryslwyn, but here the Black Mountains loomed nearer.

The English constable, Jenkin Hanard, welcomed them warmly while his wife, Elizabeth, offered refreshment in the form of a caudle, since their journey had been cold and dinner would not be served for an hour or so.

Katrine drank the hot, spiced wine, thickened with ground almonds and eggs, sitting beside the flames leaping from the central hearth. She found it delicious. Warmth spread through her and she sighed her content.

Soon, the Chevalier and Louis Dubois departed with Jenkin Hanard to inspect the herd of distinctive wild cattle which ranged the plateau on which the castle stood. The white oxen, with their long horns and black ears, were guarded against poachers as strenuously as the castle against insurgents. But the constable had agreed to allow the Chevalier to drive a couple back to Dryslwyn, there to be slaughtered for the Christmas feast.

Katrine watched the men's departure with mixed feelings. She would so much have liked to accompany them to see the herd. Yet at the same time she was reluctant to leave the warm comfort of the fire. So mayhap it was as well she had not been included in the party. Dai, too, had been left behind. He attached himself to her and sat on a stool at her feet. Myfanwy, quite content to enjoy the warmth of the fire while the men went about their business, dozed.

The little group attracted the curiosity of the regular inmates of the castle. Elizabeth Hanard and another lady came to join them while those knights and soldiers not engaged in other duties lounged about, dicing and drinking. The Chevalier had given no order for her to conceal her identity, had introduced her by her true name and title, and Elizabeth Hanard, a sensible woman of middle age and no great beauty, was full of curiosity. Trying to satisfy her hostess's good-natured interest, Katrine decided she would rather have been presented simply as Demoiselle Kate.

Raoul had decided that no harm could be done by allowing Katrine's true identity to be known. Winter had well and truly set in, making communication with England wellnigh impossible, and Hanard could not deprive him of his prize. If word should reach England, nothing could be done before spring. And, mayhap, if word of Katrine's survival should reach her guardians and others, it would be no bad thing. They

would come seeking him out and save him the trouble
of finding them. He wondered now why he had been
so keen to keep her identity secret in Carmarthen.
Had the Brecon steward known who she was he could
have done nothing about it. On the other hand there
had been time for him to report and for a Lancastrian
official to be sent to Dryslwyn to negotiate her release,
and that would not have suited his purposes. No, all
things considered, he had been right. Things were
better as they were.

Having chosen two fine oxen, they were now stalk-
ing the deer which also ranged the castle's domain,
keeping upwind. Venison would augment their table
well. He and Louis moved silently among the trees,
Hanard a pace or two behind. Hanard's huntsmen
surrounded the deer's haunt, ready to turn them back
should they be disturbed and try to escape.

A group of does stood grazing quietly in a clearing.
Silently, Raoul and Louis knocked arrows to their
bowstrings. Together, they aimed. 'Loose,' breathed
Raoul.

The arrows whispered through the air; the does
lifted startled heads but too late. Two of them fell to
the ground, arrows through their hearts.

'Excellent shooting,' praised Hanard as the remainder of the does fled into the trees.

Raoul strode forward, drawing his hunting-knife. If
the animals were not quite dead he would put them
swiftly out of their misery.

Having killed their prey, the knights left the huntsmen to skin and gut the deer where they had fallen.
Deer could not be driven like cattle, so carcasses must
be carried back to be hung in one of Dryslwyn's stores.

The cold weather would help to keep the meat fresh until the feast.

The hunting-party returned to the castle in good time for dinner. The gladness on Katrine's face when she saw him enter the Great Hall gave Raoul a strange feeling, a mixture of pleasure and impatience. He did not want her to rely on his company. He had done much to encourage this dependence in his first weeks at Dryslwyn and now he was regretting it. Because her attachment was not welcome. He had already been betrayed into showing too much concern, into indulging a natural inclination to kiss an attractive wench. When spring came she would swiftly pass out of his keeping. Ruthlessly he pushed the stab of regret aside as one of weakness, and took his place at the board with Hanard, leaving Katrine to the company of the ladies.

After the meal, prior to taking horse back to Dryslwyn, the Hanards offered to show their visitors round outside the castle.

"Twill make a pleasant stroll,' suggested Elizabeth Hanard brightly. 'You must see my pleasaunce, Lady Katrine.'

'And you must inspect the stables, Chevalier,' smiled Hanard. 'Come, don your cloaks and follow me.'

Once outside Dai stood, undecided which party to follow. Katrine went down a slope with the Ladies Elizabeth and Myfanwy while the Chevalier disappeared towards the stables, located near the gatehouse.

'Come with me,' said a rasping voice above Dai's head. 'I have something to show you.' Dai looked up into the ugly countenance of one of Hanard's older knights. A beefy hand descended on his shoulder. 'This way,' urged the knight, shifting his grip to Dai's arm and dragging the boy down the slope Katrine had just taken, which led to the inner ward. This ran behind and to one side of the castle, ten feet or so below its massive walls. At first Dai obeyed, though reluctantly. He was, after all, following in the footsteps of the lady Katrine. But at the bottom of the slope the man began to lead him towards a thicket growing on the far side of the ward, where the ground sloped away. The lady Katrine was disappearing down that same slope, but taking a narrow path much further along and was already almost out of sight, hidden by a dense growth of bushes.

'No,' said Dai, pulling up and attempting to disengage himself. 'I cannot. I must follow my mistress.' He gazed longingly at Katrine's disappearing back.

'She's with others; she won't miss you, lad. Come along with me; I'll show you some fun.'

'How?' demanded Dai suspiciously. He did not like the look of the man, who stank of ale and sweat. Not a bit like the Chevalier, who often took a bath. Dai had the job of filling the tub with hot water, so he knew.

The man's grip on his arm slackened, became subtly caressing. With his other hand he removed Dai's cap and ran dirty fingers through the lad's dark curling hair. His voice became softly persuasive. 'I'll soon show you. You'd like to be stroked a bit, wouldn't you? Like this?'

His fingers fondled the nape of Dai's neck, sending a shiver of revulsion down the lad's back. Dai wrenched his head aside, made a grab at his hat and planted it firmly back on his head, pulling it well down about his ears. 'No!' he gasped. 'Let go of me! I must go to the Chevalier!' The Chevalier's name might strike fear into his tormentor.

The man chuckled. 'You're not going anywhere, my lad, except with me. He won't mind me giving you a good time.'

'He will!' By this time Dai had begun to panic. He wasn't too young to have heard stories of what could happen to unprotected pages, even to have seen it happen, and he knew he was in trouble. He began to struggle for his freedom but his captor simply picked him up and put him under his arm. There were few men of the garrison about and those that were simply laughed, enjoying the horseplay. What harm if Jack Martin had some fun with the boy? Jack didn't like girls, but they all knew no page was safe from him.

Dai cried out, indignant at the humiliation, struggling valiantly, clawing and kicking as Martin tried to carry him off.

Down in the pleasaunce, Katrine heard his cries. 'Wasn't that Dai?' she demanded anxiously of Myfanwy.

'It sounded like him,' agreed the older woman.

'It could have been some other child,' said Elizabeth, a worried frown wrinkling her brow.

'Whoever it is seems in need of help.'

So saying, Katrine began to struggle up the slope, cursing the flowing skirt of her gown, the flapping of her cope as she tried to hurry. She was sure it was Dai and he sounded desperate. The lady Elizabeth's voice floated after her, calling to her to be careful, to wait for her.

Katrine erupted back on to the narrow ward in time to see Dai wriggle free from Jack Martin's arms. Quick as a flash he was off, darting round the side of the castle with Martin in pursuit. Men were standing round grinning, making no attempt to help the boy.

'Dai!' cried Katrine. 'I'm here! What ails you?'

Dai did not waste breath on a reply. Perhaps he did not hear her, intent as he was on escape. Martin ignored her intervention and continued his triumphant pursuit of the lad into what he knew to be a trap.

Except that it wasn't, quite. Dai, desperate, stopped short before the mass of scrub fringing the edge of the almost sheer drop to the river, looked wildly round and saw a narrow track to his left which ran along the high embankment at the foot of the castle wall. Neither the precipitous decline on one side nor the protruding bastion round which he would have to crawl daunted him. Escape from that dreadful man's repellent handling was all he cared about.

Martin cursed, hesitated, then, seeing there was no possible way the boy could pass the bastion in safety, since it ran straight down into the face of the bluff, bellowed his elation and followed. Katrine, seeing him grab the lad's collar and cuff him as Dai tried desperately to evade his persecutor, cried out in anguish. But Martin, beyond all reason, threw Dai down on the narrow path and fell on top of him.

'Help him!' cried Katrine.

She glimpsed Elizabeth Hanard puffing into sight, but none of the watchers, slowly gravitating towards the scene of such rich entertainment, seemed inclined to do more than crane their necks to see better. With an exasperated shout she launched herself to the rescue.

Gathering her cloak about her, she scrambled up a slippery bank to reach the track then made her way along it, ignoring the vertiginous, yawning emptiness waiting to receive her should she take a false step. Dai was still struggling beneath the man, who was hampered by the need to remain on the trodden earth, the only marginally level piece of ground around.

She reached his feet. Shouted and kicked his boot. He took no notice. She couldn't move round him; there was no room. But then he straddled his legs wide to keep himself from rolling and Katrine stepped between them. She leaned forward and grasped a handful of his lank hair, dislodging his round felt hat which went bounding down towards the riverbank so far below.

She didn't dare think about that. She just tangled her fingers in his greasy locks and held on tightly, tugging as hard as she could.

'Let him go!' she screamed. 'You treacherous, perverted lecher!'

Dai couldn't understand those English words, but Martin did. He cursed loudly and thrashed his legs out. 'Get off, you stupid whore!' he yelled back.

Buffeted by his flailing legs and kicking feet, Katrine lost her balance. She fell on top of the man, still clinging to his hair, but her grip had weakened. He heaved himself up and threw her off.

She could do nothing to stop herself. Screaming, she caught despairingly at each small scrubby bush she passed on her way down but it seemed nothing could stop her from bumping and rolling right to the bottom. And then, mercy of mercies, her headlong tumble stopped. It took her several dazed moments to realise that she had come to rest against one of the more thriving bushes which clung to the slope. When she looked up she could see the castle towering some fifty feet above. She did not dare to look down. She did not dare to move, even to discover whether she had any broken bones. She felt bruised, beaten all over, and she knew that the knight's spur had jabbed into her calf because the wound was throbbing painfully and she could feel a warm trickle of blood.

She could hear voices ringing out above, women's and men's, and when she looked fearfully up again could see figures lining the track from which she'd fallen. The small, huddled body must be Dai. She couldn't hear his sobs but she could imagine them. His attacker stood at bay at the point of someone's sword.

Then everything went dark. There was a rushing in her ears. She knew no more.

CHAPTER SEVEN

KATRINE roused to the sound of an anxious voice calling her name.

'Katrine! Katrine, wake up, sweeting! Are you hurt?'

Someone was slapping her face, gently but persistently. Katrine opened her eyes before remembering where she was, and when she did promptly shut them again.

But then realisation dawned. The Chevalier had come. It was his face leaning over her, his hands now chafing hers, his voice speaking to her in a tone she'd often dreamed of hearing. No trace of crisp authority, of arrogant command remained. It was filled with tender concern.

'Raoul!' she murmured.

For the first time she called him by his name but was not aware that she did. She lifted a heavy hand to touch the anxious face so near her own. 'Oh, Raoul! You came.'

'Of course I did.' Now he sounded brusque, impatient, concern a thing of the past. 'You should not have risked your life for Dai. It was a stupid thing to do.'

She shook her head, colour returning to her face rapidly as awareness of him brought sweet confusion to her senses, making her speak rapidly, breathlessly.

'I had to. No one else cared. They'd have watched and cheered.'

'Not Elizabeth Hanard,' he corrected her. 'She ordered the man Martin's arrest and sent for her husband. I, of course, was with him and came at once. But, now, can you move? Are you badly hurt?'

Bathed in delightful, languorous content—he had come personally to her rescue and spoken to her so— Katrine gingerly flexed her arms and legs and winced. 'I don't think so. My leg was damaged but it is nothing much.' The content vanished as realisation of their precarious position returned to her. 'Raoul, how did you get down here? How are we to get back?'

'Do not worry, Katrine. See, I have a rope tied about my waist with two stout men at the top to hold it. There was room for no more on that narrow track with the embankment so close behind. But do not fear. They will haul us up, with what help I can give.' His arms went round her. 'Hold tight. Are you ready?'

Katrine nodded. In his arms she felt secure, safe. Without thinking, she wound hers about his neck, pressing her face into his shoulder. Once they had arrived at the castle he had discarded all his armour. She sank into the comfort of his padded jupon, knowing that beneath it his iron-hard muscles were tensed ready to perform any task asked of them. His arms felt like metal bands, holding her to him. Trustfully, deliciously, she relaxed against him as he called to the men above.

Slowly, torturously slowly, they began to draw the double burden up. Raoul helped by digging in elbows, knees and feet wherever they could obtain a purchase. The hard ground gave little aid but tufts of coarse grass and those scrubby bushes which had failed to break Katrine's fall did provide minimal footholds at their roots.

A final heave brought them within reach of eager helping hands. For a moment Katrine was detached from Raoul's arms. She stood swaying, supported by Louis Dubois. Dai had disappeared, as had his molester.

Next instant Raoul stood beside her, breathing hard, smiling jauntily. 'Come, Katrine. I will carry you back to the hall.'

'There is no need——' began Katrine, but her objection was swept aside as her other rescuers retreated to safer ground, leaving the way clear for Raoul to swing her up and carry her to the ward, Louis following closely behind. Katrine made no further protest but wound her arms round the Chevalier's neck, only too glad to luxuriate in the intimate closeness once more.

Escorted by an anxious Jenkin Hanard and his wife, Raoul strode round the castle to its entrance, carrying her as though he bore no weight at all.

'Follow me!' cried the lady Elizabeth, and led him to the solar, where Katrine was laid gently on the big curtained bed.

'Take good care of her,' murmured Raoul as he tenderly deposited his burden and prepared to depart. 'The lady Myfanwy is with Dai, but I must tend my page and see that his persecutor is suitably chastised.'

'My husband will sentence Martin to be flogged,' said Elizabeth flatly.

Katrine shuddered. Such a punishment was severe, but surely deserved.

Raoul's hand lingered lightly, caressingly upon her

brow, his figure, his head, glowing in the radiance of the fire burning brightly in the brazier behind him. 'We must begin our journey back in an hour. Will you be fit. . .?'

He left the question unfinished. Katrine smiled up at him.

'Quite fit enough to sit a horse, seigneur. I am bruised and scratched but not otherwise hurt apart from the wound to my calf, which I am certain is not serious. But your garments are ruined,' she wailed, seeing the rents and stains marring the perfection of jupon and hose. 'You are not hurt?'

Raoul brushed at his filthy elbows and knees, at the stains marring the length of his hose, the side of his jupon. 'Nay, I suffered barely a scratch. My garments took the brunt and they can be replaced, though I shall look a sorry sight on the return journey!' This was said with a flippant, rueful laugh which tugged alarmingly at Katrine's heart-strings.

'I will tend the lady Katrine's injury immediately you have left,' promised the lady Elizabeth, giving the young knight a gentle push in the direction of the door.

'If she needs to remain I will have the lady Myfanwy stay to keep her company and come again myself to escort her back to Dryslwyn.'

'The lady Katrine would be welcome to recover here but, i'faith, I do not believe there will be need.' Elizabeth hustled him from the room and smiled archly at Katrine.'That young man shows great tenderness for you, my dear.'

Katrine pulled a face, denying the assertion, though she thought so too, for, despite his brusque manner afterwards, she could not forget those first moments when he had thought her unconscious or dead. But she could not allow herself to hope. Already she was regretting being so foolish as to luxuriate in his embrace, since now her whole being cried out to belong to him and that could never be. 'It is because I am a valuable prize, lady, no more.'

'Tosh,' responded Elizabeth roundly as she removed Katrine's cope and lifted her skirt to examine her injury. 'He may not know it but he loves you, Katrine. 'Twas plain for all to see. He nearly went berserk when he discovered what had befallen you.'

Raoul, berserk? Katrine had to smile despite herself. 'You mistake, lady.'

'Oh, it took the form of icy condemnation and curt orders which were entirely to the point, but there was no mistaking his rage and anxiety.'

'For a valuable prize.'

'You underrate your value as a woman, Lady Katrine. Charming, loving, brave. . .what warm-blooded man could resist?'

'Plenty, lady. I see no sign of devotion in Messire Louis Dubois or Sir Gruffydd or any other of the Chevalier's men—lust, mayhap, but that is different—and there was certainly none in Rhun ab Brechfa!'

'Oh, them! They lack the discrimination! And you, Lady Katrine. . .you may be his hostage, but I believe you have a fondness for the man who is holding you. What maid would not be captivated by the dazzling Chevalier, Raoul de Chalais?'

Katrine did not trouble to contradict this statement; she had already noted the devastating effect the Chevalier had on most women. Nevertheless. . . 'I like him well enough when he is charming and kind,' she admitted, wincing as Elizabeth pulled down her stocking and began to dab at her wound with a cloth wrung out in clean water, 'but he can be so cold, so. . .so autocratic and demanding!'

'He is a man of authority, child. He can be tender, too, as he has just shown. There, I think that is clean now. Particles of wool had become embedded in the wound and the spur was probably dirty. If I spread this nettle salve over it that should heal it.'

Katrine watched as the green ointment was rubbed into the nasty gash the rowel had made. 'Thank you, lady.'

'Now, if I bind it up you should have no trouble. You're a strong, healthy girl not prone to infections, I imagine.'

'No, I am not. And the Chevalier's priest has skill in herbs as well as letters.'

'Excellent. Now, my dear, mayhap you would like your surcoat removed so that my woman may clean and iron it while you rest. She already has your cope.' Like the Chevalier's, Katrine's clothes showed signs of soil and grass-stains. Mayhap the woman could improve its appearance. 'You will need to cleanse your face and hands, too, and rub savle into the scratches. Let me help you.'

Katrine allowed her outer garment to be taken off and then stumbled to the stand holding a clean bowl of water and made her ablutions. She carried a comb in the pouch hung at her waist and used it to tidy her hair. When she had finished she turned and smiled at Elizabeth Hanard. 'Thank you again, lady.'

Thrusting her thanks, aside, Elizabeth shooed her

back to the bed. 'And now I will leave you to rest. You need to recover your strength for the journey.'

Katrine lay back against the pillows, wishing that what the lady Elizabeth had said was true. That Raoul loved her. But even if he did, what good would that do? Only the lower orders could wed where they liked; such freedom was forbidden a lady born.

He could offer her courtly love and she could bask in his adoration, wedded to another or not. But that was not what she wanted. Neither, she imagined, would Raoul be inclined to indulge in such romantic folly. He was a man of action, a man of passion, not some simpering, lovesick squire willing to sit at his lady's feet and adore but not touch.

But as she drifted off into a healing sleep her dreams were all of him

The moment she saw him again those dreams shattered. He behaved with the utmost courtesy, showing kindness and concern, but in such a distant manner as to deny the warmth there had been between them earlier. There was no hint now of the tone she had so longed to hear. She might well have imagined the tenderness, the steely, possessive arms about her, the strong beating of his heart against hers.

Yet she knew she had not, that his present manner was a front, though whether meant to conceal true, deep-felt feelings he could no more afford than she, or to hide an embarrassing display of momentary unwarranted emotion, she could not tell. The latter, she supposed. For a time, while her life had been at risk, he had been overcome by the need to rescue his valuable hostage and perhaps inclined to think her dear to him. But with the crisis over he had withdrawn.

If only there weren't this strange tension between them. Then, mayhap, she could have enjoyed the easy friendship of the early days, when she had followed him everywhere as his interpreter, before the visit to Carmarthen. 'Twas then he had first withdrawn. Again after her disastrous suspicions on their return. Then she had alienated him by her reaction to his kiss. But this time she had done nothing.

Unless her response to his holding her, her calling him by his name—she had realised she had afterwards—had caused him to think her acquiescent where before she had objected to the slightest impropriety. But then surely he would attempt to make the most of her complaisance, not withdraw himself? Unless, of course, he had spoken nothing but the truth on those occasions when he had given her cause for disquiet and she truly was safe from his amorous attentions.

Her body hurt all over and her head ached. How glad she'd be to be back at Dryslwyn and able to retreat to her pallet. She wished she might never see the Chevalier again. Life under Rhun had been physically hard but at least it had left her heart and mind undisturbed by all the emotions that Raoul de Chalais roused.

The return journey seemed never-ending, but for her was lightened by the sight of Raoul's soldiers attempting to drive two reluctant oxen before them. He himself rode beside her, impersonally solicitous for her well-being, and on arrival helped her to dismount stiffly from her saddle. She could not disguise the pain afflicting all parts of her body or her need to limp. He assisted her up the steps to the Great Hall and once inside spoke.

'You may use the solar this night, maiden. The bed there will be kinder to your bruises.' When Katrine stared at him disbelievingly, he added curtly, 'You need have no fear that you will be disturbed. Take your woman with you, and Dai too. He needs a quiet night after his unpleasant experience.'

'But. . .I had not thought. . .' She swallowed hard. He thought her still distrustful and she had to put that right. 'I did not believe. . .' She couldn't put it into words but managed a placating smile. 'I was surprised, that was all, for you will need your soft bed yourself tonight, seigneur.'

'Not I.' He grinned suddenly. 'I have slept on the hard ground after receiving far worse injuries than today's bumps and scratches.' His voice softened in response to her bewildered explanation. 'Go, Katrine. Make the most of a comfortable night attended by Dorcas and Dai. I will have victuals sent in to you; you need not appear for supper.'

'I thank you, seigneur,' gulped Katrine. 'Your kindness overwhelms me.'

He made an elaborate bow. 'I am at your service, my dove, always. Until the morrow.'

Always at her service. Did he mean it? Oh, what a strange, difficult man he was! But the bed was soft and held his scent in its covers. Dorcas and Dai ran around after her, Dorcas serving her personal needs, Dai presenting the food brought in by a groom of the chamber, who also changed the linen on the bed and tended the fire. Afterwards, Katrine snuggled down in the depths of the swansdown mattress, aware that despite the change of linen Raoul's presence still pervaded the bed. Dorcas and Dai spread their blankets on truckle-beds and soon silence descended on the room, the sound of revelry still coming from the Great Hall the only thing to disturb their peace. And that was essentially an inoffensive background which soon dissolved into dreams.

Afterwards she suspected that Dorcas had put something in the posset she drank, for she slept soundly until dawn. The other inmates of the castle were already astir and she hastened to leave the sanctuary of the solar so that the Chevalier could return.

In the days that followed she quickly recovered from her experiences, as did Dai, now more devoted to her than ever. In the bustle occasioned by the approaching festivities she saw little of the Chevalier, but when she did he appeared to have devised an approach midway between the distant and the familiar. Coolly friendly, she supposed one could call it, and this she could accept. It was the feeling that they were at odds, the times when he barely spoke to her, that distressed her so.

Everyone, almost without exception, conspired to make Christmas a great event. Outside the weather might have been cold but a thin layer of snow covering the ground only added to the seasonal feeling of cheer, since within the castle it did not matter. Everyone gathered as close as they could to the hearth, where the yule log would burn during the celebrations. Overhead hung festoons of greenery and bright holly berries, which men had been labouring for days to fix to the rafters, together with the pennons of every knight present. On a plastered patch which had, originally, held some other mural, only traces of which had remained, a talented knight had painted the Christ-child in his manger with Mary, Joseph and the animals standing by.

Altogether, thought Katrine, on the eve of Christmas, viewing the result of her organisation and everyone else's labours with distinct pleasure, the Great Hall looked ready for any amusement the Lord of Misrule—a youthful knight appointed by the Chevalier for his cheeky inventiveness—could devise. Ale, mead and wine would flow freely, and dancing, singing and silly games like Hoodman-Blind would all feature, she had no doubt. And then there was the magical mistletoe, so beloved of the Celts, hung in a great bunch over the entrance between the hall screens. Much harmless kissing would go on beneath it once mass was over and the feasting began. Mass was to be read in the Great Hall itself, so that everyone might hear the solemn Latin words—few understanding their meaning but all gaining by the experience. Or so Sir Graham the priest claimed, and who was she to question his wisdom? The high table would be transformed into an altar for the occasion.

Already the celebrations had begun, the noise in the hall become loud and cheerful. Many would be suffering from the effects of drink when mass was said, but then many were seldom sober, and excessive drinking was not a sin from which one needed absolution. A long line of penitents had been confessing to Sir Graham all day, cleansing their souls and doing penance ready to receive the sacrament.

He had heard the confessions in the chapel, sitting behind a screen. The menials, archers and men-at-arms had been followed by the knights, then the ladies, herself included, then Louis Dubois and lastly the Chevalier himself.

Katrine wondered to what sins Raoul had admitted. She herself had named all the usual ones—pride because she did so enjoy wearing the new garments the Chevalier had obtained for her, envy because she coveted a fur-lined cape and boots like his, indolence because she had neglected to attend the holy offices daily and had failed to inspect the stores as often as she should so that a sack of grain had gone mouldy and there had been a panic to obtain a supply of clean rushes for the floors. Her penance had been light; a few extra minutes spent at her devotions. But she had not confessed to her greatest sin, that of resenting the power of her guardians to choose the man she would wed, of being denied the right to order her own life. Or the sin of allowing her thoughts to dally so often on Raoul de Chalais. He had insinuated himself into her mind and she simply could not dislodge him.

'You are looking forward to the morrow?' he asked now, coming up behind her, taking her by surprise.

'Naturally, seigneur,' she replied primly.

'I must congratulate you on the preparations for the festivities, lady. The hall looks quite splendid.'

Katrine looked about her with quiet pride. 'I thank you, seigneur,'

'And would you object, think it an impertinence, were I to kiss you under the mistletoe, lady, since it seems to be a custom here?'

She looked up at him, shocked into silence. She had already decided that she would avoid passing under that bunch of glaucous green berries were he anywhere in the vicinity. Just in case. For she dared not think what effect another of his kisses would have on her.

His green gaze held a whimsical light, half serious, half taunting. She had made a fool of herself in the past over nothing. She would not be so caught this time.

'Of course not, Chevalier,' she said airily, keeping the sudden *frisson* in her tightened nerves under control by sheer will-power. 'Everyone will be doing it, will they not? And you, surely, will be kissing all the ladies?'

His smile told her he appreciated the neat way she had turned the tables. 'Not all. Only those who smell as sweet as you.'

'I have an advantage now, seigneur. I may bathe whenever I choose. I did not smell as sweet when I served Rhun ab Brechfa, but through no fault of my own.'

'You would condemn me, my dove, for eschewing those who are less fortunate? And will you willingly allow every ragged scullion to touch your lovely lips with his?'

Katrine's bold glance dropped. Her shoulders sagged a little. She scarcely noticed his veiled compliment, the endearment which cut through his studied, cool friendliness and would normally have brought resentment to her heart. She was not his dove; he was simply mocking her. 'No, seigneur, I would not. Neither of us will be troubled by such as they. They would not presume—they know their places. So do the archers, the men-at-arms. But some of the knights. . .'

She allowed her sentence to trail off. Some of the knights stank. Most of them kept themselves less than fresh.

'And they,' murmured the voice above her head, 'may wash as oft as they choose. As may their ladies, though many do not take advantage of their good fortune. Mayhap you should abide by my rule.'

'Kiss only those who smell as sweet as you? Would that I had the choice, seigneur. Being a woman, I do not.'

'Neither,' he told her seriously, 'do I. If I truly kissed only those I wanted to, the others would take offence. So you see we shall both have to suffer. But, since tomorrow we shall feast and 'twill be a celebration, for once it must be endured.'

Katrine nodded. He would do his duty, just as she would do hers.

'But now,' he observed, 'it is time for you to seek your couch an you are to rise fresh for early mass.'

'Aye, seigneur. I will bid you a good night.'

He bowed with scrupulous politeness. 'Until the morrow, Lady Katrine.'

Together with the Chevalier, Louis, Myfanwy, Gruffydd, other senior knights and their ladies, if they had one with them, Katrine took her privileged place on one of the benches ranged across the hall. Everyone else would stand, or mayhap squat on the fresh, sweet-smelling rushes which, after the festivities, would be as contaminated with spilled ale, bones, bits of gristle, spittle and dog-droppings as the old marsh which had been cleared out the previous morning.

Those who had slept in the Great Hall had kept up their drinking and dicing until dawn, she suspected, and some were still slumped on the floor in a drunken stupor. The servitors had imbibed what they could, even if it were the dregs left by others. And fornication had probably been rife, judging by the dishevelled state of the women. But with the Chevalier in command the revelry would never be allowed to get out of hand, of that she was convinced. Any rioting or fighting would be nipped in the bud long before it could cause real trouble, and the feasting would not degenerate into an orgy.

After the service Katrine tried to slip away to her room. She was tired to the bone after days of hectic activity and needed to finish her sleep before the carousing and feasting of Christmas Day got under way. So immediately the blessing had been pronounced Katrine edged towards the screens, trying to ignore the bunch of mistletoe hanging above the entry and slide out before anyone saw her.

It was not to be. The first to claim a kiss was Yves the cook, closely followed by an emboldened Morgan—both scurrying back behind the screens and along the passage to the sanctuary of their busy kitchen, both men equally redolent of stale cooking smells and ale. But she did not object to their salutes. She had come to know them well over the last weeks as chatelaine and their kisses did not offend her, they sealed a pleasant working relationship.

But before she could make good her escape she was accosted by a loutish drunken English knight, Sir Baldwin, who held her fast and and would not let her go. His kiss went on and on, suffocating her, forcing her to struggle for her freedom, her breath. A group of his peers had gathered around them, some urging him on, others demanding their turn. They meant no real harm, Katrine knew that—they wouldn't dare—

but she found the man and his kiss utterly offensive. If he didn't release her soon she would faint from revulsion and lack of air.

The cries of the crowd around them diminished. She didn't know why until a well-known voice drawled, 'My turn, I believe.'

The men melted away, leaving Sir Baldwin to face the Chevalier alone. Not that the Chevalier was breathing fire or issuing theats. Just that his presence demanded instant withdrawal from anything he claimed as his. And, subtly, he was implying that Katrine was his, for that moment at least.

He touched his knight on the shoulder, drawing attention to his presence. The man lifted his head, releasing Katrine's bruised lips. She gasped for air, her face scarlet. Sir Baldwin blinked, his expression suddenly mulish.

'I haven't finished,' he muttered, his head so clouded by drink and lust that he failed to see the green ice in Raoul's eyes.

'I think you have, *mon ami*,' murmured Raoul. 'I, your commander, say so.'

Now the man did realise who was accosting him. Sullenly, he thrust Katrine from him. 'Have her, then,' he muttered, and laughed, a harsh grating sound that left no one in doubt of his scorn. 'I can find a better armful among the menials.'

'One who will suit your tastes better, no doubt.' Scorn had entered the Chevalier's voice now. 'But,' he declared, his words ringing round the hall, 'the lady Katrine pleases me.' He bent his head and kissed her, not hard, because he had seen her bruised and swollen lips, but nevertheless lingeringly, allowing no one to doubt his enjoyment.

Katrine, already trembling, felt her body melt into his as she clung to him for support. He smelt wonderful, of herbs and wine. But what was he now saying?

'The lady Katrine is mine. My hostage, my woman. Come, Katrine. Let us retire to my solar.' Then she heard the breath of a whisper in her ear. 'Trust me, my dove.'

Releasing her, taking her small hand in a strangely reassuring clasp, he led her the length of the hall to the wooden steps leading up to his private chamber. As they began to climb a small rustle of movement and murmur of speculation ran round the company. Looking down from the gallery, Katrine saw vague faces turned up to watch but a mist seemed to have risen between them and her; she could see nothing distinctly. Could not think. Could not bear to imagine what the Chevalier meant by his words, his action.

Was he about to go back on all he had promised? His woman, he had said. That implied—— But her mind shied away from what that implied. Something she could long for, something she could never, in honour, be.

The moment the door of the solar closed behind them Raoul dropped her hand.

'I was going to my chamber,' she told him, her voice unsteady. 'To rest and change before the feast.'

'Things became rough sooner than I had thought,' he remarked conversationally.

'I did not mind the cooks,' murmured Katrine, ashamed to find that her throat had constricted and she found it difficult to speak at all.

'No, their kisses were honest festive fun. But it you wish to avoid such horseplay as Sir Baldwin's in the future I suggest you enter and leave the hall by this route, at least as long as the festivities last and the mistletoe remains hung. Though now I have laid claim to you you should be safe from serious molestation. Should any ill befall you the perpetrator would have me to answer to. They knew that before. This morn, their knowledge has been reinforced.'

'That. . .that is why you said what you did?'

'Of course. My dove, you did not doubt me again?' He shook his dark head at her, chiding rather than exasperated. 'I told you to trust me. When will you ever learn?'

'I—I am sorry.'

Mayhap it was herself she no longer trusted, since she wanted nothing more than to throw herself into his arms and seek his protection, now and always. But it seemed he had no further designs on her. He had opened the door leading to the tower stair.

'Rest well, my dove. You should be safe enough in your chamber.' He touched her swollen lips with a slender finger, wiping off a spot of blood which had oozed from a small split. 'Sir Baldwin deserves to be horsewhipped, but it is better not to rouse his enmity. Others would take his part. I cannot afford a split in the ranks of my men. But he will lead the next detail to keep watch on Rhun. That should cool his ardour.'

His fingers still lingered at her lips. Astonishing herself, Katrine kissed them before darting away to the sanctuary of her room.

* * *

The feasting went on almost without break for the twelve days of Christmas. Katrine enjoyed the troupe of tumblers who had braved the severe weather to be with them, and were no doubt glad of a warm roof over their heads, and the antics of the fool, who was a bit of a magician too, bringing pennies and even hens' eggs from people's ears and mouths. And, when he returned to the floor after bounding up the dais to lean over the table to retrieve a pebble from the Chevalier's broken nose, he produced, from the air itself, three of the Chevalier's precious playing cards.

Everyone gasped and Raoul glanced anxiously from the pack which lay before him on the board to the cards the man must have taken without anyone noticing. He held out an imperious hand and, having had them returned with a flourish which set all the fool's bells tinkling, looked carefully to see that they were not damaged before acknowledging the fool's clever trick with a wry smile.

''Tis well for you you did not harm my cards,' he observed. 'I brought them with me from Gascony and they are rarely to be found in this country. I would find it difficult to replace them.'

'But not impossible, lord,' said the fool, bending so low that the bell on his cap brushed the floor, several others about his person tinkling prettily. 'In some of the great households fools who are more foolish than I lose all they own gambling upon the turn of a card.'

'Or the toss of a dice. You are a wise man, Sir Fool. But sometimes,' Raoul murmured, almost to himself, 'one needs must gamble.'

The man's eyes darted from Raoul to Katrine,

sitting beside the Chevalier as usual and little realising how often her eyes strayed to watch him, not knowing that Raoul, for all his cool detachment, often let his gaze linger on her face with something like regret in its green depths.

'Aye, lord, all men must gamble upon the lady of their choice. Will she love him? Will she be faithful? Or will she bring wealth, position perhaps, but trials and tears to sour his enjoyment of them?'

Raoul frowned, while Katrine held her breath. Surely the man had overstepped the mark, even for a fool, licensed to say what other men would not dare. For Raoul had declared her to be his woman, although only she knew he did not mean it.

'You think marriage a matter of love, Sir Fool? Then you are a greater fool than I had thought.' The words were rapped out and the fool bowed again.

'Or a philosopher, lord.' The man gave his idiot laugh, a pretence, Katrine knew. It took a clever man to entertain by acting the fool. 'That thought amuses you? No? Then I must cudgel my poor brain for something that does.' And, having struck his head a resounding blow, he went off into what must have been his usual routine, prancing, jangling his bells, reciting comic poetry, poking fun at well-known nobles, making naughty allusions, pulling grotesque faces, falling over, being pathetic, being jolly—anything to make his audience laugh.

He succeeded well. At the end of his performance Raoul rewarded him with a golden noble, choosing to pass over the matter of the man's impertinence, while others of his audience threw lesser coins. He must consider himself well-paid, thought Katrine, for he

had collected as much for his solo performance as the
four tumblers had for their act.

The entertainers remained until after Twelfth Night
and the company often danced to the sound of
Myfanwy's harp. It was, altogether, the happiest
Christmas-tide Katrine had ever known. For she
allowed herself to relax, to enjoy Raoul's company, to
bask in his attention, however reluctantly it was given.
Having claimed her for his own, he had had to pretend
that she was.

CHAPTER EIGHT

AND after Twelfth Night the pretence had to be
maintained. How could he suddenly ignore her again,
with so many people watching? Since Myfanwy and
the knights' ladies who shared their chamber knew
that she slept in her own bed every night, the whole
castle must already be wondering at the Chevalier's
restraint, and mayhap his chivalry impressed them.
She knew his actions were dictated by her need for
protection, that any desire briefly shown had been
merely to tease.

But somehow she could never feel entirely easy in
his presence, especially when passing through the solar
on her way to the hall. Despite this embarrassment
she had to do so, both for appearances' sake and for
the greater comfort the route offered her. At that time
of the year the inner ward became an inhospitable
place, treacherous underfoot, full of draughty corners
and biting winds. Not to mention the rain which fell,
washing away the snow and bringing a damp chilliness
which penetrated to the bone.

Naturally, she made very sure to knock loudly
before entering what was, after all, the Chevalier's
private apartment, where he slept, washed, bathed
and did all the things a man needed to do. Not that
his privacy was undisturbed; how could it be in a place
where privacy was almost impossible and certainly not
expected? Louis shared the chamber and the huge

bed, while Hugues, Dai and Louis's squire slept on pallets on the floor. It was not, therefore, only the Chevalier she was likely to disturb, but a roomful of male creatures, all or any one of whom might be there at any time.

So she waited for an answering shout inviting her to enter whenever it became necessary to pass through the chamber, as it did early every morning, late in the evening and several times in between.

One bright and breezy morning in March she knocked eagerly, for the Chevalier had returned from Carmarthen late the previous evening and she had not spoken to him since. Hearing no response, telling herself she would soon find him in the Great Hall, she thrust the heavy studded door open, walked in, shut it behind her. Halfway across the floor she drew up short, arrested by a sound from behind the heavy bed-curtains. She should have gone on—whoever was there had privacy enough—but something stopped her.

She did not consciously think. Instinct took her to the bed, made her sweep the curtain to one side and gaze down upon the figure lying there, the covers thrown back to reveal a broad, well-developed chest sprinkled lightly with dark, downy hair, sparsely fleshed ribs above a taut, iron-hard abdomen, the muscles flexing with each shallow breath, the whole glistening with sweat, the perfection marred only by scars left by several wounds.

His hair lay in damp disarray upon his forehead. Horror kept Katrine still and silent for a long moment. Then Raoul began shaking. His teeth would have chattered had he not clenched them, knotting the muscles round his blue, unshaven chin. He turned his face away and she saw his fists clench as he fought the malaise which held him in its grip.

Undoubtedly, he had a fever. Where were Louis, Hugues, Dai? Why weren't they here, looking after him? With a little cry Katrine came back to life. Her hand went out, stroking the wet, tangled mass of his hair back from his forehead, feeling the burning heat, looking for signs of plague, of injury, of anything to explain his state.

'Seigneur,' she cried. 'Seigneur, you are ill! Now you are shivering, you must keep yourself covered.'

She leant over to pull the covers over him. Her hand brushed his bare skin just as a convulsive shudder shook his body. An answering tremor ran through her, but she ignored it and met his feverish gaze with steady eyes.

'Katrine,' he muttered, then, in a stronger voice, 'Go away. Leave me.'

How could she? She could do no such thing, except to fetch help.

'What is it?' she demanded.

'Nothing. Leave me; I shall soon recover. I am not dying, merely suffering from a chill.' He swallowed with evident pain. 'I sent the others away. You must go too. . .'

The normally forceful voice trailed off. His eyes, last seen so clear, so brimming with life, resembled dull, unpolished jade. Behind his irritable command Katrine sensed anxiety. Despite his airy assurance, he feared his affliction to be catching, some plague he had caught during his trip to Carmarthen which he could pass on to others.

'If I go it will be to fetch Sir Graham,' she informed him firmly. 'He should be able to reduce your fever. Like you, I do not think it serious, seigneur; you show no other symptoms, except that of a sore throat. But your linen should be changed, you should be bathed and given a curative potion.'

'Don't fuss,' he snarled.

'I'm not fussing,' said Katrine sharply. 'Just doing the sensible thing.' While she was speaking she had found a cloth and dipped it in water from his ewer. Although he was still shivering he had a fever, and cold water was the thing. 'You will find it more comfortable an you will allow me to bathe your face.'

She did not wait for his permission but began to wipe the sweat from his forehead. He seemed to lack the strength for further argument. His eyes closed. A tremor ran through him as the cold water added a new, painful chill to those already afflicting him but he did not complain. She thought she caught a faint sigh as the temperature of skin and cloth adjusted to each other and her ministrations became more comfortable. Katrine wiped away the clammy sweat from his brow and moved on to touch his eyes and cheeks, but the cloth caught on the stubble on his chin and she could do no more than dab.

'You should allow the barber to shave you,' she informed him sternly. ''Twill make you feel better.'

His hand emerged from beneath the covers to catch her wrist. 'I feel better already, my dove,' he informed her untruthfully, since he had begun to sweat again. 'I thank you for your concern. But tending me does not form part of your duties. Go, if you must, and fetch

Sir Graham. But not, on any account, the surgeon. I will not be bled,' he declared fretfully.

He was determined to send her away. Katrine struggled with resentment but his grip induced the strange effect that his touch always had on her, bringing pain, weakness, a thrilling joy that made her want to melt into his embrace. Sternly, she pushed the feeling away, shook her wrist free.

'I will fetch Sir Graham,' she said tightly.

Katrine stalked out, feeling ill-used and defiant. He might at least have been grateful for her concern.

She found Sir Graham working at the accounts in his small chamber near the chapel and quickly explained her errand.

'I'll go to him at once,' he promised, jumping to his feet and picking up the scrip and small chest in which he kept his remedies. 'A fever, you say? With an aching head and a sore throat?' At Katrine's nod he smiled. 'There seems to be an outbreak of that malaise in the castle this morning. I have already treated two of the men who accompanied the Chevalier on his mission to Carmarthen and I fear it will spread.'

'You think it is the same thing?'

'I believe so. But I do not consider it serious. Rest assured 'tis not the plague. I see no reason why they should not all recover. The Chevalier is a strong, healthy young man. He can be in no danger.'

He hurried away to tend his patient, smiling reassuringly at Katrine as though he could sense the anxiety she was trying to suppress. She hadn't thought the fever serious but you could never really tell, and sometimes such things could take a sudden turn for the worse.

Katrine escaped the infection, despite her determination to nurse the Chevalier. For which he did not thank her. He proved a fractious patient and several times that day and the next Katrine swore to herself that she would leave him to suffer. But she couldn't, and by the third evening he declared himself better, ready to resume his duties the following morning.

Everyone else was in the hall at supper. Katrine had left the table early in order to make sure he ate the victuals sent up to the solar. His appetite had been poor and he needed sustenance to help him recover his strength. It had frightened her, seeing the Chevalier brought so low.

To her surprise she found him sitting in his chair by the brazier, wearing a robe which he drew more closely around him as she entered. The dishes on the table by him had been scraped clean, the flagon of wine almost emptied.

'You are feeling better!' she exclaimed, smiling happily to see him looking so much more his usual self.

'Aye, my dove, I shall be about my business again on the morrow.'

'So soon?' She moved across to him, her heart beating rapidly. Over the last days he had been rude and disagreeable every time she had come near him. But she wanted to feel his forehead to make certain the fever had quite gone. 'You should give yourself time to recover properly.'

As she spoke she reached out to put her hand on his brow.

'Enough!' he said forcefully, and caught her wrist

before she could touch him. 'I will not be mollycoddled any longer!'

As always, his touch brought all her latent feelings for him to the surface. Her eyes met his, the message of her helpless surrender writ in them plain as the charge on his shield.

It was too much. His breath caught, he gave a groan and dragged her down to sprawl on his lap. His gown, never secure, slipped open as his arms drew her tightly against his chest.

The heat of his body penetrated the layers of Katrine's clothes. She felt the hard thrust of him against her thigh. Embarrassed, she tried to struggle away but he was too strong for her.

'Raoul,' she gasped. 'Let me go!'

The sweet scent of her, her gentle touch had been sending him crazy for days as she had hovered over his bed. Now she was in his arms the feel of her soft body pressed against his broke the last of his ebbing self-control. He tightened his grasp.

Something deep inside Katrine seemed to blossom and burst; she gave a groan which came right up from her depths as he swept her up and carried her to his bed.

He threw off the impeding gown and her eyes searched his naked body, taking their fill of his male beauty. This was no time for embarrassment or shame. Feverish excitement gripped Katrine as he came down beside her and his mouth burnt a path over her eyes, her cheeks, her forehead, to her ear, her neck, the throbbing pulse at its base. When it met the obstacle of her clothes he simply removed them, managing buttons, untying laces, with an expertise which might

have shocked Katrine had she been in any fit state to
remark it.

But since that first instinctive moment of resistance
she had sunk into a daze of desire, beyond fear,
beyond rational thinking about anything at all except
that Raoul wanted her. The teaching of her childhood,
her own scruples were burnt away in the all-consuming
flame enveloping them both, bonding them together,
forging them into one being.

Raoul's strong, clever fingers sought out all the
secrets of her body, sensitising it in ways she had never
dreamed possible. Their lips fused, his tongue tangled
with hers and she moaned her surrender. The fiery
trail of his kisses reached her breasts and Katrine
gasped again as new, delicious shafts shot to the core
of her. Her arms tightened about his sweat-slicked
shoulders, her fingers tangled in his already tousled
hair, her hips moved beneath him, urgent, demanding,
innocently offering him her virginity without thought
or question, for she had never dreamed love could be
like this, so overwhelming, so ravishingly sweet. He
was hers and she was his. Nothing else mattered.

His fingers probed, found what he needed to know,
and he moved above her, urgent to take that which
she so freely offered. But in that fateful instant he
looked down into her drowning eyes, saw the inno-
cence and vulnerability he was about to ravish, and
reality burst upon his fevered senses. Beneath him lay
a young virgin, for all her enticing sensuality. A
violent shiver racked through him as he brought his
passion under control. He prised their sticky bodies
apart and rolled away, groaning in frustration and
despair.

'Go away, Katrine,' he rasped.

Katrine felt as though a pail of cold water had been dashed over her. Suddenly aware of her shocking nudity, she reached out blindly for her garments, seeking to cover her shame. Trembling so much that her fingers would not obey her commands, she struggled to dress, missing the attentions of Dorcas. Now the heat of passion had receded, the enormity of what had nearly happened overwhelmed her.

She had almost allowed the Chevalier to deflower her. She must have been mad! And he—he must have been weakened by his fever. He had almost broken his word never to harm her.

But not quite. She should be thankful that he had retained enough self-control to stop. But gratitude could not overcome her sense of loss; it was as though something precious had been wrenched from her grasp. She felt disorientated, confused, adrift in a sea of sensation with no way to find her direction.

Because she could not cope with all the emotion seething within her she turned it into anger. It was far easier to condemn him than to wrestle with her true feelings for the man lying with muscles tensed, breathing harshly, but otherwise quite still. Not looking at her. How dared he ignore her after what had happened?

Fully clothed again, even if some of her laces remained loose, she dragged shaking fingers through her hair and drew a deep breath. 'Would I had left you to die!' she stormed.

'I told you to leave me alone,' he retorted harshly, his back firmly turned. 'You have been tempting me for days. You received no more than you deserve, my dove.' His voice suddenly rose. 'For God's sake get out of my chamber before you completely destroy my honour!'

'Honour!' she snorted. 'What honour?'

'Just go away,' he snarled, settling more determinedly into the bed, drawing the covers up to his ears. If she didn't go soon he wouldn't be responsible for his actions.

Katrine went—back to her chamber, thankfully empty still. But it would not be long before Dorcas came up, or Myfanwy and the others. She must compose herself before they arrived. She sank down on a chest, wrapped her arms about herself and shivered.

She had thought Raoul too ill to think of her as a woman, though she had been very aware of him as a man as she had tended him. They had seldom been alone together. Louis had found himself another bed while his friend was sick, but visited the solar to report on the day's events and try to cheer the patient, but Dai and Hugues had come creeping back, and Raoul had not sent them away again, so they had nearly always been there when she had visited him. She had issued numerous instructions regarding the care of the patient and, she thought wryly, they had probably resented her interference as much as Raoul. Why hadn't she seen that she wasn't wanted? She'd been too pigheaded, knowing only that she must be near him.

But he had been aware of her, and his command of himself had been diminished by his sickness, enough to allow him to respond to the surge of desire she had felt thrusting up at her as he had sat her on his lap.

With the result that he had awakened in her such a clamorous response that she would never be quite the same again. Not so innocent, for a start. She had felt the full force of a man's passion, seen him about to take her. And not been afraid. Had, in fact, wanted him to.

How wonderful it had been in his arms! Her cheeks burned at her memories. He had so nearly taught her the lesson she longed to learn. And she had rewarded him with anger and scorn. Because she had not known how else to react. He'd almost despoiled her, hadn't he? And then, when she'd shown herself completely willing, he had stopped. No wonder she had been angry—with him, but with herself, too. How could she have allowed. . .?

Because she loved him.

Of course he was right, they could not in honour lie together, but the knowledge that she tempted him so severely afforded her extreme satisfaction. If he truly desired her then mayhap. . .

But then, like a crash of thunder in her ears, she realised that they would have to face each other again. There could be no avoiding him. She would have to apologise or life was going to be most awkward. As well as frustrating.

The next day, as he had predicted, Raoul was up and about again, looking pale and barking at everyone. His men forgave him even as they grumbled, understanding his ill-temper as impatience with his own weakness. Several more people went down with the fever, including Hugues. Some it attacked more violently than others, but none died except for one elderly servant, who succumbed because his lungs became inflamed and he couldn't breathe. The funeral proved a sombre occasion but his was the only death in the castle that winter and everyone thought that a good reason to rejoice. The Chevalier had brought them through in much better case than anyone had expected. Better than Rhun ab Brechfa had managed, for there had been several people, both young and old, who had died of the cold or fevers or some other ailment during his time.

Katrine had reverted to her old route across the inner ward again. For all its convenience, she could no longer face slipping through the solar. It held too many embarrassing memories for her, and besides, it seemed vital that she did not come face to face with the Chevalier. Or sit next to him at meals. She feared he might insist, but he simply eyed her with cynical amusement and shrugged, implying that if she chose to hide herself among the other ladies he had no objection. Mayhap he too suffered from embarrassment. He had cause. And, of course, both had to endure the gossip as people whispered behind their backs, speculating as to why they now so sedulously avoided each other.

But she had been wrong to berate him when, after that first moment of instinctive protest, she had succumbed so willingly to his passion. He would have stopped had she insisted.

She knew she should seek him out to apologise but she could not steel herself to do it. Embarrassment kept her as far away from him as possible. She had behaved like one of the harlots the men kept in the gatehouse. Mayhap he was disgusted with her, for he made no attempt to approach her, even when he was fully recovered and apparently restored to good humour.

In the end they met, quite by chance, in the stables. Word had come through the previous day that Prince Henry had commanded the Chevalier to take his company to Aberystwyth, one of the two castles still remaining in Owen Glendower's hands. Once they fell, the rebellion would finally be over. Prince Henry himself meant to conquer Aberystwyth, leaving Harlech to the Talbots. The various contingents of his army would muster there in April.

Consequently there was much to do to be ready to march. Raoul was back to his old, vital self, planning, organising, leaving nothing to chance.

Katrine would celebrate the sixteenth anniversary of her birth at the end of April. It seemed the day would be spent in a tent outside the walls of Aberystwyth unless Henry could force its surrender quickly, which seemed unlikely. For she would accompany the Chevalier. He had made that abundantly clear, issuing clipped orders from his position on the dais.

Katrine had hidden her hurt and disappointment. She could not truly regret what had occurred between them, but it had destroyed the old camaraderie. She would be travelling simply as his hostage, not as a friend. But she would be riding Paris.

A smile of anticipation curved her mouth as she approached the stables. She had grown fond of the palfrey over the winter and it seemed only prudent to see for herself that he was fit for the long journey. March was blowing itself out in fine style and she had gathered her golden hair into a black caul and flung a cloak about her shoulders to keep out the chill of the wind. It swirled about her as she entered the dim barn and caught on a splinter so that she had to unsnag the woollen thread. Inside, most of the stalls were empty, for the company was training hard. She had thought to find the place free of men except mayhap for a stable-hand or two. Therefore, confronted by a tall figure leading a great warhorse, she stopped in dismay.

He halted equally abruptly. His horse whickered a greeting. From a nearby stall Paris added a blow of delight.

The confrontation was so sudden that Katrine had no time to hide her feelings. The light was behind her but, even so, Raoul could see the leap of joy in her luminous eyes before confusion took over and golden-tipped lashes swept her cheeks, hiding their expression from him.

His face was in what light filtered in through the door, and for a fleeting instant Katrine glimpsed a spark of fire in the green depths of his gaze. Confusion overwhelmed her and she veiled her own eyes from him. But suddenly she knew. She had to bridge the gulf before it became a chasm impossible to cross. For even if Raoul could never be her lover she could not bear for him to be her enemy. The last week had been agony and the next few would be the last shared with him. She must have something precious to remember when she was wed to Lionel d'Evreux, or whoever else her guardians chose for her. She would never love again. No one else could ever compare with her Chevalier.

When she raised her lids to look at him again the

fire had disappeared from his gaze, yet he made no attempt to push past and leave her. He stood there, as rooted as she. And so their eyes met and held. Hers pleaded for forgiveness. His suddenly softened.

'Ride with me,' he invited.

Only when he took hold of it did she realise that her hand had gone out in supplication. His fingers enfolded hers, relaying their warmth to her heart.

'Oh, yes!' she agreed instantly.

Raoul called an instruction to a figure lurking in the dimness behind him and her palfrey shifted expectantly as the groom began to tack him up. She was not dressed for riding but that did not mean she couldn't, and she would not risk keeping the Chevalier hanging about while she went to change. He might get tired of waiting. She moved forward to pat Thor's nose and the big horse snuffled her hand, looking for a titbit. She had brought some lumps of sugar broken from the loaf for Paris. The two horses would have to share it. Raoul did not speak and neither did she. They stood in silence for the few moments it took for the groom to change the halter for a bridle and strap her side-saddle on the palfrey's back.

Out in the yard the groom held the horses' heads while Raoul, hands clasped as a stirrup for her foot, helped her into the saddle. He leapt into his own without aid and led the way from the ward.

Still silent, they crossed the bailey and made for the path leading down to the floor of the valley. Much of the flooding had gone now, though the river was still high. The water meadows would soon dry out for summer grazing but were still too soft to ride on so they kept to the road. Katrine knew the Chevalier

would not take her far without an escort because of
the danger. A rebel strike he did not expect, but
footpads and vagabonds lurked everywhere. He wore
his sword and she trusted him to defend her from any
attack launched within sight of the castle. Few, however desperate, would dare to show themselves so
near. What he could not defend her from was the
gossip their unchaperoned ride would raise.

Scattered trees, copses and thickets sprang up everywhere. Raoul set off at a canter towards one of the
larger stands of trees. Katrine's cheeks bloomed, her
eyes sparkled. The horses responded willingly, enjoying the outing as much as their riders. Raoul wore a
cap sporting a long feather in its band. His cheeks
took on some colour as the wind whipped them. But
although he rode easily his face bore a sombre
expression.

He slowed the pace as the trees approached, turned
aside and took a path leading into the wood. Katrine
followed without question. She guessed he was seeking
privacy, some place where they would be unobserved.
A trembling excitement gripped her.

He stopped in a small clearing mere yards from the
road but well-screened from it. He dismounted
quickly, tied Thor's reins to a convenient branch and
returned to help her down. But Katrine had already
slipped to the ground and tied her own reins to a
sapling. At that moment his touch would be impossible to bear.

Would he ever break the silence? Could she? It was
becoming oppressive. She must do what she had
always known she must. She cleared her throat.

He had stopped a yard or so away. Not quite

looking at him she said, 'Forgive me, Raoul—for the things I accused you of. I was angry and upset. I didn't mean them.'

'You owe me no apology.' His tone was abrupt. ''Tis I who should apologise for my behaviour. And I never thanked you for your care. It was no part of your duties.'

Katrine risked looking at him and gave a tremulous smile. 'So you told me, seigneur. But I took no notice.'

'Mayhap I should be more like Rhun ab Brechfa,' he mused, his eyes at last holding something of their old, mocking twinkle. 'You obeyed him in everything.'

Katrine shuddered. 'I did not enjoy being whipped.'

Raoul ground out an oath under his breath. 'Forgive me for reminding you. I had intended my remark as a joke.'

'I know, seigneur, but the memory is too painful for me to treat it so. But now—I would like to begin again, to forget everything that has passed.'

'Everything?'

Katrine bit her lip to stop it trembling. Her blush gave her away. 'It is better so.'

'Mayhap.' He did not sound as though he believed it. He gave a short, self-mocking laugh. 'Huh! But I must confess the feel of you in my arms haunts me. Can you truly forget those moments we shared, Katrine?'

'I must,' she whispered, not meeting his eyes.

'And I,' he said seriously, 'must remind you that you are in my power. I hold you hostage.'

'But——' Katrine felt completely confused. 'You promised on your honour!' she whispered.

'Ah, yes. My honour. I promised that I would never

harm you and I will not. But, my dove, were we wed——'

'Wed?'

Katrine's incredulous cry cut across what he had been about to say.

'Wed,' he repeated firmly. 'You will wed me before we begin the journey to Aberystwyth.'

Katrine clenched her fists over her pounding heart. Her agonised gaze pierced through him. 'But that is impossible!'

'Not at all,' he retorted, absolutely calm, completely sure of himself. 'Sir Graham will perform the ceremony at any time I choose.'

'I know that! But I am promised——'

He lifted his brows. 'You are not betrothed, my dove. You have said so.'

Her fingers twisted together, squeezing her arms against her breasts as she tried to control her agitation, her breathing. Did she really want to marry this man? Yes! cried her pumping heart. No! warned her rebellious spirit. Not like this, under duress. For what choice would she have were he to insist? In her distress she called on the power of those she most resented for help. 'But my guardians would never agree.'

'They will not know until it is done.'

'And when they find out they will use every device to have the marriage annulled!'

He shook his head. 'There will be no legal loophole. You are above the age of consent.'

Calmer suddenly, she gazed at him, her clear grey eyes pleading for an explanation. 'Why, Raoul? They are powerful men. Do you wish to challenge the King himself?'

Why, indeed? Such an action could ruin his chances of recovering his Gascon lands. King Henry might sequester Katrine's estates. Raoul scarcely knew the answer himself. He desired her, true, and, provided she retained it, her dowry was huge. But he had been making his own enquiries, and in Carmarthen he had received his answer. Lionel d'Evreux remained unwed, unbetrothed. To snatch her from the arms of a d'Evreux! That would be ultimate triumph. To present her as his wife. Unattainable. Their prize gone, their pride trampled underfoot. His foot. There could be only one honourable response. A look crossed his face that made Katrine quail—an expression of such feral glee that she shivered and stepped back.

'What is it?' she whispered.

He peered at her down his distinctive nose. 'What is what?'

'That look. . .as though you would delight in killing someone.'

'What if I would?' He shifted his feet to plant them wide and a twig snapped. His chin lifted arrogantly; his tone matched his stance. ''Tis no concern of yours, my dove.'

'If I become your wife——'

''Twill still be no concern of yours. I am a soldier. I have killed many men.'

'In battle, yes. But methinks this is a different matter. I cannot wed a man intent on murder. I asked you why you wished to marry me and that look was your answer. You wish to use me in a matter of vengeance. Is that not so?'

Raoul considered the small figure standing defiantly

before him, her head thrown proudly back, her dove-grey eyes challenging him despite her obvious distress. He was reminded of that first day, when she had been brought forward for his inspection and he had felt the first stirrings of admiration and desire. Now he knew the depth of the passion she had to offer and desire had become almost an obsession to possess. She was necessary to his plan and he wanted her. What better reasons could he have for wedding any wench?

He answered her demand with prevarication. 'Mayhap. You are useful to me, that I will concede. But as to murder, I wonder you should imagine that could ever be in my mind.' And then, suddenly, the Chevalier she knew emerged, smiling wickedly, irresistible in his charm. 'But, Katrine, most of all I desire you. And I cannot in honour take you unless you are my wife.'

They had been standing facing each other like enemies. Now he stepped forward to lay his hands on her shoulders. 'I want you, my dove,' he murmured, 'and I think you do not find me offensive. We could deal well together, you and I.'

He was close, too close, as he bent his head and claimed her lips. For an instant Katrine resisted the exploratory warmth of his mouth, wondering whether she could indeed bear to wed a man intent on some unknown vengeance. But then his kiss deepened, his tongue probed and once again her body opened to him like a flower.

Her resistance ebbed. She clung to his strength and was lost. She loved him. Mayhap, as his wife, she could turn him from his purpose.

He broke off the embrace at last, satisfied with her

surrender. 'You will wed me,' he said. It was neither a question nor a command. Simply a statement.

'Yes,' whispered Katrine.

She might be his pawn, but he was her king. She would defend him and cherish his honour to the last.

CHAPTER NINE

THEY were wed two days later in the Great Hall, with almost everyone present. Raoul wanted no hole-and-corner affair which could be doubted later. Afterwards they and a few others—Louis and Myfanwy among them—retired to the chapel where Sir Graham celebrated the nuptial mass.

The announcement of their betrothal had brought forth mixed reactions from the inhabitants of the castle, though most were not surprised.

'I knew it!' Myfanwy had cried, kissing Katrine. 'I knew you had had a lovers' tiff!'

'So you have been caught at last,' Louis had teased Raoul.

'Caught?' Raoul had laughed. '*Mon ami*, it is I who have done the catching! The little Katrine was most reluctant to agree to our union.'

'But she adores you! She has been looking wretchedly unhappy since you began avoiding each other after your fever, but now she is radiant.'

The ready wrinkles had appeared in Raoul's forehead as his brows lifted. 'You think so, *mon ami*? A childish hero-worship, no doubt, born of gratitude for her deliverance from Rhun's clutches, which she will soon outgrow.' But of which he had taken full advantage. The frown deepened.

Louis had regarded his friend gravely. 'Do not break her heart, Raoul. She does not deserve that.'

Raoul's face had immediately cleared. There was little likelihood of that. 'Do not concern yourself, Louis. When this is over we shall deal well enough together. Better than most couples, I vow.'

Even to Louis he had not admitted to the spell his hostage had cast upon him, for his friend had already accused him of softness where she was concerned. Nor would he admit that Katrine's reluctance had been born of propriety, of fear of her guardians, mayhap of what the future would hold, rather than an aversion to bed with him. But bedding was one thing, love another. If anyone even suspected that love existed between them, however wrongly, he would become vulnerable.

But he did naught to prevent the feasting or the normal rituals of marriage being performed afterwards. The ceremony of bedding would reinforce his claim to Katrine should it ever be in doubt. As would the removal of the stained sheet the following morning.

Louis, Hugues and Dai had all moved out of the solar before Katrine was led there by Myfanwy and the other ladies. Katrine knew she could not avoid the embarrassment of being undressed, bathed, scented and put naked into the big bed to await the boisterous entry of Raoul and his attendant knights, and so she made the best of it. Few women had the privilege of privacy in which to lie with their husbands—the act was natural, a part of life, and she had seen and heard it many times since her capture by Rhun. That it would also bring her great pleasure Katrine was no longer in doubt. She was nervous, of course she was, and she would rather not have been the object of so many knowing eyes, but she was excited, expectant, too. Raoul de Chalais was her husband in name and soon he would be so in fact. She could not wait for the moment when they were left alone together.

He came, doffed his gown and slipped into the bed beside her. A shiver shuddered through Katrine as she felt his warmth, remembered that other time they had lain in this bed together. She was scarcely aware of the priest reciting the blessing, the loving cup being passed to them, the ribald jokes which flew about far above her head. But the pungent aroma of the herbs Myfanwy scattered over the bed, reputed to aid fertility, made her nostrils twitch, and brought home to her that soon she might be bearing the Chevalier's child. This time the thrill that ran through her was of a different kind—a soft, expectant feeling that threatened to bring tears to her eyes.

The bedding parties did not in truth remain long. Louis led the move to pull the curtains about them and retreat, and the others followed, returning to the Great Hall to continue with the feasting.

Feeling awkward now they were at last alone, Katrine slid further down into the bed, her loose hair spilling over the pillow like golden silk. After her flock-filled pallet the mattress felt like swansdown. Mayhap it was—she'd thought so once before. But more likely it was just chicken feathers. The pillows, too. The linen sheets caressed her body, the fur-lined blanket had no harsh fibres to stick through and prick her skin. Memories of the comfortable beds she had enjoyed as a child returned, to bring sudden tears to her eyes. So much that was harsh and unwelcome had happened to her since her father's death. But now here she was, sharing a comfortable bed with the man she loved. If only he had wed her for love instead of expediency she could have wished for nothing more.

Raoul sat up and swept the curtains aside. Their privacy would be complete without the screen they provided and he wanted light, the warmth of the fire to heat their skins. He turned with a smile to look at his bride.

'Tears, my dove?'

Surprise, perhaps anxiety, lurked in Raoul's voice, making her blink. He could not want a weepy bride! He would think her reluctant and that would never do. He desired her and mayhap, one day, she could make him return her love. Meanwhile she must be grateful for what she had. Katrine turned to him, smiling mistily, and admitted to part of the reason for her tears.

'I was remembering,' she said. 'I have not known such a comfortable bed for many years.'

He leaned up on one elbow to trace the line of her full mouth with an abrasive finger. It felt like hers had been before he had come and rescued her from harsh drudgery. No soft, gentleman's hands, his, but strong ones, hardened by the tasks he shared with his men. Yet they were sensitive, too. The touch of his finger was feather-light—it seemed too light to cause the melting weakness afflicting her limbs. The glow from several flickering candles softened his features: his chin had lost its determined thrust, his mouth its stern line. His eyes, so often changing from limpid, sparkling pools to chips of green ice, now looked soft as moss, but she expected that before long they would change again, to burn with the flame of desire she had seen there once before.

'Poor little maid,' he murmured, bending to touch her forehead with his dry, warm lips.

She reached up to touch him, as he was touching her, running a finger down the length of his nose. 'How did that happen?'

He laughed. 'When I was a squire. An accident, a blow in training. I have since had to come to terms with my ugly looks.'

Her eyes sparkled up at him as she hit his chest. 'Raoul de Chalais, you know very well your looks are not ugly! You are fishing for compliments!'

'Well, my nose is deformed.'

'Flattened and bent, but fascinating.'

She was flirting with him and he did not seem to mind. Emboldened, all traces of tears banished, she touched a scar on his shoulder. 'And this?'

'Ah, that. Pilleth,' he informed her succinctly. 'A defeat.'

She caught the bitterness in his voice. 'But surely through no fault of yours, Chevalier.' She reared up to kiss the scar before she pushed the bedcovers lower. 'This too?'

'No. Shrewsbury. A victory.' He sighed, as though in resignation. 'They are all mere scratches. An you demand a tally of all my scars, we shall be occupied all night, my dove. They were all acquired in training or in skirmishes, not battles with a name to locate them.'

She traced the line of seamed flesh covering his ribs and felt his muscles contract beneath her finger. 'Like the fight from which Rhun fled?' she demanded thoughtfully. How soon would this rebellion be over? How soon would he be safe? Never, she supposed. He would always answer the King's call to arms.

'Similar.' His voice had thickened, for her exploring of his wounds was exciting him beyond bearing. She was a jewel indeed, his dove, for she seemed to know by instinct how to please him.

Katrine felt his flesh rear against her and allowed her hand to stray to touch it.

'No!' He snatched her fingers away and took them to his lips. '*Ma dame*,' he protested hoarsely, 'you are very forward for a virgin.'

'Am I?' Katrine had decided to abandon all her reservations about this marriage and all her inhibitions, too. She knew not what the future held, but these moments were theirs, to be enjoyed to the full. She *was* proud, she *was* bold, when circumstances demanded. And her new husband, having forced her into matrimony, would not have things entirely his own way. But still, she did not wish to offend him. 'Did you not like my touch?' she enquired anxiously.

'My dove, I adored it, but it was too soon, unless you wish me to cause you pain. For you are virgin; I needs must be careful.' And controlled, he added silently.

As he spoke his hand began to gentle her, smoothing the length of her from shoulder to thigh and incidentally pushing the covers down about their feet. She sighed, remembering how he had kissed and caressed her before, and reached up to wind her arms about his neck. 'Teach me what to do,' she whispered, pulling his head down so that she could kiss the bridge of his broken nose.

'My lovely dove,' he murmured, his breath catching in his throat as he looked at her body, rosy in the glow of candles and brazier, at her abundant hair spread on the pillow like a halo.

Rousing this virgin was so easy. She seemed to blossom and flower beneath his hands and lips, and her eager breath fanned his neck as he parted her legs and rose above her. 'Now, my dove,' he breathed, 'do not be afraid.'

Katrine was not afraid. She anticipated his thrust and rose to meet it. The pain was slight but something seemed to explode within her as she gave a joyous shout and clasped him close. 'Raoul,' she cried. 'Oh, Raoul!'

'Bear with me, my sweet. It is not over yet.'

And the exquisite pleasure went on and on. Raoul nursed his own response, giving her time, knowing with absolute certainty that she was his, that she would warm his bed better than any other woman he had known. He need not have scorned to wed a virgin. And when his own release came she held him tight; he could feel her kisses smothering his neck and shoulder as she sought to give expression to the deep emotions possessing her.

His shuddering stopped and he lifted his dead weight from her, rising to his elbows, to look down into her face. Her eyes were heavy with passion and he knew she had not achieved full release. He bent to kiss her mouth, whispering, 'Next time 'twill be better for you.'

Her response was eager, her hands everywhere on his back, pressing his buttocks to her. He was still inside her, and to his astonishment he felt himself harden. How could it be, so soon? She was a witch.

She had felt his response and whispered, 'Oh, yes. Again, please!'

He moved slowly, languorously, long, caressing strokes which brought little sounds of pleasure from her. She locked her legs about him as though she would never let him go, pressed him into her, urging him deeper, ever deeper, and at last he felt her muscles quiver and knew she was about to spin out of control. He drove to his own completion until they lay, locked together in a private cocoon of shared ecstasy.

At length he rolled from her and gathered her into the crook of his arm. 'My wife,' he murmured, smoothing the golden hair away and kissing her fore-head. 'No one can take you from me now.'

There was a sort of triumph in his voice which Katrine vaguely mistrusted. He had been so intent on making their union indissoluble, not because he loved her but because he had some private vendetta in mind. Yet surely he must feel something for her or he couldn't have been so wonderful just now, making her his wife, a true woman, in such a breathtaking manner.

For the moment she refused to worry about his motives. She would take what he had to give and be grateful. In return she would love him as she hoped to be loved herself. One day.

She drifted into sleep, a smile of deep contentment on her lips. Raoul watched, glad she was his, wishing he did not have to use her. But she would not be hurt.

She could not love d'Evreux; she did not even know the fellow.

His conscience cleared, he too fell asleep, his wife still held securely in his arms.

He awoke early. The candles had guttered out, the brazier no longer glowed. He could feel her warmth pressed against him; she was still curled in his arms, one of which had gone to sleep under her weight. He shifted gently, not wishing to disturb her slumber, yet the feel of her had already awakened his desire. But he must not. She would think him insatiable and mayhap, at the moment, he was. His eyes were used to the dim light and he could see the pale oval of her face, the lashes fanning her cheeks, the rise and fall of her small, perfect breasts. He had never wanted a woman more.

She made a small sound and came awake. For an instant she looked bemused, wondering where she was. But only for a moment. She turned to him, pressing herself against him, touching him, knowing now exactly how to rouse him. Not that he needed any rousing.

Their union came quickly, sudden and climactic. Neither uttered a word, just made sounds of pleasure and fulfilment. When it was over Raoul rolled her over on top of him and held her there, her breasts pressing down into his chest. She smothered his face in kisses, her hands holding his head, fingers threading through the dark strands of his hair. He closed his eyes and let her young ardour wash over him, so innocent, so intense, somehow so healing.

But total healing could only come with retribution.

He knew that. The hatred he had nurtured for almost all his life ran too deep to be remedied by any other means. So he must use her to that end.

Sounds of bustle about the castle reached their ears. The servants were astir, tending the fires, putting up the trestles, sweeping, cleaning, doing the hundred and one things necessary to the life of Dryslwyn. Grooms would be mucking out the stables under the direction of his master of the horse. Every man in his company was mounted, or they could not have followed Rhun so deep into Wales. Barns had had to be erected in the bailey to house the lesser horses and the mules. They would be leaving the comparative security of their winter quarters shortly to make the long and difficult journey to Aberystwyth.

'I trust you will not find the journey to Aberystwyth too arduous, my dove,' he murmured, removing a strand of her hair which had caught in his mouth. His head was enclosed in a scented golden canopy as she bent over him. he did not wish to move, but knew he must. 'The horses are well-fed and strong, but I'll warrant you have never camped out on campaign before.'

'Nay, husband, how should I?' She teased his nose with her lips. 'But I shall gladly share the hardships with my lord.'

'Ah, my dove!' The mocking intonation had left his use of the endearment. He might almost have called her his love. Katrine's hands tightened on his head and her lips found his rugged, seductive mouth. 'Your presence looks like to make the journey a pleasure,' he said as she lifted her head and he rolled from under her. 'I must rise,' he added, pulling the curtains close about the bed. 'Hugues will be here soon. I will dress in my wardrobe and send Dorcas to you here.'

Katrine put out a hand to stroke the arm holding the curtain. 'Kiss me, my husband.'

He shook his head. 'I dare not,' he growled wryly, 'else 'twill be time for dinner ere I rise!'

He withdrew and Katrine was left alone in the darkness of the bed. She stretched, feeling pain in all the muscles she had never known she had. But the night just past would remain in her memory all her life. Nothing could take the joy of it from her.

She was curled into a ball, dozing with a smile curving her lips, when Dorcas came.

'Well, my lady,' she said as Katrine woke again, 'I have no need to ask whether you enjoyed your nuptial night!'

Katrine blushed. She'd thought herself past it, but she was not. She ignored the remark as she slid from the high bed. 'I must bathe,' she said. 'Did you order hot water?'

'Indeed and to goodness, so I did.' Dorcas sounded offended that Katrine should even suspect of her such neglect of duty. ''Twill be here in the twinkling of an eye.' Dorcas eyed the stained sheet with a satisfaction which would have been comical were it not so embarrassing. 'I'll take this,' she declared, whipping it from the bed, 'and show it to the ladies.'

The proof that she was no longer virgin, that the marriage had been consummated. She had heard that many men found themselves impotent on their wedding night. The smile returned to her lips. Raoul had not let her down. Nor she him. Provided she could sleep in his arms each night she would gladly endure any discomfort that the projected progress might impose.

A few more nights in this bed and then she would be sharing a pallet in Raoul's pavilion. The prospect excited her. She thought she might enjoy being part of a campaign, joining with all the other lords and their retinues to answer Prince Harry's call. There might be fighting but she hoped not. The King's guns were being brought round by sea to pound the castle's walls. Aberystwyth would soon fall. And then the army would disband and they could go home. To Huntershold or to Gascony scarcely mattered any longer.

But first Raoul had to settle his private quarrel. She did not know what it was or what part she was to play in it. But, whatever it was, she hoped it would be over quickly.

The Chevalier had decided to travel via Rhun ab Brechfa's retreat in the hills.

'Must you?' asked Katrine with a shudder.

'He must be made aware that we know where his stronghold is. And, by the terms of our agreement, he must be given the opportunity to ask for his pardon of the Prince of Wales. He must therefore make his way to Aberystwyth an he wishes to seek audience with the Prince.'

'What of Dai?' asked Katrine uneasily.

Raoul squeezed her shoulders and gathered her to him. They were alone in the solar and had just made love.

'I shall insist Dai remains with me,' said Raoul quietly. 'The boy is terrified of his aunt and uncle. His father too, I imagine. I will come to some agreement over him. If Rhun wants his pardon badly enough he will agree.'

'Could you not leave him here?'

'Nay, he would be most hurt! To be left behind with the old and infirm, the babies!'

'Will you not leave a garrison, seigneur?'

'A small one, for appearances' sake. But the south is quiet. Rhun's was the last spark of opposition here. I foresee no danger of attack and 'tis now Jenkin Hanard's task to see Dryslwyn defended, since 'tis an outpost of Dinefwr.'

'Keep Dai close by you,' murmured Katrine. 'I do not trust Sir Gruffydd where the child is concerned. He did not take Dai's reappearance at Dryslwyn kindly and at heart he still owes allegiance to Rhun.'

'I will, my sweet; I know the danger. Between us Louis and I and our squires will keep close watch on Dai. Once we reach Rhun's I will warn the page not to wander.'

'I doubt he will wish to,' murmured Katrine drowsily. A hard day's preparation followed by lengthy, passionate lovemaking had almost overcome her.

Raoul tucked her head under his chin and murmured, 'Rest now, my dove.'

But Katrine was already asleep.

They set out to join the Prince. The days passed, mostly bright and chilly with showers to dampen their progress. Many of his men by now knew the way to Rhun's stronghold and Raoul had brought an old retainer from Dryslwyn, who claimed to know the mountains well, to lead them to Aberystwyth. They travelled through verdant valleys, followed rushing streams, but always the mountains were there, towering over them, their summits stark and majestic. No wonder the Welsh loved their country, Katrine thought. It was beautiful.

As they neared Rhun's stockade men seemed to rise from the ground to meet them. For an instant Katrine's heart leapt to her throat but then she recognised the leader of the lance keeping watch on the Welshman's movements.

Consultations followed before the column formed up again, to include those who had been keeping watch. Rhun had not stirred from his stronghold recently. Stores had arrived by mule-train, probably from Carmarthen, like their own.

A herald rode ahead, his horn hung with Raoul's arms, blue and red with the two silver bands, tasselled with gold. As usual, the knights rode with their lances vertical, pennons flying in the breeze. An impressive cavalcade.

Before the gates of the stockade the herald sounded his horn and halted. Challenged, he shouted his message. The Chevalier Raoul de Chalais and his party had come in peace and asked that the lord Rhun ab Brechfa and his lady would receive them.

Scurrying footsteps could be heard behind the pales of the perimeter fence. It seemed a long time before the gates opened and Rhun's herald bade the Chevalier and his companions welcome.

Who should accompany their commander had already been decided. Dai would remain outside the stronghold, protected by Sir Hugh Layfield, who, after Louis, was Raoul's most senior knight. Raoul had thought it politic to allow Sir Gruffydd and his lady to accompany him, particularly as Katrine was to do so as his wife. And, of course, Louis and Raoul's trusted guards, without whom he seldom moved in this hostile land.

Rhun and Eiluned stood before their door ready to receive them, Dafydd a pace or two behind. He had grown in the past months but looked thin and unhappy. His eyes darted among the Chevalier's followers, searching for Dai, perhaps. Rhun looked as heavily disagreeable as ever, still as broad as he was tall, his thin, angular wife as sharp. They appeared an ill-assorted couple, Katrine had always thought so, but they shared a similar cast of mind. The winter spent amid the Welsh mountains had soured rather than improved them. Katrine could not bring herself to smile a greeting. The scars they had left on her were still too new.

However, they extended every courtesy to their guests, though Katrine suspected it a little and knew it to be grudging on Eiluned's part.

Raoul exerted his charm. Hostility might be hidden beneath the surface of their exchanges, but old enmities often changed to friendships and he would rather have Rhun friend than foe. Whatever he might protest, he could not entirely blame the man for defending his homeland against what he considered to be its oppressors. His father had done the same, and, although Raoul's own loyalty to the English King was absolute, he could sympathise. What he could never forgive was the treatment meted out to Katrine. But, in the interests of peace, he could force himself to ignore it.

Rhun, of course, showed cynicism about the marriage.

'What I failed to achieve because of my son's death, you have, Chevalier,' he said, his smile barely concealing his chagrin. 'I must congratulate you on your conquest. The little Katrine——' he turned to bow to her where she sat on his other side '—has blossomed and you have acquired her fortune. Unless, of course, the legality of the marriage is questioned.'

'Its legality is beyond question.'

'And has been consummated?'

'Beyond doubt. As several witnesses will testify.'

'And your relationship cannot be said to fall within the degrees of affinity which the Church proscribes and considers incestuous?'

Raoul smiled. 'Impossible, my lord.'

'One can never be quite certain what the clerics will dredge up from the records if required. However, if what you say is true, then the King, her guardian, has only one option left an he wishes to oppose the union. To sequester her fortune. Your lands, I believe, are already lost?'

'That is so, my lord Rhun. 'Tis to recover them that I seek to serve Prince Henry well.'

Katrine had followed the exchange with mixed feelings. Raoul had an answer to every objection to their marriage, which cheered her. But he had not attempted to challenge Rhun's implication that he had wed her for her fortune. She swallowed her disappointment and reminded herself that she had expected no less. Why else had Lionel d'Evreux been offered as a prospective husband? But Raoul had had another, darker reason for marrying her. A reason he would not divulge to Rhun or even to her.

Meanwhile, Raoul had assumed his easiest, most confident manner as he assured Rhun that he could anticipate no reason why their alliance, a *fait accompli*, should not be accepted by his wife's guardian.

But Katrine could read beneath the assured surface. He had assessed that danger and found his other reason for marrying her more compelling. He was willing to risk his own fortune and hers in order to gain his ends.

But surely, surely, he would not risk the delicate, developing relationship they had established, throw away the delight they found in each other, the passion they shared? If, in pursuit of his vendetta, he threw away both their fortunes, would he still want her?

She shivered. Probably not, since, although he wanted her passionately, he still did not love her. The relationship meant little to him apart from the physical satisfaction he found in it. But it hadn't happened yet. Until it did, she must hope.

Rhun thanked the Chevalier for diverting to inform him of the gathering of Prince Henry's forces before Aberystwyth Castle. He promised to proceed there with his own contingent within the next few days.

He did not question how Raoul had discovered his dwelling among the hills. Mayhap he thought Sir Gruffydd had guided him there. Or mayhap he had known he was being watched from the surrounding hills. Nor did he show distress upon learning of the investment and inevitable surrender of Owen Glendower's last strongholds, receiving the news impassively.

Raoul refused an offer to lie within Rhun's hall that night, preferring instead to return to his camp, which had been made without its gates.

'We shall be astir early, my lord Rhun. We cannot impose such inconvenience upon your household,' he excused himself and his companions. 'I shall look forward to meeting you again before Aberystwyth.'

'You may depend upon it, Chevalier. I have few men to bring with me but I shall come. Obtaining the King's pardon is important to my future and to that of my family.'

'You must return my nephew Dai to us,' put in Eiluned abruptly. 'I know you have him in your retinue.'

Katrine's eyes strayed to Gruffydd Gethin. He must have managed a quiet word with her.

'I regret, *madame*, that will be impossible,' said the Chevalier smoothly. 'I have promised Dai Prys that he may remain with me as my page. Later he will be trained as a squire, either in my household or in that of a great magnate. Surely neither you nor his father could wish for a better future for him?'

'In an *English* household!' hissed Eiluned.

Raoul's stance became imperious. 'England, Aquitaine or Wales, wherever he serves he will owe allegiance to the English crown.'

'Do not insist, my dear.' Rhun had assessed the cost of wresting Dai from the Chevalier and found it not worthwhile.

'May I go with Dai?' piped up Dafydd eagerly, then flinched as he saw the strength of his mother's wrath.

Eiluned spoke from behind clenched teeth. 'You

may not. You will go where you father and I send you, my son.'

'You will travel to Aberystwyth with me,' rumbled Rhun. 'Your future will be decided there.'

Dafydd subsided, not displeased by that promise.

'I wish they had allowed Dafydd to join Dai,' said Katrine later as they sat, just within the shelter of the pavilion but within reach of the heat of a fire, consuming the cooks' offerings. Morgan had agreed to join the campaign and had quickly learned the art of cooking on the march. Yves had spoken of pay and booty, and what self-respecting cook wished to remain to feed the few left behind in Dryslwyn? Besides, a strange alliance, even friendship, had grown up between the two men. The challenge to outdo each other kept them both in lively spirits and the Chevalier and his men well-fed.

'Patience, my dove. I will try to arrange something at Aberystwyth.'

Katrine grinned widely but her eyes were soft. 'They will both be your slaves for life.'

Raoul shook his head. 'I have no desire for slaves. Loyal followers, yes, but not slaves unable to break free if they so desire. Those days are past, in this land at least. One of the many reasons I prefer to serve England's Henry rather than the French Charles.'

'And I, husband? Am I not tied to you by bonds it is impossible to break, subject by law to your will? As your wife I am your possession, just as a slave would be.'

The soughing of the wind, the crackling of the fire, the general noise of the camp made their conversation quite private although Louis Dubois, the Gethins,

Layfield and others were supping within normal ear-shot. Hugues and Dai had crept near the fire, toasting their feet.

Raoul's lips twisted wryly. What she said was true in law. Some men beat their wives into absolute submission. But Katrine knew she need never fear that. His smile suddenly turned mischievous before he straightened his features.

'An you continue to please me, my dove, you have nothing to fear,' he informed her solemnly.

But the mischief still lurked in his eyes. Katrine pouted. 'And if you tire of me, seigneur? And once I have served your mysterious purpose? What then?'

She was half serious. He took her hand, greasy though it was from the wing of roast fowl she had just consumed. His own was no cleaner. 'I dare swear, my sweet wife, you will always find some way to overcome my wishes an they do not tally with your own. Your record so far has been prodigious.'

Katrine stared at him. 'I have obeyed you in everything!'

'But my wishes have often been formed against my better judgement, to accord with your liking. I cannot think why,' he added, as though surprised himself, 'but from the beginning of our acquaintance I have felt constrained to protect and please you. I do not imagine that will ever change.'

Katrine's heart lifted. Were that true, there was hope yet. He must at least feel a fondness for her. 'I shall always do my best to please *you*, husband,' she promised huskily.

CHAPTER TEN

Days later they emerged from the embrace of the mountains to see the Irish Sea spread before them. A freshening breeze had whipped up crests to scatter the surface with white, like chicken feathers blowing across a giant undulating cloth. Above, clouds scudded before the wind, their shadows ceaselessly changing the colour of the cloth from grey to blue to green, dappling it with dark and light.

Katrine had seen rivers, had glimpsed the wide estuary at Carmarthen, but never before had she viewed the sea itself, stretching to the dark, sharp line of the horizon with no other land in sight.

As they joined the coastal path leading to Aberystwyth she drew rein, stopping to feast her eyes. Near the shore small ships plied to and fro, their sails bellied with the press of the wind driving them forward, while further out a convoy of larger ships ploughed through the swell. Even from that distance Katrine could see the glint of metal helmets, the flash of streaming pennons.

Beside her, Raoul held his hand up to shield his eyes against the glare as he concentrated on the larger ships heading north. 'See the leopards on their sails?' He glanced at her and grinned. 'King's ships, carrying the cannon to Aberystwyth. Come!' He signalled the men behind to move forward again. 'We must make haste. The attack must soon begin.'

190

The company donned full armour to enter the Prince of Wales's camp the following day. Impressive they looked, too, thought Katrine proudly. Especially the Chevalier, of course. Close to, he appeared even more splendid than had that distant figure encircling Dryslwyn while she had watched from the tower. How long ago that seemed now! Yet in truth 'twas only six months. Six months in which she had grown from rebellious if subdued child to experienced woman. A woman who knew that whatever happened in the future she would somehow survive. And would have her memories. But Katrine could tell by the suppressed excitement in his manner, the eagerness with which he examined the banners and pennons flying over neighbouring camps, that Raoul expected his moment to come soon. The moment he had been anticipating throughout the winter. The moment when her part in his schemes, mayhap her future, would become clear.

She hoped it would not take too long. She hoped it would never happen. How could she bear to lose him? And what if he was killed?

Then, she would be given to some other man as wife. She knew that with quiet resignation. Mayhap she would even find a kind of happiness with someone else. But it could never be the same.

They were directed to make their camp beyond the castle and within sight of the sea. Above them towered the great curtain walls, set upon a mound and protected on the seaward side by a rocky bluff and on all sides by the ditch encircling the ward. Once upon a time there had been an extensive outer ward occupying the headland down to the water's edge but the sea had almost demolished the fortifications there. And so the castle was cut off from revictualling or reinforcement from the sea. But Henry's cannons could be landed near by with ease and drawn into position by teams of oxen.

Katrine remarked on the enormous size of the camp, which stretched out in every direction, swamping the small town which had sprung up under the walls of the castle.

'Everyone will be either here or at Harlech,' shrugged Raoul, dropping to lounge on his folding chair, his long legs stretched out before him. He had just returned from a reconnaissance, having reported to his immediate commander in the field. 'Those who have fought in Wales before wish to be in at the end.'

'Is Lionel d'Evreux here?' asked Katrine in a small voice. How would it feel to face the man who should have been her husband by now?

'Oh, yes,' replied Raoul, and the chilling smile on his lips sent an uneasy shiver down Katrine's spine. 'He is here, as is his cousin, Giles d'Evreux, Marquess of Thame, one of the Prince's senior commanders.' He gave a sardonic smile. 'Their pennons fly near Prince Henry's. He sits before the barbican gate, while we are to guard the entry on this side and watch it well, for there is a sally-port beneath the north-west tower, giving sheltered access to the ditch. Henry is girding the castle with a ring of steel to contain and watch the defenders while the cannons pound the walls. Once they are in position and have made a breach we shall attack.'

Katrine's nerves tightened. If only she could understand her husband! If only there need be no fighting! She shifted her position on the chest she was using as a seat, threaded her fingers together and clasped her hands in her lap, concentrating on the immediate problem rather than the one she dreaded most. 'Will you tell them I am here?'

'All in good time, my dove.' He draped an elbow over the back of his chair. 'We have scarcely arrived. I have yet to decide whether 'twould be best to approach a representative of Lancaster first. Many of his vassals are here and, of course, Harry, his son. An I could gain audience with the Prince. . .' He let the sentence die away as he mused.

Katrine watched her husband, her uneasiness growing. For the first time she sensed indecision in his manner. Not lack of purpose, but doubt as to the best way of achieving his aim. And he was gazing at her almost as though she were not there, his eyes narrowed in a steely glare, seeing beyond her to some resolve she could not divine.

But still determined to delay the announcement of her survival. What possible objective could that serve? Unless. . .but no. His quarrel could not be with the d'Evreux family. He had no personal knowledge of them. She must not allow her imagination to run away with her.

She straightened her back. 'I cannot see why you should not inform them immediately. What game are you playing, husband?'

He did not smile. 'No game, my dove, of that you may be quite certain. But,' he mused, 'I must proceed with care.' He seemed to come back to himself, to realise her presence as something more than that of a mere cypher. 'Would you be happier lodged in the town?' he asked abruptly.

Katrine studied him, her own eyes narrowed now. Much of Aberystwyth had been evacuated, the townsfolk not wishing to be caught up in a bloody battle. Camp-followers and other hangers-on had found billets in the empty dwellings. 'You wish to be relieved of my presence, seigneur?' Her tone bit. She could not understand his attitude and she would rather be angry than hurt.

'It might be more convenient for you so.' He saw the outrage on her small face and suddenly smiled, the old, irresistible Raoul emerging from behind his grim thoughts. 'And more congenial,' he added, 'but if you do not mind the close proximity of more than a thousand rough men-at-arms and archers, the noise and bustle of an army encampment, then I shall look to my own comfort and keep you by my side.'

'Where I belong. Not among the riff-raff who follow in the army's train. Congenial?' she scoffed. 'A roof over my head would be poor compensation for the company I would be forced to endure there.'

'You would have Myfanwy, Dorcas and an escort. And I would not desert you, wife.'

'Myfanwy? Does she wish to leave the camp?' She had not thought of Myfanwy's wishes.

Raoul shrugged. 'I do not know. But she would naturally accompany you if you wished to seek shelter elsewhere.'

'And,' she said flatly, 'you would visit me, as duty demanded.'

'And inclination,' he demurred softly, his look bringing the colour to her cheeks.

But she would not be so beguiled. Katrine paused

an instant and then asked sharply, 'If I remain here, shall I be free to move about the camp?'

A new frown descended on his brow, one of thought, not displeasure. 'I cannot see why not, an you do not go alone. Dorcas at least must accompany you, a guard too. Otherwise I should fear for your safety.'

Katrine nodded, satisfied. 'And must I avoid Lancaster's men and members of the d'Evreux family?'

He considered her, his attitude still tense despite his indolent posture. A smile returned to his lips, one which made Katrine uneasy. 'Nay, wife! I shall not inform them yet, but should they discover who you are 'twould suit my purpose well enough.'

'How?' demanded Katrine.

'That, dear wife, you will doubtless discover. All in good time.'

He was toying with her, Katrine thought furiously. And she would not play into his hands. She would avoid the Lancster and d'Evreux camps, make no attempt to contact them. Let him play his game without help from her. Her inheritance was probably already lost. But, dear Mother of God, do not let her lose him too!

'I shall remain here,' she told him firmly. 'A wife's place is by her husband's side.'

He rose to his feet and pulled her to hers. 'A true soldier's wife,' he murmured as his arms went about her. 'But if a battle looms, then you must obey me instantly and retire to a more secure place. I would not wish to have your safety preying on my mind while I fought .'

'Then I would go, husband.' She pressed her fore-head against his shoulder. 'But I pray there will be no need for battle to be joined. The castle must surely surrender.'

'We must wait and see what the cannon can do.' He lifted her chin and gazed deeply into her dove-grey eyes. 'Do not fret, my wife. Trust me. No harm will befall you.'

Maybe not. But 'twas not herself she worried about, she thought, surrendering her lips to his kiss.

Early one morning, escorted by Dorcas and one of Raoul's most trusted men-at-arms, Katrine passed through the busy camp towards the area on the out-skirts of the town set aside for military drills. She walked past farriers with their blazing fires, the sound of red-hot iron being beaten into shape ringing in her ears, and dodged the mounts of knights and squires as they travelled between the encampments or mayhap made their way forward to do their turn at sentry duty. Suitable buildings had been requisitioned for the storage of supplies and of the ammunition for the guns which had now been manhandled into place. Already the camp had become used to the daily cannonade as great iron balls were flung at the massive walls erected so long ago by the Normans. So far man's weapons had made little impact. Yet nature, using the power of the sea, had long ago reduced the outer defences to rubble. Raoul and others like him were impatient. If no breach could be made there would be little alterna-tive to a long and tedious siege.

Until that day Katrine had confined herself to walk-ing along the shore, savouring the fresh breeze off the sea, watching the small boats scurrying to and fro like beetles or birds, depending on whether it was oars or sails that powered them through the waves. The life of the camp had gone on all around her, noisy and bustling, with Raoul coming and going as his duties dictated and the question hanging so uneasily between them ignored.

For the nights were filled with delight, and neither wished to lose the physical joy they found in each other. If this interlude was all she was to have, then Katrine wanted nothing to disturb the peace between them. She dreaded the coming confrontation between her husband and her guardians and the man she had been intended to wed, but even more she dreaded the moment when Raoul made his move against his enemy. Whoever he was. She still did not know.

Today, relieved of picket duty for the while, the Chevalier was drilling his men in weapons practice, sword, mace and battle-hammer, wielded both mounted and on foot. Other captains were exercising their men in similar fashion, while mounted knights charged along the lists in practice courses. A tournament was being arranged for the following week and those intending to enter were keen to practise their skills. Beyond, right on the outskirts of camp, lay the town's butts, and there archers practised with their longbows. It was ironic, thought Katrine, that the longbow had originated in Wales, that King Richard's archers had been mostly Welsh. Now, like the Welsh lords, those men were divided, some shifting their loyalty to the King, whoever he might be, some backing the uprising because they remained loyal to the usurped Richard's memory or perhaps because they wished to free Wales from the English yoke. Motives on all sides were very mixed. Katrine had been surprised to discover so many Welsh lords in Prince Harry's camp. Rhun, when he finally arrived, would find himself in excellent company. Many of his compatriots had changed sides several times over the years.

And young Prince Henry had grown up. She had seen him in the distance, a slender, commanding figure with his brilliant surcoat quartered with the leopards of England and the lilies of France. At sixteen, when he had been given nominal charge of his father's army in Wales, he had been too young to take real command and so had been given older, more experienced men to guide him. Henry Percy, known as Hotspur, had been one of them until he had defected to the rebels' side, plotting with Glendower and Mortimer to overthrow King Henry and divide the realm between them as regents under the kingship of the young Edmund, Earl of March. But the King had rushed to Shrewsbury to the aid of his son and Hotspur had been killed in the battle that ensued. Now the Prince was twenty, experienced, able to lead the army himself. Raoul was only three years older, and he could have done just as well, Katrine was convinced, had he been a son of the King instead of a rebel Gascon lord. What her husband had achieved from such meagre beginnings brought a lump of pride to her throat.

Katrine walked to the edge of the field and stood for a moment watching the busy scene, hearing the dull boom of cannon-fire in the distance, an intermittent background to the more immediate sound of metal clashing with metal, of thundering hooves and wild whoops coming from the nearby tilt-yard.

Raoul, it appeared, was engaged in a furious encounter with Louis, both men wielding their massive, shielded broadswords with untiring skill. Both the Powys horse Raoul had taken from Rhun and his destrier, Thor, stood near by, their necks dark with sweat but nevertheless tossing their heads, eager to throw off the restraining hand of a groom. Raoul must intend to use them again or he would have sent them back to the stables.

Prince Henry himself, she suddenly noted, was preparing to run a free course with a knight mounted on a beautiful grey horse, so pale in colour that it was virtually white. She did not know the man or recognise his pennon, but then she knew little of the lords gathered to support Prince Harry, certainly not enough to recognise their coats of arms, their banners, pennons, or badges. But she decided to remain and watch for a while. The object of the exercise was to break a slender lance against the opponent's tourney shield, not to knock the man from his saddle as in some forms of joust. A solid strike would shatter the specially designed lance and score a point.

A dais had been erected near by, with benches set upon it for the use of such as herself as well as others with a more professional interest in observing the army preparing for battle. There was a vacant seat if the lady on the end would be prepared to move along a little. But as Katrine approached she realised that the young woman, her face striking under an elaborate heart-shaped head-dress, was splendidly attired, obviously a person of consequence, accompanied by other ladies in addition to servants and guards. The attendants sat on straw spread on the ground while the retainers stood at ease, their pikes pointing skywards.

Katrine advanced somewhat diffidently, unsure of the reception she could expect from such an exalted personage. Despite her newly acquired wardrobe it must be obvious that she was young and of lesser degree. If the lady made no move to shift then Katrine would have to remain standing, for she could see no other seat available. She did not really mind, though it would be more restful to sit. Poor Dorcas would be forced to stand in any case, unless she chose to join the other servants on the ground.

The lady looked round as Katrine drew near. She did not look too formidable and Katrine ventured a respectful curtsy and a smile.

One lovely, arched brow rose above eyes so dark that they appeared black. Katrine, stunned by the other woman's sparkling beauty, the creamy skin, wide cheekbones and small, cleft chin, blushed and prepared to retreat. But the other's eyes in their nests of lashes shone with good nature, and a ready smile tipped the corners of her generous mouth.

'Good morrow, mistress. You seek a seat?'

'Aye, my lady, but——'

The woman was already moving, urging her companions to do the same. 'Come, sit by me.'

Her eyes were on the ring encircling Katrine's finger, a ring that Raoul had produced without explanation, although it looked old, like a family heirloom. Booty of war, like herself? she had wondered as he had placed it on her finger, surprised that it fitted as

well as it did. As she took her place on the bench and
folded her hands in her lap she touched it, self-
conscious under the other's gaze.

'I have not seen you here before, mistress,' went on
the lady. 'You are here to watch your husband,
perhaps?'

'Aye.'

'As am I. Which knight is yours, lady?'

Katrine sank down gratefully. At least she had not
been taken for a common soldier's wife. 'The one
there, my lady, mounting the bay destrier. His coat is
part red, part blue, with two silver bands.'

'Ah, yes! A splendid knight; I have watched him
oft.' Katrine expected to be asked why she had not
been to the practice fields before and was relieved
when she was not. Instead, 'What is he named?' asked
her new acquaintance.

'Messire Raoul de Chalais, a chevalier from
Gascony.'

'The Chevalier?' The lady looked surprised,
amused. 'I have heard much praise of a knight known
as the Chevalier. He took Dryslwyn castle last
autumn, I believe?'

'He did.' Katrine felt unable to enlarge on that
statement.

'I had not heard that he was wed.'

Katrine shifted her feet nervously. ''Tis less than a
month since. Just before we set out from Dryslwyn.'

'You were there with him!' A clear, joyous laugh
rang out. 'You are a woman after my own heart, my
dear. I travel almost everywhere with my husband.'

'Who is, my lady?' ventured Katrine. Someone
important, she had no doubt.

'He is over there, running a course with Prince Henry. Giles d'Evreux, Marquess of Thame.'

Stunned, Katrine swallowed hard. 'You are the Marchioness of Thame?' she managed to utter.

'Indeed, but there is no need to look so shocked, my dear.' The other smiled wryly, acknowledging the young girl's awe at discovering her station. 'Bring your knight to our pavilion to dine. I believe my husband has yet to meet the Chevalier, there are so many lords and knights here, but I am certain he would like to acquaint himself with so enterprising a young man. Will you come?'

'I thank you, my lady. I must abide by my husband's wishes, but undoubtedly he will be delighted to accept your invitation.'

Katrine hardly knew how she got the words out. But she judged them to be true. He had seemed to think such an acquaintance would further his devious plans. She had vowed not to assist him, but fate had overruled her design. She had to accept. How could she turn down such a genuine invitation, so warmly given, without giving offence?

The young Marchioness, who looked not a day over five and twenty although Katrine suspected her to be nearer thirty, possessed a brilliance which Katrine envied. Watching her husband break his lance against his prince's shield, love and pride shone from those dark, fathomless eyes. She clapped her small hands together in delight.

'My husband made his fortune in the lists of Europe while he shared Henry of Bolingbroke's exile there. Young Harry will have a difficult task to beat him.'

'But competing with the Marquess must be excellent

practice for him,' murmured Katrine, wondering how Raoul would fare against so formidable an opponent. Mayhap next week's jousting would provide the answer. 'The Chevalier, too, survived for some years by his prowess in the lists,' she added.

They watched, breathless, as twice more the two horses thundered towards each other. On both occasions it was Prince Harry's lance which broke. Lady Thame looked put out.

'How could he?' she muttered to herself.

Having completed his contest with his prince, the Marquess rode towards his watching wife. As he approached he removed his helm, revealing the close-fitting chain-mail hood and gorget beneath. Grey-blue eyes set in a strong, handsome face smiled warmly at the Marchioness.

'Pippa, my love, are you not chilled, sitting there in this wind?'

'Nay, my lord,' returned his wife, rising to her feet. 'I am warmly wrapped. But you allowed Harry to win!' she accused, scowling at her gorgeous husband ferociously.

Giles threw back his head and laughed. 'Do not allow him to hear you say that, my love; he will count it treason! Nay, wife, he won fair and square. That young man will shortly outdo us all. He has developed unusual skill in arms and has the makings of a great leader in battle.'

His wife frowned the more. 'I pray such talents are not needed once this rebellion has been finally put down. I would not have you constantly on campaign, Giles. I do not wish to be parted from you, and our children need us at home.'

Giles shook his head, his eyes thoughtful. 'You are missing them, my love? So am I. Nothing would please me better than to see the end of fighting, but Harry will be sorely tried to find a purpose an there is no call for his services in the field.'

Katrine could scarcely take her eyes from the Marquess's commanding countenance. A gold-tipped moustache and wisps of matching beard showing round the edges of the encircling mail told her his colouring was fair whereas Raoul was dark, but both had that air of natural authority, the indefinable charisma which made men follow them unquestioningly, though in Giles d'Evreux it had matured into solid authority. In ten years' time she could imagine her husband as just such another. Philippa d'Evreux—for that must be her new acquaintance's name—was a lucky woman. Particularly as there seemed to be a deep affection between the two, despite Philippa's apparently furious accusation. Katrine suspected it had been made more to tease than in anger.

Philippa suddenly remembered Katrine's presence. 'Husband,' she said, 'may I present the lady of the knight Raoul de Chalais, who is known as the Chevalier?'

Katrine got hastily to her feet and made a deep curtsy. Still mounted on his beautiful white charger, Lord Thame inclined his head in acknowledgement. 'Your husband has made quite a name for himself, lady.'

'I have invited both to dine with us, Giles. You do not mind?'

'Of course not, my dear.' He inclined his head towards Katrine again, at the same time gathering his reins in readiness to move off. 'I shall look forward to making your husband's acquaintance anon. Until then.'

Both women watched his departure towards the stables. Turning her eyes away at last, Katrine realised that Raoul and Louis were preparing to break a lance or two together, Raoul mounted on Thor, Louis on the Powys horse, which Raoul had given him before leaving Dryslwyn.

'Look, my lady,' she said. 'The Chevalier breaks a lance with his lieutenant.'

Philippa watched with evident interest, and as Raoul's lance splintered against Louis's shield she laughed.

'Our husbands must be persuaded to joust together, I think. They would be well-matched. But now I must go. I look forward to seeing you later.' Her eyes sparkled and her smile warmed Katrine's heart. 'We shall become friends, I think.'

'You do me too much honour, my lady,' mumbled Katrine, curtsying deeply, overcome by the other's kindness, wishing this delightful woman were not related to Lionel d'Evreux.

'Nonsense, child!' said Philippa. 'Come!' She glanced around, gathering her ladies, the maidservants and her guards about her with her eyes. Then, with a casual wave of her hand, she departed, leaving Katrine feeling nervous and apprehensive. She could not avoid telling Raoul of the invitation. Could not escape his inevitable confrontation with Giles d'Evreux, the senior representative of the d'Evreux family present.

What would be their reaction when they discovered her identity?

Raoul smiled, a peculiar smile, half grim, half mischievous, when Katrine told him of her chance meeting with Lady Thame and the invitation to join them at their board.

'So, my dove,' he mused, 'your careful avoidance of their camp served no purpose after all. How did you name yourself?'

Katrine silently fumed. He had known of her tactic and said nothing. Now he was amused that her careful keeping of herself to herself had only, in the end, resulted in the meeting she had been trying to elude. His question had been posed in a lazy tone of enquiry but his eyes watched her intently.

'As your wife only. Did you wish for more?'

'Nay, sweeting.' He seemed to relax. 'They will discover your identity soon enough. And, mayhap, wonder why you did not tell such close relatives of your once prospective husband who you were.'

'You forced me into marriage. I decided to allow you to bear the brunt of their wrath.'

'Forced, my dove? I did not perceive any great resistance on your part. In fact, you appeared only too eager to share my bed.'

Katrine's colour rose. He was right, curse him! But he had no need to embarrass her with the memory of her easy surrender. 'I protested most strongly that I was not free——'

'But you were. Never forget that, my dove. No betrothal had taken place. I prevented your ever becoming a d'Evreux bride, true, but you were mine by right of conquest and you needed the protection of my name. If any one of them chooses to challenge me on the matter I am more than ready to defend my actions.'

A small, satisfied smile played about his mobile lips. Something quite startling became clear to Katrine in that moment.

'You wish to be challenged!' she cried.

The smile widened but there was something chilling about it. 'Mayhap I do,' he acknowledged. 'But now we must prepare ourselves for this visit to the d'Evreux camp. For my sake, my dove, make yourself as beautiful as possible. Wear your most becoming gown. I wish our hosts to see you at your best.'

'Only my best could possibly be good enough for *you*, seigneur. Dorcas!' The woman was just outside the tent, chatting with the guard. 'Bring me the green sarsenet kirtle and the saffron velvet surcoat.'

Katrine's scathing tone pricked Raoul's conscience. He was using her, an innocent, little more than a child, to further his cause. She did not deserve such treatment, but he had no other weapon to use against his enemies.

'My dove!' He reached out and caught her as she flounced across towards the flimsy silken partition which shielded their sleeping quarters from the remainder of the pavilion. Dorcas entered and moved towards the chest which held Katrine's gowns. Her presence did not deter him. Hugues and many others were always within earshot. No one would dream of inerfering between husband and wife, and if they all knew a little more of his private affairs than he would prefer then so did every servant of every master or mistress he had ever known.

'My dove,' he repeated, looking down into her mutinous face with something like compassion, 'to me you always look perfect. I see you, not the clothes you wear.' He bent his head and kissed her firmly clamped lips, lips which nevertheless trembled while tears shone like diamonds in her eyes. 'But others do not know your inner beauty as I do; they see only the outside, beautiful enough by all accounts——' he wiped an escaping droplet of moisture which threatened to trace a path down her cheek '—especially when you are angry and have jewels in your eyes. But I wish my wife to look like the high-born lady she is, worthy to wed the highest in the land.'

'But whom you, a mere knight, have snared.'

Katrine's voice shook. How easily he could seduce her with tender words and a kiss! Yet some vestige of pride made her continue to protest. To hit his pride where it would most hurt.

But he seemed not one whit put out. He smiled again. 'Aye, my dove. And I wish the world to know it. Believe me, I have my reasons.'

'So you have always said, yet I, your pawn, am still in ignorance of your design. Can you not tell me, husband?'

It was a last plea for understanding between them. Raoul recognised it but had held his revenge so close to his heart for so long that he felt unable to break his silence, even to his wife. Only Louis had any inkling of what he was about and 'twas better it remained that way.

Sadly, he shook his head. 'Trust me, my dove. All will resolve itself shortly. You will not have long to wait for your explanation.'

Katrine tugged herself free of his hold. 'I will do your bidding and change,' she informed him tightly.

CHAPTER ELEVEN

KATRINE'S stomach churned as they approached the Thames' splendid pavilion. Since it was pitched at some considerable distance from their own, Raoul had insisted that they ride, to save themselves a lengthy walk from which they would probably emerge both tired and covered in mire.

Both horses were, of course, caparisoned and tacked up with their best ornamented saddles and bridles and other horse furniture, the leather cut and decorated with shining metal studs, her palfrey's head-stall hung with tiny tinkling bells and last used by the lady Eiluned. Heads turned as they passed by with Hugues and Dorcas riding behind and an escort in their wake. As Raoul had no doubt intended, thought Katrine dourly. He was making a show. She had a dreadful feeling that his purpose was about to unfold.

But how could the fact that he had deprived Lionel d'Evreux of his bride have anything to do with his own personal vendetta? She kept telling herself that it couldn't have—he did not know the family; he had said so often enough. Lord and Lady Thame had shown no sign of recognition. Yet she and her connection with the d'Evreux family seemed to be central to his schemes.

Her mind whirled as she was helped to dismount on the edge of the Marquess of Thame's camp and the horses were led away. His pavilion stood in the centre

of his retinue's tents, surrounded and guarded, just as
Raoul's only on a much grander scale. The pavilion
itself, gleaming scarlet in the spring sunshine, was four
times as big as the white one she shared with her
husband. While Hugues, Dorcas and the escort were
taken off to be fed elsewhere, they trod forward,
ushered by a sergeant-at-arms, to be received at the
open flap by a man she took to be a steward. She felt
softness under her feet as she stepped into the warm,
cosy atmosphere engendered by sunlight filtering
through the red silk and looked down in astonishment
to see a patterned carpet spread over the ground.
Even indoors she had never known such luxury. She
had heard it said that in the East they were used so,
but here such beautiful things were treasured as coverings for chests or mayhap to be hung upon a wall.

A large board supported by trestles stood in the
centre of the space, laid ready for the meal. Silver
gleamed upon the linen cloth and even the trenchers
were of pewter. But signs of war intruded. Weapons
stood piled in one corner and armour hung from
perches set in the timber posts.

So absorbed was she in the pavilion's appointments
that she scarcely noticed the group of people gathered
on the far side of the table. But now their hosts
detached themselves to come forward to welcome
them.

Raoul was greeted by the Marquess of Thame with
warm courtesy, which Raoul apparently returned.
Lady Thame drew Katrine forward and they were
both introduced to the other members of the party;
some of the ladies Katrine had seen earlier, some
knights, one other visiting lord. But as they took their

seats at the board Katrine's eyes followed the massive figure of the man who might have been her husband. Lionel d'Evreux. A knight in his own right and heir to Richard d'Evreux, the second Earl of Wenstaple.

Tall and muscular, like a tree-trunk, she thought, he was fairer even than his cousin of Thame but without any sign of the intelligence which shone from both Giles d'Evreux's eyes and even those of Lionel's brother, younger than he by a year, who was introduced as Sir Edward d'Evreux but addressed by everyone as Ned, and who was visiting his relations from the camp of the magnate to whose affinity he was attached. Ned was dark, like Raoul, and his devotion to his cousin Philippa shone from his grey eyes every time he looked at her, which was often. She, Katrine noted, treated him with affection and tolerant understanding, no doubt waiting for the day when Ned married a woman who could return his love. Ned, Katrine decided, would make a more worthy heir to the d'Evreux inheritance than his slow-witted brother. She looked from Lionel to Raoul. And smiled to herself. Decidedly, she would rather be the Chevalier's wife. But had she never met Raoul and been given the choice between the brothers she would have chosen Ned. He bore an elusive resemblance to her husband. Before the latter had acquired his broken nose, of course.

Lord Thame had seated the Chevalier on his left, with the other noble lord on his right, and the other knights, including Lionel, seated beyond the visiting lord, with Ned taking the place at the end of the board. Next to Raoul sat Philippa d'Evreux with Katrine on her other side. The Chevalier and his wife had been accorded the courtesy of honoured guests. Beyond Katrine the other ladies filled the side of the table and the seat at the end facing Ned. No one sat opposite, of course, for that was where the servitors worked while squires, including Hugues, stood behind their masters ready to be of service to them.

With the meal well under way the Marquess dispensed with meaningless pleasantries, ignored the bawdy jokes coming from one end of the table and the discussions of dress from the other and asked Raoul about his siege of Dryslwyn. Raoul launched into a lively account of his chase after Rhun ab Brechfa and his investment of the castle; of his entry under a flag of truce to demand its surrender.

'And 'twas given?' asked Giles as Raoul paused.

'Aye, after some parley. I found,' Raoul went on, just a little too casually, 'that the lord Rhun held a hostage there, one worth a rich ransom, who would constitute part of my prize.' A smile touched his lips but did not reach his watchful eyes. 'She was his prime bargaining counter. In return for her person I gave my word to assist Rhun to obtain a pardon, for she is King Henry's ward and Rhun had kept her safe.' He leaned forward so that he could see Katrine sitting beyond his hosts and indicated her with an airy flap of his hand. 'Behold the lady Katrine Lawtye, heiress of the late Earl of Huntershold, who is now my wife.'

He could not quite keep the triumph from his voice. Katrine sat quite still, staring sightlessly at the hands clenched in her lap. Her mouth had gone quite dry. Gasps of astonishment ran along the table like fire. Everyone was leaning and staring. How could Raoul do this to her?

The Marchioness's hand covered hers. 'My dear,' said Philippa in a clear, firm tone, 'we are so thankful that you are alive. We had never quite given up hope of your survival.'

Katrine dared to look up, glancing at Philippa before seeking the eyes of her husband. But his were assessing the Marquess, who sat back, his gaze narrowed as he assimilated the news. Then Lord Thame stirred and his smile, slightly wry but warm nevertheless, was turned on her.

'Indeed, my lady, we are all delighted. You must know that my family had a special interest in your fate?'

Katrine could only nod.

'Then why are you wed?'

The sudden demand came from Lionel as he slammed his fist down on the board, making the silver shiver and the trenchers jump.

'Easy, Lionel,' murmured Giles warningly. 'We have not heard the bones of it yet.'

'But she was promised to me!' Lionel's eyes were popping out of his head in his anger. He glared at Katrine as though he would like to shake her. He did not appear to see her except as the object of his rage. 'You should have wed no other! I have waited faithfully these six years for you to return! I will not have you stolen from me now!'

'Come, brother.' Ned's calm tones came from the end of the table. His eyes had been on Katrine, noting her anguish, the pleading looks she directed towards her husband. ''Twas an excuse to avoid other betrothals and you know it. You have no desire to wed the lady Katrine or any other. And,' he added forcefully, 'you were never betrothed.'

Lionel reddened. Ned, it seemed, had the knack of making him feel foolish, inferior, had unmasked his inner feelings, and his resentment showed.

He repeated, sullen now, 'I will not have her stolen from me!'

'Ned has the right of it, cousin; she was never fully yours and could not, therefore, be stolen from you,' observed Giles coolly. 'You must accept the situation.' He turned chilly eyes on the Chevalier. 'I assume the marriage is unassailable?'

'Absolutely, my lord.' Raoul's smile deepened. He was enjoying himself, Katrine thought. There was steel in his narrowed green eyes as he confronted his host. 'But do not think the Huntershold fortune lost to your family, my lord. I am more your cousin than is Sir Lionel.'

Another ripple of astonishment ran along the table. Philippa glanced quickly at Katrine's wide, incredulous eyes. 'You did not know,' she whispered—a statement, not a question.

'No.' Katrine forced the word out, her mind reeling. 'Can it be true?'

Giles's calm tones, his raised hand, restored order and silence to the table.

'How say you so? You are a Gascon, are you not?'

'Aye, my lord. But we share a common ancestor— Baron William d'Evreux, Lord of Wenfrith. Mine is a bastard line as,' Raoul added deliberately, 'is yours. Your father, Thomas d'Evreux, Earl of Acklane, is my great-uncle. As is—or was until his death—his half-brother, Sir Lionel's grandfather, Richard, first Earl of Wenstaple.'

Giles showed his first real emotion. He drew a deep breath. His hand clenched about his cup. 'Stephen's grandson?' he wondered.

'Precisely, my lord. So, you see, I have kept the Huntershold fortune within the family.'

And this, thought Katrine despairingly, was why he had wed her. Why she had been so essential to his plans. She knew now that it was his family he wished to revenge himself upon, so strongly that even preferment, her fortune, their happiness mattered little to him. This man she did not know. Did not like. But he was the husband she loved.

Lionel broke the tension by banging his fist down again and lurching to his feet.

'You lie!' he shouted.

Raoul rose gracefully to face him. 'I can assure you that I do not. But you have impugned my honour, Sir Lionel. I shall hold myself ready to meet you whenever and wherever you wish.'

Katrine's hands jerked in her lap. Her mouth opened but no words came. She could do nothing to stop this madness.

But Giles could. He did not bother to rise. 'Lionel, apologise!' he snapped. 'I will not have a guest—nay, a *cousin*—insulted at my table. Apologise, I say!'

His voice rang out, his authority absolute. Lionel blinked, his slow mind grappling with his emotions: disbelief, anger, pricked pride, impotence. For he could not gainsay his powerful cousin.

He gave a stiff bow in Raoul's direction and

growled, 'I am ordered to apologise and so I must. No doubt you speak the truth.'

Raoul bowed, his easy movement in sharp contrast to Lionel's stilted gesture. 'This time,' he said softly, 'I will accept your apology.'

Giles spoke again. 'Enough of this foolishness! Your fame has gone before you, Chevalier. We are proud to welcome you into the family.'

Raoul looked slightly taken aback by this speech of welcome. 'Mayhap I, my lord, am not so proud to belong to it. My wife and I will take our leave. Come, wife.'

Katrine doubted whether her legs would support her. She pushed herself up, using the edge of the table to help her, then looked helplessly at Philippa, who had been so kind. 'Forgive me, my lady, and him for his lack of civility. I know not why. . .'

Philippa nodded, her dark eyes sad. 'You love him,' she observed, very softly. 'Have faith, child. All will be well.'

'Thank you,' murmured Katrine. 'And the Marquess. I would not for the world——'

Raoul's impatient tones cut across her words. 'Do you come, wife?'

The men had stood as she did. No one protested, no one spoke. In a daze, she curtsied to Giles, whose face wore a heavy frown, walked to the opening and preceded her husband from the pavilion.

The horses and servants had been held near by. As Hugues, who could not hide his incredulity at his master's revelations, helped her to mount, she looked despairingly at Raoul's taut face.

For him the matter was far from finished.

Back in the pavilion she dismissed Dorcas. Hugues remained tactfully outside, keeping an eager, inquisitive Dai with him. Everyone knew trouble when they saw it.

Katrine turned to face her husband. Her voice shook but she spoke with precise clarity. 'That was unforgivable. You used me and abused the Thames' hospitality. I thought you an honourable, courteous man, Raoul de Chalais. It seems I was mistaken.'

Raoul simply threw her a contemptuous glance. 'I owe no d'Evreux courtesy or honour!'

'Nor your wife, it would seem, Sir Raoul.'

She had never called him that before, the formal English title which no one ever seemed to use. The bitterness in her voice seemed to touch him. His eyes lost their fierce glare. He sighed. 'Nay, wife, I did not mean to hurt you. You have suffered enough from Rhun ab Brechfa.'

Her voice still shaking, she said, 'You said you meant me no harm. When you wed me I believed you felt something for me, but now I know you did not.' She saw him start forward and raised a hand to ward him off. 'Oh, yes, your body desires mine, my lord husband, as it might that of a whore, but otherwise you can feel nothing for me or you would not have used me as you did. I have been a fool. You wed me simply to flaunt your conquest in the faces of those you consider your enemies. I could understand a desire to acquire my inheritance and accept it, for I have never expected any suitor to disregard its value, but I cannot even imagine why you should so hate your family that you are ready to gamble the restoration of your lands in Aquitaine and the acquisition of my estates here in order to exact revenge. What have those people ever done to you?'

'Sit down, wife.' He spoke abruptly, pointing to the chest, and Katrine did not argue. Her legs would give way soon enough if she did not. Only anger was keeping back the bitter tears stinging her eyelids. She would not let him see her bent and beaten. She lifted her chin and stared into his sea-green eyes, which at that moment held little expression. He did not sit himself, but paced the small pavilion like a caged tiger.

'What have they done to me? you ask. Nothing.' At her gasped interruption he turned to her, his upper lip curled almost into a snarl. 'Not to me, my dove. But to my grandsire. The Stephen, blood-brother to his father, whom Giles d'Evreux so correctly named.' He slammed his fist into his palm. 'Why did they not appear ashamed when they discovered who I was? I was forced to throw their welcome in their hypocritical faces!'

'You did that well enough.' Katrine surprised herself with her calmness. 'But why?'

'Why? Why? You keep asking me why. Very well, I will tell you.' He flung himself into his chair and stared hard at her lovely, stiff, vulnerable face. Remorse at the pain he had inflicted on his innocent wife churned his stomach. She was wrong; he did feel something for her beyond his raging desire. But even for her he could not deviate from the path he had set himself.

The need for vengeance had been festering within him for as long as he could remember. Ever since, as a child of barely eight years, his mother Louise had told him the story as she had lain dying of childbed fever after the birth of yet another stillborn babe.

When he had gone to his father, demanding that he do something to right the wrong done to his maternal grandfather, Antoine de Chalais had merely shrugged. 'We have only your grandmother's word for the truth of the story,' he had said, 'and she had it from her husband, who could not substantiate the facts. I cannot see that it would serve any purpose to rake up that old history now.'

But Antoine had had no personal involvement. He had wed Louise to obtain a substantial dowry which, presumably, Raoul's grandfather Stephen had provided. Raoul had been unable to shrug off the injustice as easily as his sire.

His grandmother had been a prize of war, he knew that much. Such marriages seemed to run in the family, he thought as he continued to watch his wife's face. When he spoke it was more gently than he could have imagined a few moments since.

'Lionel d'Evreux's grandfather, Richard, the first Earl, hounded his half-brother Stephen, my grandfather, from England at the time of the Great Plague. Stephen was forced to earn his living as a mercenary on the continent. There, he met my grandmother and wed her.' No need to go into details irrelevant to the reasons for his hatred. 'In 1367, after fighting for England in Spain, Stephen returned to his own country to attempt to heal the breach with his kin. But Thomas d'Evreux, his full brother, killed him. The d'Evreux family persecuted and then killed my grandfather,' said Raoul bitterly. 'Mayhap now you can understand my need to avenge his memory.'

The words hung in the air between them as Katrine tried to assimilate their meaning.

'Thomas was not hounded from the country. He bears the d'Evreux name,' she said at last. 'His son has become Marquess of Thame. There must have been a reason——'

Raoul cut in, 'Thomas was a mere child at the time Stephen was driven away. Eleanor, Richard's wife, took him under her wing. Otherwise. . .' He let his words trail off, lifting his shoulders in an expressive shrug.

'It was all so long ago,' muttered Katrine, not quite knowing what to think. 'The people concerned are all dead.'

'Thomas is not, although he is an old man now. The Marquess is the one I would like to kill. That would cause Thomas the grief he deserves.'

'Raoul,' begged Katrine with a shudder, 'you must not speak so. The Marquess is renowned as a man of great valour and humanity. He is in no way responsible for his father's deeds. And how did Thomas kill his brother? Why?'

'That I do not know. The fact is enough.'

'For you, mayhap, but not for me! I beg you, husband, try to discover the truth of the matter before you take any more rash action!'

'The truth? God's teeth, woman! Think you they would say the truth an it did not suit them?'

He sprang to his feet, angry again, his normally clear thinking curdled and clouded by his obsession. Katrine could see it eating away at him like a maggot in meat, poisoning his whole personality. What had become of the splendid Chevalier, the stern but fair commander, the cheerful companion, the considerate husband, the passionate, gentle lover?

She made one more attempt to reason with him. 'They seem like honourable people. Trusted by the King.'

'Twas no use, she could tell. Raoul had come to the moment he had been waiting and planning for for so long and nothing would deflect him.

'The Marquess is the man I would like to challenge,' Raoul mused, 'but methinks he will give me no cause. But Lionel is easily provoked. He is the heir of Wenstaple. 'Twould cause consternation in the family were he to die by my sword. In fair combat, of course.'

Katrine swallowed, suddenly deadly afraid. Lionel towered over even the tall Chevalier. Was twice as stout. Sheer strength could bring him victory.

Raoul's teeth flashed in the dimness of the tent. 'His brute strength against my skill and cunning. 'Twould be a fair challenge, do you not agree, wife?'

Dully, Katrine stared into his grinning, reckless face. 'Supposing he kills you, seigneur?'

'Then you would be a widow, wife, free of a husband you despise for wishing to take vengeance for an old wrong.'

Before Katrine could reply an urgent blast on a horn interrupted them. Instantly, Raoul transformed into the knight she knew.

'My watchman is sounding!' he cried, snatching up his arming cap, pulling it on his head and covering it with basinet and mail gorget as Hugues, answering the call too, ran into the pavilion to strap his knight's breastplate into place.

'No time for more,' cried Raoul, pushing aside the

armour intended for feet and legs, snatching up his heavy sword and running from the pavilion, strapping a vambrace to his sword-arm. 'An attempt to break out!'

His camp had become a chaos of running men and stamping horses as Louis, Gruffydd and other knights rallied their men and raced to reinforce those of his company on picket duty by the sally-port. His commander came charging through, ready to order up reinforcements from other companies should they become necessary. But this might only be a diversion to weaken some other point. All the gates and entries, their own flanks and backs, must be guarded with undiminished vigilance and strength. Throughout the camp the call to arms had been sounded.

There were enough men on duty to prevent an initial attempt at break-out or relief, Raoul had said. Katrine watched him ride off to join them, the others at his heels, her heart pounding with excitement and fear.

Both the surgeon and Sir Graham were following. Expecting to have to tend the wounded, she thought, Sir Graham mayhap ready to hear last confessions and to administer the last rites.

Dear Lord, keep him safe, she prayed. He is not bad, just confused, idealistic. In the matter of his feud against the d'Evreux family she felt so much older and wiser than Raoul. He was in truth still a rash, hot-headed young man, in most respects aged beyond his years by his trade, his ability to lead other men. Yes, he was a strong, charismatic man, a strategist, a fearsome fighter. But, lacking the security of a respected family line, feeling denied his birthright, he was seeking to restore the balance in the only way he knew.

She must find help before he did something rash, stupid, ill-conceived. Philippa. Lady Thame. Tomorrow forenoon, when the men were occupied in feats of arms. For she had to believe that Raoul would return safely today.

But she could not just wait here for him. Even as the thought entered her head Myfanwy came in through the opening, followed by Dorcas and Olwen. And at the same moment the distant, tangled sounds of shouting, clashing metal and the wild neighing of frightened horses intensified. Katrine and Myfanwy looked at each other, both stricken by the echoing sound of fierce fighting.

'I must see what is happening. Will you come with me?' Katrine asked.

Myfanwy nodded, her face white. 'If there are wounded we may be able to help.'

'I will come too, my lady,' offered Dorcas.

Olwen said nothing but followed her mistress as the party set off towards the skirmish. Dai was nowhere to be seen and Katrine guessed he had followed Raoul and Hugues. If necessary he would hold the horses while the others fought on foot.

'We must not venture too near,' said Myfanwy. 'We must not get in the way.'

Katrine nodded. She felt exhausted, mentally and physically, sickened with worry. What a day. Everything seemed to be happening at once. But through it all she knew nothing, could think of nothing, except her need to be near Raoul. To save him if necessary, if she could. Because she desperately loved the man

he truly was. Despite the aberration of hate and
vengeance. Despite the way he had used her. In many
ways she could understand.

It did not take them long to reach a point from
which they could see the fighting, which was taking
place beyond the strip of rocky headland where once
the outer bailey had been. The defenders must have
hoped to break through the defensive line and ride
north to Glendower's hide-out in the Snowdon range
to seek help. At a casual glance it looked like a
tournament, with teams of knights fighting each other.
But here the weapons were not protected, the swords'
blades, honed to razor-sharpness, the swinging maces'
spiked balls and the terrible battle-hammers able to
inflict fearful wounds. Men already lay dead and dying
beneath the horses' hooves.

A solid phalanx of Raoul's men-at-arms stood
shoulder to shoulder across the enemy's narrow escape
route between sea and camp, ready to stop any of the
castle's defenders who might break through.

She saw Dai, standing clear of the fighting, hopping
from foot to foot in his excitement and anxiety, his
eyes fixed on the broad shoulders of the Chevalier.
He clasped a broadsword to his chest, longer than he
was tall. Raoul's spare weapon, she thought, no doubt
thrust at him by Hugues before the squire himself had
followed his lord into the midst of the fighting, Raoul's
banneret steadied high with one hand while he fended
off attackers with the other.

With Hugues at his shoulder, Raoul seemed to be
holding his own as the fighting swayed back and forth.
Even as she watched, his immediate opponent toppled
from his saddle and Raoul's sword slashed down to

finish the man off before he could cut at Thor's stomach or Raoul's own unprotected legs.

As the defenders were driven back towards the castle a few supporting arrows flew from the battlements above but the range was extreme. Raoul's archers returned the fire, the arrows mostly clattering harmlessly against the castle's walls but sufficing to keep the defenders pinned down, inhibiting their aim.

The commander had brought other knights and men in support but it seemed they would not be needed. Two of the party from the castle attempted to gallop back across the old outer ward to safety, only to be struck down by archers. Raoul and his men had held the attempted break-out, prevented any man from escaping to send word for help—not that Glendower would be able to muster much assistance—and had decisively won the day. Those enemies not dead were throwing down their arms.

Katrine breathed a heartfelt sigh of relief. Raoul, Louis and Gruffydd were safe, and it looked as though Raoul's force had sustained only light injuries—a few cuts and no doubt many bruises. Several of the enemy lay dead or dying in pools of blood. The surgeon and Sir Graham moved forward to tend those still living, friend and foe alike.

The excitement had stirred the entire camp, not least its commander-in-chief. As a weary but victorious Chevalier led his men from the field the Prince of Wales rode to meet them, the commander at his side.

'That was well done, Sir Knight.' His clear tones rang out as he studied Raoul's banneret with its fox's head imposed across the silver bands, his gaze intent.

'I do not recognise your arms or badge. What is your name?'

Raoul had dismounted and now bowed his knee to the young Prince. 'Raoul de Chalais, my liege, from Gascony.'

His commander intervened. 'Sir Raoul is known as the Chevalier, my lord, and regained Dryslwyn for your father the King.'

As the Prince looked at him with new interest Raoul said, 'I had that honour, Your Grace.'

Harry nodded. 'I have heard of your courage and initiative, Chevalier. I shall not forget.'

The Prince walked his horse on to move among the victorious soldiers, smiling and congratulating until he came upon the prisoners. Then his expression hardened. 'Keep them safely confined,' he ordered, his voice imperious. 'We will show clemency an they swear allegiance to their true Sovereign Lord.'

With that, he was gone. Raoul mounted again, not quite so easily as usual. Katrine followed him and his company back to the camp along a route lined with cheering men-at-arms and archers who seemed to have gathered from all around now that the emergency was over. Dai walked proudly at Thor's head, his face shining with happiness.

Gruffydd's face remained impassive. He had fought well, but Katrine wondered at his inner thoughts. He could not have enjoyed crossing swords with his countrymen.

Back in the pavilion Hugues helped Raoul to remove his armour. It was only then that Katrine noticed the red staining the Chevalier's hose. And the way his left arm hung limply at his side. No wonder

he had allowed Dai to lead Thor back! A little maggot
of worry gnawed at her insides. On the other hand,
she was not at that moment in charity with her
husband, however courageous and skilled he had just
shown himself.

'You are hurt, husband,' she said matter-of-factly,
moving towards him, keeping her concern from her
voice. 'Allow me to tend your wounds.'

''Tis nothing, my dove.' He looked down at his
thigh, at the blood soaking into the blue wool. 'A
mere scratch, I believe.' But it burnt like fire and he
had lost much blood.

'And your arm?' There was no sign of blood there,
thought Katrine thankfully, but then frowned.
Mayhap 'twas broken, to cripple him for life.

'A blow to my shoulder. 'Tis bruised and numb, no
more. Hugues can see to me; he has done so in the
past.'

Katrine smiled at the squire. 'Then I will help you.
We will need fresh linen and salve for the cut. Mayhap
a sling for the arm.'

'Warm water and a cloth, my lady,' said Dorcas at
her elbow.

'Thank you. Find some linen to make a bandage
and bring the salve.'

Hugues had already stripped the Chevalier of his
hose and untied the strings holding his braies at the
knees. The linen undergarment was already slit and
sodden with blood and Hugues chopped it off with his
knife, exposing the wound.

Another scar to add to those she had already discovered. Katrine inspected the gash, choking down
the nausea that the sight brought. A clean cut, but

deep enough to warrant several stitches to keep the
edges together.

Hugues stood up. 'I'll fetch the surgeon,' he said,
confirming her own view.

Raoul sighed. 'I suppose you had better,' he agreed.

Later that day, the wound cleansed, stitched and
bandaged, Raoul lay on his pallet watching Katrine
prepare for bed. Katrine felt his eyes upon her and
knew he was wondering whether she would move her
own pallet back to its normal position beside his,
where they could share the same coverings and lie in
each other's arms.

She did not look at him as she gathered another
blanket and skin and made for the pallet where it lay,
several feet from his though still behind their screen.
His wounds were only an excuse, she knew that. The
fact was that she could not bring herself to share his
bed while the question of his family feud hung
between them.

He watched but said nothing as she dismissed
Dorcas and lay down, pulling the blankets close about
her neck. She would have nothing else to keep her
warm that night.

CHAPTER TWELVE

RAOUL was up and about again the following day, limping slightly, his arm stiff, but otherwise his normal, vital self. He went to the practice field to supervise the training of his men, although he did not take an active part himself.

'Must be feeling it more than he will admit,' observed Louis with a grin. 'But do not worry, my lady; the Chevalier always regains his strength quickly. He will be quite recovered in a day or two.'

Katrine nodded. She had gone to the field again, hoping to see the lady Philippa, but been disappointed to find both her and the Marquess absent. She had spotted Ned with his lord's contingent in the distance and noticed Lionel d'Evreux standing quite still, scowling at the Chevalier, his fair brows knotted low over his eyes. He had turned his head and the scowl had grown even deeper when he had seen her. That one would not forgive or forget easily, thought Katrine with a shiver. He would chew it over in his slow mind, his bitterness at what he imagined he had lost growing. If only she could have passed on to the Marchioness what Raoul had told her. Then mayhap his relatives might have understood his attitude. But they remained in ignorance of the source of his hostility and so would not understand his uncivil behaviour.

Two days passed and Raoul was mounted again, testing the strength of his arm and leg. Katrine had

still not encountered the lady Philippa and guessed
that after Raoul's behaviour there would be no further
invitation to the d'Evreux camp.

That night, as she prepared to go to her pallet,
Raoul stopped her. Hugues and Dorcas had both left
to find their own beds. Raoul had been sitting watching her for some moments, making her nervous under
his scrutiny. Yet the feeling was still there, that she
could not easily lie with her husband until his strange
mood had left him, his feud with his family been
settled or forgotten.

'Your pallet should be beside mine, wife. There was
never need for us to sleep apart.'

Katrine studied her feet, the pink toes peeping from
beneath the chamber-gown she had been about to
throw off. 'I would rather it remained where it is,' she
said stiffly.

'How so, wife?'

Raoul's voice was soft, but she could feel the steel
behind it. He knew she was avoiding close contact
with him and had decided to challenge her over it. She
forced her answer out, still not meeting his eyes.

'I do not know you in your present mood, seigneur.
You are a stranger to me. I have no wish to lie with a
stranger.'

'A stranger?'

Raoul's voice held a hint of incredulous laughter.
He had not shouted or berated her as she had feared.
Katrine gathered her courage.

'The man I married was honourable, courteous,
showing mercy even to such as Rhun ab Brechfa. He
possessed all the attributes of a true knight.'

Her voice faltered to a stop as he took her shoulders

and turned her fully towards him. He put a finger under her chin and lifted her face to his. 'And now I do not? Look at me, Katrine.' But she kept her eyes down, concentrated on the dark curls of hair on the muscular chest showing in the gap of his gown. 'I'll brook no disobedience, wife. Look at me, I say!'

His voice had sharpened. Reluctantly, Katrine lifted her eyes to meet his. 'My family relationships are my own business,' he went on curtly. 'That which lies between us is both yours and mine. The other is no affair of yours.'

''Twas not until you made it so! Until you used me to taunt those you wish to hurt. And what will you do next, husband? Think you 'twill not affect me, your wife? Had you not wed me, but demanded a ransom for my return, then 'twould indeed be no concern of mine.'

He sighed and moved his hand to cup her chin and caress her soft cheek. ''Twas how I intended it to be, my dove. But——' he shrugged and a wry, self-deprecatory smile touched his lips '—I cannot regret my decision to wed or the weeks we have shared as man and wife.' His voice hardened as though to compensate for the weakness he had just shown. 'And I will not allow you to deny me that pleasure we have found together. Whether your pallet is moved or not, tonight you will lie with me.'

As he spoke, before she could move or protest, he swept her into his arms and strode to his bed. She saw the wince of pain as his bruised shoulder took the strain, his thigh the extra weight, watched the beads of sweat break out on his brow. But the Chevalier was a hard man; he would do what he must regardless of pain or weakness. She found herself on the pallet, her gown somehow gone, his too as he came down to her.

The air was chilly on that April night but the shiver that ran through Katrine had nothing to do with the cold. He would spoil the joy between them but she could not resist. He had the right, and she would not plead. He took her with speed, with urgency, showing her who was master, ignoring any pain his wound gave him. Yet as his strokes quickened, mounting to his climax, all the old sensations washed over Katrine. She gritted her teeth and clenched her hands at her sides, determined not to give him the satisfaction of knowing he had brought her pleasure despite everything. It was the only way she could think of to register her protest.

If he noticed, he made no comment. He left her for a moment to drag her pallet next to his own, then lay beside her again. Katrine had turned her back. She did not wish him to see or feel the tears wetting her cheeks.

So, although they lay together, Raoul need not have bothered to shift the bed for all the closeness left between them. He could feel her warmth, smell the delicate odour of her body, sense the rigid resistance radiating from her tensed muscles. Release had come to him at the cost of considerable pain but had brought no satisfaction. He longed to take her in his arms again, to gentle and woo her back, to receive the passionate outpouring of response in which he had learned to lose himself. Instead he lay cursing the fate which had made her an essential part of his plans and his own foolishness in indulging his need to sample her attractions. He had convinced himself that to wed her would make his revenge more sweet, but it had been self-deception. He had wanted her and been unable to find another way to have her. And, once wed, he had discovered in her the one woman who answered all his needs.

She had turned against him because of his purpose. But he would not be deflected by sentiment. Honour demanded that he avenge his grandfather in the only way he knew how. Soon. Soon he would spread knowledge of the d'Evreux dishonour, for all should know. He could no longer demand a ransom from them for his wife's return, but he could demand honourable satisfaction from one of their number. Lionel would do.

Katrine discovered that the Marquess of Thame had left the camp on some errand for Prince Harry and was expected back that day. Tomorrow, therefore, she could hope to find his wife watching him. In rather dispirited mood she walked towards the sounds of shouting, of scraping metal, pounding hooves and roars of encouragement, wishing it did not remind her so much of the real battle which had been fought only days earlier. But she wanted to be near Raoul, for she was fearful of what he might do. Last night he had seemed so set in his purpose, determined to let nothing interfere. He had thrust his wounds aside, although she knew they still gave him pain.

When his altercation with Lionel d'Evreux came she had been half expecting it. D'Evreux had been standing rather as before, glowering, challenging simply by his presence. Raoul rode up to him, leapt from his saddle and gave a mock-bow.

'You seem displeased by something, Sir Lionel. It cannot surely still be annoyance at my stealing your hoped-for wife, for you had no legal right to consider her yours. Mayhap 'tis that you would not have me acknowledged as a member of the illustrious d'Evreux family?'

He was taunting Lionel, trying to make him lose his temper, an easy enough design on the evidence. Katrine watched the blood rise to Lionel's face, the way his great fist clenched on the hilt of his sword, and bit her lip in anguish. She wanted to shriek at Raoul to stop it, but knew he would disregard her cry. He looked easy, almost casual, but they stood near enough for her to see the knotted muscles along the line of his jaw, making it ripple and his chin jut forward.

Lionel seemed momentarily at a loss for words. Then he bared his teeth and spat, 'I apologised because my cousin demanded it, but I still say you lie! Such as you can be no kin of mine!'

'Oh, no, my dear Lionel.' The familiarity was like a slap across the face. 'I do not lie. My grandfather,' he said clearly, his voice ringing out for all to hear, 'was hounded from England because his half-brother Richard feared his presence might prejudice his own hold upon Wenfrith, since he had long been absent and given up for dead. And years later, after my mother's birth, when he returned to seek reconciliation in England, your cousin's father killed him—on what excuse I do not know. But kill him he did.'

A buzz of excitement ran through the bystanders who heard, and others, sensing something dramatic about to happen, drew near to listen. Who was this

upstart with the nerve to challenge the reputation of
the d'Evreux family? It was doubtful whether many
believed the Chevalier's wild accusations, but when
Lionel shouted, 'A pox on you, sir! I will defend my
family's honour!' and threw down his glove, a sigh
echoed over the ground. This promised fine sport
indeed!

Raoul bowed low, an ironic smile curving his lips as
he picked up the glove. 'All arms,' he decreed.
'Mounted, with lance, mace and sword.'

'Very well.' Lionel's supreme confidence appeared
unshaken by the Chevalier's choice of weapons. 'I say
we meet here in the field at noon.'

'Agreed.'

Katrine's heart was pumping, her hands shaking.
Noon, when most of the camp would still be at table.
Except that knowledge of the challenge would spread
like wildfire and the combat would not lack an audience. But it must not take place! She must stop it! It
was madness. Raoul was injured; he must lose against
a huge, stalwart knight such as Lionel d'Evreux. Even
superior horsemanship and skill could not save him
against such odds.

Wildly, she searched her mind for something to do
to prevent the meeting taking place. One thought
filled her mind. She must find Philippa d'Evreux and
seek her help. In her husband's absence she could
surely do something, speak to the Prince, have the
combat forbidden. Such a conflict must surely be
against his wishes. Even without Lady Thame's help
the news should reach Prince Henry; the entire camp
would be buzzing before long; mayhap he would. . .
But no, without her special pleading he might decide

against intervention. And Katrine knew she simply had to do something, however unlikely it was to succeed.

Both Raoul and Lionel had gathered supporters about them. Louis was talking to Raoul. By the serious look on his face mayhap he was attempting to dissuade him from his rash plunge into deadly danger. She couldn't tell, but no one seemed concerned to keep her informed. With a broken cry of anger and desperation she turned on her heel and began to run through the camp to the Thame pavilion.

She did not hear Dorcas's startled exclamation or her call to the guard, who had been absorbed in the drama taking place close by and had not noticed his mistress's departure. Aware of nothing but her desperate desire for speed, Katrine soon outstripped them, and the busy life of the camp ensured that many of the men and animals thronging the narrow pathways cut her off from her maid and bodyguard.

When a horse nudged close and a voice hailed her she looked up in annoyance, wishing only to be allowed to proceed without hindrance. But, seeing Sir Gruffydd Gethin smiling down at her, she relaxed enough to acknowledge his greeting.

'May I be of assistance, my lady?' he asked, his expression concerned. 'You appear to be in somewhat of a hurry. I could take you up behind——'

Katrine did not wait for him to finish but stopped to grip his horse's girth. 'Thank you! Help me up,' she panted. 'Take me to the Thame pavilion—quickly, I beg.'

'Immediately, my lady.'

She did not see the twisted, satisfied smile on

Gruffydd's face as he lifted her up behind him. 'Hold on,' he instructed, and dug his spurs into his horse's sides.

The beast started off at a canter, scattering anyone in its path. Katrine closed her eyes, leaning against Gruffydd's back, feeling the hardness of metal beneath his surcoat, struggling to regain her breath. Thank the Virgin Gruffydd had come along. She would have reached the lady Philippa in a state of collapse else.

Gradually it dawned upon Katrine that the sounds of the camp had diminished and that they had been riding for too long without arriving at their destination. She opened her eyes, took one look about her and tightened her grip on Gruffydd, the beginnings of panic churning in her stomach.

'This is not the way!' she gasped. 'You have left the camp! Take me back immediately!'

Over his shoulder, shouting above the pounding of his horse's hooves, the jangle of its harness, Gruffydd said, 'I regret, my lady, that I cannot do that at the moment. I am taking you to see Rhun ab Brechfa, who is camped not far from here, watching the English army from a distance, deciding when to make his presence known. He will, I am certain, be delighted to renew acquaintance with you. Particularly as you are now the Chevalier's beloved wife.'

The sneer in his harsh voice sent a new chill through Katrine. Gruffydd had something in mind, and whatever it was boded no good for either her or Raoul. He must have remained with them, biding his time, keeping in contact with Rhun, ready at any moment to betray their trust. And Myfanwy. Did she know? Did she share her husband's disloyalty to those who had shown her nothing but kindness since Rhun's departure? Somehow Katrine doubted it. She believed Myfanwy had become attached to her in the intervening months. Myfanwy would not connive at anything which would harm her.

Gruffydd must have acted on the spur of the moment, seeing her alone for once and obviously in distress.

'You must take me back,' she pleaded. 'I must see the Marchioness of Thame. My husband. . .'

Her voice trailed off. 'Twas no use entreating Gruffydd; he had no mercy. He had simply spurred his horse to a faster gallop, a speed at which she knew she would be badly injured if not killed were she to throw herself from its back, as she longed to do. She gripped Gruffydd's surcoat all the harder and clenched her teeth in sudden determination. She would see Gethin suffer for this!

Five minutes later—or was it more?—tents came into view, set in a pleasant meadow by a stream with distant mountains as a backcloth. Gruffydd was clearly known there, for the challenge as he approached was perfunctory.

'A visitor for the lord Rhun,' he shouted in Welsh. 'Is he in his pavilion?'

'Not at the moment, Sir Gruffydd; he's over by the village to see about victuals, but he should not be long.' Katrine doubted the villagers would have much to offer Rhun, and guessed that what little they did possess would be commandeered rather than paid for. That was Rhun's way. 'He'll be pleased to see you an you bring news,' added the guard.

There was no possible way to escape from here,

surrounded by Rhun's men. When Gruffydd drew his mount to a halt before the spacious pavilion, which was charged with scarlet Welsh dragons, she slid to the ground and tried to compose herself to wait until Rhun returned. Agonising as the delay was, she determined to face her old tormentor with as much courage and pride as she could muster. Gruffydd pushed her inside the tent and then went off, having instructed the guard to make sure she did not leave before his master's return.

The pavilion was adequately but not lavishly furnished. Katrine could see no sign of Eiluned's presence, though a small pair of boots and a child's wooden sword she recognised of old indicated that Dafydd had come with his father. But none of that was important. The realisation that through her own stupidity she had been carted off and was now held here, when so much depended on her freedom of movement, rose as gall in her throat.

She began to pace about the bare ground inside the tent like a caged animal. Waiting was worse than any physical torture, for although time seemed to be passing on leaden feet it was in reality speeding by. Rhun's men were being served with their dinner despite their lord's absence and the sun was already high in the sky. The forenoon was well advanced; it must be approaching the vital hour of midday. She jumped to her feet again, unable to contain her anxiety. She had never felt so helpless in her life. 'Twas no use cursing Gethin, though she did, for to do so relieved her feelings. But all she could see in her mind's eye was Raoul, injured and operating below his normal splendid power, being crushed by

Lionel d'Evreux, whose size and strength seemed to grow in her imagination with every passing minute.

She heard the sound of hooves and rushed to the flap. A quick exchange of voices followed and then Rhun appeared before the opening, Dafydd just behind him.

Dafydd cried, 'Katrine!' and ran forward, the pleasure on his face stretching Katrine's taut nerves, bringing tears to her eyes.

She gathered the boy to her and laid her face on his dark hair. 'I'm glad to see you again, too, Dafydd. Though I wish it were not here and now.'

'How is Dai?' asked Dafydd anxiously.

But his father, ignoring Katrine, interrupted the reunion by demanding of Gruffydd, who had appeared at his side, why he had come and, more particularly, why he had brought Katrine.

So it had not been planned. Katrine found comfort in having that confirmed.

'My lord,' she began urgently, before Gethin could respond, 'I beg of you, allow me to return to Prince Henry's camp immediately. Your knight has abducted me at a most inopportune moment and when my husband hears of it he will be greatly displeased. He will demand reparation.'

If he was still alive to demand anything. Katrine battened down the unruly thought, refusing to give way to her increasing despair. Because she had been so troubled she had run through the camp unguarded. Gruffydd had seized his chance and brought her here. For what purpose she could only speculate.

Until he said, 'The wench is normally well-guarded, lord—Dai Prys too. But today I came across her alone

so brought her to you. Her return in exchange for
your nephew, lord. I thought it a worthy bargain which
would gain you a measure of revenge.'

So that was it. She gathered her wits together. 'And
who will then speak with Prince Henry for you, my
lord Rhun?' she cried, her brain sharpened by need.
'Certainly the Chevalier will not, an you bargain with
him so, break your given word. And who will accept
Dafydd into his household an it is known you have
betrayed another knight's trust?'

Rhun stood, feet planted in the way she remembered, arms crossed over his breast, eyeing her with
speculation and no little animosity. She saw his first
instinctive glee subside as expectancy turned to doubt.
He lowered his chin to his chest and his eyes to the
ground at his feet. After a moment's silent thought he
turned to Sir Gruffydd.

'The wench speaks sense. Seizing her will have done
more harm than good, you fool. God knows how
much damage your stupid act will have begot.'

'But, lord, I sought only to serve you and our
cause——'

'Our cause is dead,' broke in Rhun heavily. 'Have
you not seen it, man? Glendower holed up somewhere
among the foothills of Snowdon, Harlech and
Aberystwyth invested by forces too strong to challenge. I must make my peace with King Henry or live
out my life a condemned man, so, much as I hate his
hide, I cannot afford to displease the Chevalier, who
has undertaken to speak for me.'

'But what of your nephew, lord?' demanded
Gruffydd desperately, seeing himself held at fault for

an action he had considered inspired. 'Your lady urgently desires his return——'

'The question of Dai will have to wait,' said Rhun heavily. 'I have more important matters to deal with first.' He turned to Katrine. 'I myself will return you to your husband, lady. I assure you, your abduction was not of my seeking.'

'Then please hurry!' cried Katrine. 'You do not understand, lord; the Chevalier is in dire danger, and if he dies so too do your hopes of clemency! What time is it?'

Rhun snapped his fingers for his horse to be brought forward again, together with Dafydd's pony. 'Bring a mount for the lady,' he ordered. To a man who had emerged from a nearby tent in answer to his shout he said, 'Clerk, have you the hour?'

'Aye, lord.' The man poked his head back inside his pavilion and emerged again to report, 'The sand in the glass indicates there is a quarter hour to go to noon, lord.'

Katrine gasped. Time had flown! Every second was precious and her mount had not yet come.

'Am I to accompany you, Father?' asked Dafydd eagerly, seeing that his pony had been brought forward with his sire's mount. 'I should like to see Dai again.'

Rhun scowled, noted the presence of the pony and gave an exasperated shrug. 'I suppose so. 'Twill do no harm for you to be seen in Prince Henry's camp. I must secure your future. We will move in to join him on the morrow. I will make the arrangements while I am there. Come, my lady, here is your horse.'

She would have to ride cross-saddle, but that did

not daunt Katrine. The guard helped her up and Rhun himself led the way from his camp at a canter, followed by Gruffydd, Dafydd and herself.

'Please hurry,' she heard herself gasp. 'The contest is due to begin at noon, and I must stop it.'

Rhun gave her a curious look but said nothing, though he did increase their pace slightly, which meant that Dafydd's pony had a struggle to keep up.

When they at last reached the camp Katrine knew she had come too late. The shouts and cheers from the practice field told her that Raoul was already engaged in battle with his d'Evreux cousin.

CHAPTER THIRTEEN

THE tumult increased as they drew nearer, Rhun
passing through the checkpoints without hindrance
because of the company he was in.

It seemed as though the entire camp had abandoned
their dinner to watch the contest. Katrine urged her
horse forward through the crowds still making their
way towards the spectacle until at last the field came
into sight. They had scarcely begun; their heralds were
still shouting the challenge and counter-challenge. She
forged on until she reached the low palings protecting
the area, where she reined in and sat quite still, her
eyes fixed on her husband, who was mounted on his
splendid Thor, both man and beast protected by
armour, Thor pecking impatiently at the ground,
Raoul controlling him with one hand, sitting imperiously upright in his fighting saddle. His head and face
were enclosed in his huge tourney helm, which was
surmounted by a plume and a distinguishing crest
fashioned in the likeness of a fox's head.

Reluctantly, her misted gaze turned to Lionel
d'Evreux. He too was well-mounted, he too wore full
armour and looked every bit as splendid as his
opponent.

'Lady Katrine!'

Hearing the voice calling from near by, Katrine
dragged her eyes away from the combatants. 'Twas

Lady Philippa, as she'd thought. She slid from the saddle and made her way to join her.

Katrine's face had lost all colour. All the blood seemed to have drained from her body, leaving her lethargic, defeated. Nothing could stop the combat now. Both parties were too committed to the engagement.

She could feel Philippa's anxious eyes on her and essayed a smile, at the same time making a slight, clumsy curtsy, all she could manage in her drained state. 'My lady. You have come to watch the spectacle,' she said flatly.

'Reluctantly, and with extreme anger. How could the Chevalier be so offensive to Lionel, taunting him until he could in honour do nothing else but defend the good name of d'Evreux? But sit down, my dear.' She waved one of her ladies away to make room for Katrine on the dais. 'You look fit to fall, and by the look on your face I doubt you had aught to do with it.'

'No, my lady. . .'

The two knights were ready, sharp, metal-shod lances levelled, the first course about to be run. No joust, this. No shields on which to break a lance. No barrier to prevent the horses from charging into each other.

Katrine closed her eyes as the crash came. A sigh passed round the crowd. She looked again to see both men still mounted, turning to prepare for another pass. She expelled her held breath and went on with what she had been about to say. 'I tried to come to you for aid to stop it, but I was prevented. I know your lord is away but I thought you might be able to petition the Prince of Wales. He would surely not wish such a combat to take place within his army.'

'He would not, and had he been here I would have enlisted his aid, but he too is absent from the camp today. No one else will lift a finger to prevent the madness. But I am happy to find that you do not share your husband's unaccountable determination to seek a quarrel with us.'

'You do not understand, my lady,' whispered Katrine, gripping her fingers together, making herself watch as the two destriers charged towards each other again. This time the crash was tremendous. Both men swayed in their saddles and she gave an anxious gasp as Raoul slipped sideways, almost losing his seat. He just managed to regain his balance but his lance had broken against Lionel's breastplate. He had nothing but a stick of wood with which to meet his opponent's next charge. Unless he used his mace—but the spiky ball on its end could surely not be counted a defence against a long, deadly lance.

'What is there to understand, Katrine?' demanded Philippa roundly, compelling her attention again. 'I thought the Chevalier a splendid knight until he began his assault upon the family he claims to be his. But now. . .'

She let the sentence trail off and Katrine tried once again to gether her wits, for unless she could make the lady Philippa understand Raoul would die despised and unmourned by those he had sought to destroy. For Lionel's strength was already telling. Despair clutched at her heart. Raoul must lose the combat.

'I do not agree with what my husband is doing, my lady,' she managed to utter huskily, 'but neither can I condemn him. He has his reasons—good ones in his eyes.'

'Lionel said something about wild accusations against his grandfather and my husband's father, the Earl of Acklane.'

'Aye. Raoul has been taught that Richard, who later became the first Earl of Wenstaple, arrived home from Crécy when all thought him dead just in time to see his father, William d'Evreux, die. Stephen, William's natural son by a villein's daughter, lived on the manor, respected by the people, expecting to take over the title and estates despite being a bastard. So Richard hounded him from the country, afraid of the competition.'

'Nonsense!' exclaimed Philippa, outraged.

''Tis what he believes, my lady.' Katrine's voice strengthened. 'And, further, when Stephen returned from Spain after Najera, where both he and his full brother Thomas had fought, he came to England to make his peace, only to be cut down by the Marquess's father.'

'He has been fed lies,' averred Philippa grimly. 'But if that is what he sincerely believes, then——'

She cut off abruptly as the horses once more thundered towards each other, Raoul's broken lance pointing determinedly at Lionel's breastplate. With only yards separating them Raoul threw down his useless weapon and swung his mace. Taken by surprise, Lionel had no time to change his plan of attack. Raoul swerved Thor at the last moment. Lionel's lance grazed the side of Raoul's armour and then was caught by the merciless descent of the barbed ball, which shattered the shaft. Raoul had swung the mace with both hands, using incredible strength considering his bruised shoulder, thought Katrine, feeling his agony as a sharp stab of pain in her own body. A huge 'Ahh' sighed round the field as Lionel's splintered lance fell to the ground. Thor pounded away, Raoul still swinging the heavy weapon, yelling his defiance.

Raoul had already wheeled his horse, and Lionel was not slow to do the same. Their approach to each other this time was more wary, for speed of attack would be of no benefit while wielding a heavy mace.

The combatants circled each other. Blows were struck and parried, accompanied by grunts and shouts, each one which landed thudding dully against the other's armour. Lionel's strength seemed indomitable and Katrine, wincing at every blow, wondered how much longer Raoul could endure it. But a roar rose from the crowd as, sweeping aside Lionel's weapon, Raoul swung again with incredible speed and landed a resounding blow on Lionel's helm, knocking it askew, unsettling his balance so that next instant a further massive blow to his shoulder sent Lionel crashing to the ground.

Raoul leapt from his own saddle, picked up Lionel's mace, hurled it to the end of the arena and sent his own soaring after it. Hugues and Lionel's squire both ran forward to capture the horses and lead them away. With a rasp of metal, Raoul drew his sword, detached its scabbard from his belt and threw it aside.

Lionel was on his feet, struggling up despite the heavy armour he had affected. Raoul wore lighter protection because, as he had explained to Katrine, it gave him more agility. Lionel's helm had come off completely during his fall, but his head and neck were still covered in mail. With an expansive gesture Raoul threw off his own helm, for he also wore a hood of mail beneath, and swung his weapon challengingly before his opponent.

'God save them both,' murmured Philippa, anxious for her cousin, who had quickly drawn his weapon and taken up an aggressive stance. 'I would have nothing happen to your knight, Katrine, but the Earl of Wenstaple will not easily forgive the death of his heir.'

The two men had already crossed swords. ''Tis my husband who will die,' said Katrine, her despair almost overwhelming her. 'Lionel is too strong for him, for the Chevalier is weakened by injuries received only days ago in the King's name. My lady, is there nothing we can do?'

'Nothing. Your knight chose to challenge, despite his enfeebled state. He must bear the consequences, and so must you, my dear, although for your sake I wish it could be otherwise.'

'See,' whispered Katrine after an interval of fierce exchanges which made the arena ring to the sound of clashing steel, 'Raoul is tiring. He is limping—dear Mother of God, he is down on one knee!'

Both she and Philippa leapt to their feet. ''Tis his leg,' gasped Katrine, jumping down to the ground and running forward to grip the palings until her knuckles whitened. 'His leg has let him down.'

Philippa's hand rested on her arm. 'He is up again, my dear.'

Both women remained standing after that, unable simply to sit and watch as tension mounted. First one and then the other knight gained ground before being forced to retreat. And then, as though by mutual consent, the combatants parted for a moment, both panting, drawing rasping breaths. The heavy sword hung limply in Raoul's hand. Katrine saw a trickle of blood running down his cheek where it had been nicked. How long could it go on? she wondered in anguish. Raoul's strength was visibly ebbing. He was white as the linen bandage about his thigh and swayed slightly as he stood. Yet even she could tell he was the better swordsman. Faster, more accurate with his thrusts, more skilled in his defence. Where Lionel appeared to plod, Raoul, despite his handicap, seemed to dance in this grim ritual of death.

And then Raoul looked beyond Lionel and saw her. For an instant, as his eyes focused, she thought she saw something like relief flood across his features. Their gazes locked, hers wide-eyed, anguished, his startled, momentarily uncertain, then blazing with something she could not understand. He lifted his sword in salute, his teeth flashed in a mocking, jaunty smile and he leapt forward into the fray with a shout.

Raoul attacked quickly, using all the tricks he had acquired over the years of tournament, joust and battle to overcome his opponent's defence. He knew his strength was going, none better. It was vanquish now or face defeat. He locked his sword-hilt with Lionel's and with one last gigantic effort twisted and thrust. Lionel's sword spun from his hand and the impetus of Raoul's attack, the fact that his leg gave way beneath him, threw them both to the ground. Raoul was up on the instant, wincing with pain but otherwise ignoring it, his sword poised above Lionel's face, the only unprotected area of his body easily available to him.

'You die!' he uttered fiercely, standing triumphantly astride his fallen enemy. With great deliberation he raised the point a foot or so, holding it there, savouring his moment of vengeance.

'No! No, Raoul! No!' screamed Katrine, and turned urgently to Gethin and Rhun, standing near by. 'Lift me over the palisade,' she begged.

Katrine's scream carried clearly above the throaty roar of the crowd, penetrated the savage fury deadening Raoul's senses, the red haze of blood-lust clouding his vision.

Katrine. A wave of sheer relief swept over him, as it had done at first sight of her. She was safe. Lionel had denied kidnapping her, and mayhap in that at least d'Evreux had spoken the truth. He stood over his enemy like an avenging angel, seeing no flicker of fear in the blue eyes staring up into his, merely anger and annoyance. And confusion as to how near-victory had turned so suddenly into defeat.

The young man had courage, of that there was no doubt. He would never ask for quarter.

And then Katrine was beside him, tugging at his arm. 'Raoul! Listen to me! Lionel's death will achieve nothing! Have mercy, I implore you!'

His adversary had fought with honour and accepted death with courage. Raoul felt his antagonism drain from him as the fever of the fight abated. And he knew, with a clarity no words could have expressed, that if he killed Lionel d'Evreux, as was his right as victor, he would lose the respect of his wife. The wife he had thought he had lost but had by some miracle regained. Mayhap her recent withdrawal of warmth and passion would become permanent. Until this moment he had thought vengeance all he desired, the answer to all his problems, that once achieved it would fulfil all his needs. That afterwards he would be free to resume his life, to recover his estates, to wed and found his own branch of the ever-spreading d'Evreux dynasty.

Katrine had changed all that. Sight of her had spurred him to victory. Yet vengeance would be small reward an he lost her. A future without her suddenly looked bleak, empty, not worth the living were she not to be part of it.

He made a sudden movement and a gasp went up. Lionel's eyes were upon him, his lips moving as though in prayer, certainly not in supplication. And then a deep sigh echoed over the field as Raoul's sword dug into the ground by Lionel's ear.

Raoul turned to his wife. He was breathing heavily and his words came out on gasping breaths. 'You ask for mercy, my dove. You have it, and anything else you desire that is in my power to grant.'

Her radiant smile was the last thing he saw as he crumpled into oblivion to lie beside his vanquished enemy. But he heard an echo of her anguished cry before the darkness completely engulfed him.

He came to as he was carried into his pavilion. The sound of Katrine's stifled sobs seemed to accuse him. He had never meant to cause her so much pain.

The surgeon had accompanied them back, treatment not being urgently required on the field but the old wound in Raoul's thigh needing attention. Hugues tended his master, removing his armour. Blood had soaked Raoul's nether garments beneath the chausses, the long stockings of mail which would have protected him had he been wearing them on the day the castle's defenders had essayed a sortie. The slash had broken open, some of the stitches torn away.

'You are a fool, Chevalier,' chided the surgeon as he threaded his needle with some small animal's gut. 'You should have rested until the wound had healed.'

'You are the fool,' retorted Raoul roundly, if rather less forcefully than usual. 'I had and have no time to coddle myself. Doubtless 'twill heal again.'

'An it does, 'twill be through the care of your lady, Sir Knight, not through your own common sense! She has seen the wound kept clean, has replaced the soiled bindings with new. No doubt she will continue so to do. An you wish to keep your limb, mayhap your life, I advise you to submit to her ministrations with good grace and to rest your leg until the wound has properly healed.'

Raoul grunted, paused a moment, his mouth clamped against pain as the surgeon drove the needle through his flesh. 'I would do much to please my lady wife,' he admitted rather breathlessly as the surgeon tied a knot, 'but I will not be coddled like a babe!'

'No one is asking that of you,' declared the surgeon, his needle piercing Raoul's flesh again as he made another stitch.

Raoul gritted his teeth, the muscles around his jaw knotted as he fought the pain. Katrine was tearing linen into strips, head lowered, trying to contain her distress. That she should be so upset both irritated and comforted him. Irritated him because he could not stand being fussed, comforted him because it must mean she cared for him a little. And he needed her to care for him.

'There,' said the surgeon, having added more stitches to his handiwork. 'That should do it. It looks a little angry, but so would I had you mistreated me as you have your wound! Have you the salve and bindings, my lady?'

''Tis Sir Graham's salve,' whispered Katrine. Her hands were still shaking with shock and relief, although she had managed to control her sobbing. 'He is an excellent apothecary.'

'So I believe.' The surgeon smoothed it on lavishly before binding the muscular thigh with speed and dexterity. 'Leave it for a couple of days undisturbed, unless you have reason to suspect it of suppurating. Call me immediately if you are concerned. And watch out for fever.'

'Thank you, Sir Surgeon.' Katrine swallowed. 'I will do as you say.'

'I trust your spouse the Chevalier will, that's all,' muttered the surgeon as he departed.

'Hugues!' shouted Raoul the moment the doctor had gone. 'Help me up from this accursed pallet!'

'Nay, lord!' cried Katrine. 'You must rest!'

'I'll rest, my dove, but sitting, not lying like the vanquished rather than the victor! Come, Hugues— you too, Louis. Help me to my chair. Yes, my dove, I'll put my foot up on a stool and rest my leg, for in truth it pains me too much for much else. Thank you, Dai. But I will not lie abed. What happened to Lionel d'Evreux?' he demanded abruptly.

'He left the field with the Marchioness of Thame,' Louis told him.

'Would that either the Marquess or the Prince of

Wales had been here to prevent the encounter!' cried Katrine.

'I thank God they were not! I needed vengeance, my dove, and I suppose I have it and must be satisfied. Although he lives, Lionel was defeated—and the world knows,' he added in a scathing tone, 'in how much honour the name of d'Evreux may be held in the future!'

'You needed justice, not vengeance, husband. That was why I tried to find the Lady Philippa. I thought she could appeal to the Prince of Wales. I did not know he had left the camp.'

Raoul regarded her through narrowed eyes. 'You were not with her, or so 'twas said by the Marquess's sergeant-at-arms, and I could not dispute the point. Dorcas and that stupid guard of mine, God rot his soul, said you had disappeared into the crowd. We searched everywhere for you without success.'

'Your husband was quite distraught, my lady,' said Louis, ignoring the black look thrown at him by his friend.

'I am sorry to have caused you concern,' said Katrine drily, 'but *I* was distraught at the thought of the stupid challenge you had provoked and accepted. I ran through the crowd to find her without thought for my personal safety.'

'My challenge was far from stupid, wife. And I thought it all the more jusitifed when I accused Lionel of abducting you to dishonour me and to claim you for himself were he to conquer. Not that I intended to die, my dove,' he added with a touch of his old arrogance.

'Lionel did not touch me. How could you accuse

him without proof? It seems to me you lack all judgement when dealing with any member of the d'Evreux family, my husband!'

Raoul chose to ignore that comment but asked sharply, 'Then where were you?'

Katrine hesitated. She knew Rhun had entered their camp and waited outside for an interview with the Chevalier. There was no evading the truth.

'Do not punish the guard, husband. 'Twas not his fault he lost me. I was hurrying through the camp to the lady Philippa when Sir Gruffydd rode up. He offered to take me up to speed my progress, so naturally I accepted. However, I soon discovered that he had no intention of taking me to her but rather to Rhun ab Brechfa, who is encamped at some little distance from here.'

'God's teeth! I'll have the knave's head for this!'

Raoul went to leap to his feet, but Louis' hand on his shoulder kept him in his chair.

'Rhun is outside,' said Katrine quietly. 'He brought me back immediately he heard of my presence in his camp, although unfortunately he was absent on my arrival and time was lost. Gruffydd wanted to enable him to regain control of Dai Prys, but Rhun now wishes for nothing but to make his peace.'

The boy, sitting at the Chevalier's feet, gasped. 'I do not wish to return,' he cried. 'Please do not make me go!'

Raoul's hand patted the lad's head. 'Have no fear, my boy.'

'He is also looking for a lord willing to take Dafydd into his household,' said Katrine.

'I am certain a bargain can be struck,' mused Raoul.

'But I do not wish to see the man now. It will do him good to sweat a little.'

'He intends to seek permission to join the siege of Aberystwyth on the morrow, husband. He believes he will be welcomed.'

Raoul nodded. 'He will be.' He gave a bark of sudden laughter, his eyes gleaming with all his old humour. 'An I am not myself thrown from his army on Harry's return!'

'Do not jest, Chevalier!' reproved Louis.

'No jest, my friend. If Thame's displeasure carries any weight after the Prince learns of his family's dishonourable history, then I may be banished from his sight. But there is no need for Rhun to know that! As a man of honour I will keep my word to him to the best of my ability. But not today. Tell him to delay his entry into the camp until he is sent for.'

'Could Dafydd stay?' piped up Dai pleadingly.

Raoul considered. 'An his sire permits. You wish to renew your friendship with him, eh?'

'Aye, lord.'

'Then you know what to say, Louis. Begone, make my peace with Rhun and convey my thanks for the safe return of my wife. Keep Dafydd here to visit with Dai an you are able. As for Sir Gruffydd——'

'I will deal with him,' said Louis grimly.

Raoul nodded, and a glance passed between the men. 'I thank you, my friend. Hugues, Dai, accompany him.'

Alone with his wife, Raoul inspected her grave face. 'You do not look pleased, my dove. Yet I spared Lionel's life for your sake.'

'For which I thank you, husband.'

A small smile touched her colourless lips. She looked so wan that Raoul frowned, increasingly annoyed by her attitude.

'Will nothing satisfy you, wife? Do you still question my judgement?' Katrine shook her head, a negative gesture which meant merely that she did not wish to argue, for her eyes were lowered; she would not look at him. 'What more do you want?' he demanded angrily.

Katrine forced herself to look at him. She so badly wanted to throw herself into his arms, to feel his solid body, warm and vital, pressed against hers. Did he not understand how being forced to watch him risk his life for some ancient and possibly imaginary wrong had crushed her own spirit? How the entire episode, his use of her, his vindictiveness, had shown her a side of his nature that she could not comprehend, let alone admire? The gulf that his deeply nurtured desire for revenge had opened up between them seemed to widen rather than close, for despite the quarter granted Lionel he still regarded his victory a justification of his cause. And Lionel would always suffer from the knowledge that he had failed to defend both himself and the name of his family against Raoul's accusations. Killing him might have been kinder than sparing him to live in shame and dishonour. Mayhap she should not have intervened on his behalf. Yet had Raoul killed his defeated opponent, she thought wretchedly, she would have found it difficult—nay, impossible—to think kindly of her husband again.

She gathered the last of her reserves together. She must sort out this muddle if she wished for any sort of future happiness. 'I would like you to meet with the

Thames, with Lionel d'Evreux too, to listen to their side of the story and make your peace with them. They are in no way to blame for any sin their forefathers may have committed.'

Raoul snorted. 'Do you think me a woman that I should resort to women's ways?'

Katrine shook her head, this time looking at him, a wistful smile breaking out to illumine her face. 'I know that is not so, my husband. You are the Chevalier— valiant, brave, just, honourable, loyal, one who readily shows pity to those less fortunate than himself. Which is why I would beg you to live up to your knightly virtues and hear what your kin have to say. The lady Philippa believes you have been misinformed. Surely you should, in justice, hear what they have to say?'

'Justice is what I meted out today!' snapped Raoul. 'But. . .' He paused as her face fell, then went on, 'I have no fear of meeting my kin, even of listening to their excuses, though I doubt I shall find them acceptable. Should they desire my presence, I will attend them in their pavilion. I will not,' he said, flashing her a look full of cynical amusement, 'force them to grovel and come to me.'

'That,' said Katrine sharply, 'was not worthy of you, Raoul!'

'God's teeth, woman, have I not done enough today? Grant me a little peace in which to recover!'

'I thought,' retorted Katrine sweetly, 'you had no desire to rest. But allow me to help you to remove your gambeson and support you to the bed. You have shown your valour, husband. There is no need to prove anything more — physically. I will bring you your supper here.'

'You will do no such thing! I will eat with everyone else. Neither will I retire to my pallet. But——' he grinned somewhat wryly, with a confiding look which tugged at her heart '—an you have something to soothe bruises I would welcome your ministrations. I must confess my body feels as though it has been beaten to a pulp!'

'All those blows you exchanged!' muttered Katrine grimly and without showing too much sympathy. A few bruises were no more than he deserved. 'Lionel's head must be ringing yet!'

'Mayhap. Are you going to help me off with this garment or not, wife?'

He had risen to his feet. Katrine unlaced the padded tunic he normally wore as some protection, which was essential under armour to absorb the blows and stop chafing. With his shirt removed as well the extent of the damage done by Lionel's mace became apparent. Katrine caught her breath. The great, ugly red patches almost covering his body were already turning black and blue. His armour had prevented savage cuts and lacerations but the blows must have been brutal to inflict so much damage.

Raoul saw her look of horror and chuckled. 'D'Evreux's bruises will be worse, that I'll warrant!'

Katrine said nothing, but brought out some soothing oil of lavender and began to massage it into his skin.

As she worked she became aware of Raoul's quickened breathing. Her soothing strokes had, all unconsciously, become caressing. She changed the rhythm, making it jerky, rubbing hard to work the oil into his skin. She moved round to tend his ribs and powerful hands caught at her shoulders. As Raoul's mouth descended towards hers she closed her eyes, steeling herself not to let him sense how much she needed him. She could not respond yet, not until he had made his peace with his family.

And if he never did? The question tore at her as his lips claimed hers and the kiss deepened, became demanding, Raoul ruthless in his determination to elicit a response from her frozen lips. He forced them apart, but she kept her teeth clenched together against his seeking tongue. Shaking, almost swooning with the intensity of her emotions, Katrine stood unresisting, apart from that denial of the freedom of her mouth. She wanted so much to comfort him, to offer sympathy and understanding, but that must wait. First he must show those same emotions to Giles and Lionel d'Evreux.

And if he never did? The same question probed at her mind again. If he never did, things could never be quite the same between them, but time would heal the worst of the present heartbreak. She must try to understand what drove him, to accept him as he was. Love him for himself, not for the man she had thought him to be.

Raoul's hands shifted and his arms pulled her to him, so tightly that she could feel the erratic rhythm of his heart beneath her hands. 'One day, my dove, you will come to me freely and with passion, as once you did. That I swear.'

He meant he would conquer her resistance. He was probably right, Katrine admitted to herself. She could not fight both him and her own emotions for long. But for the moment she must not weaken. The issue was too important.

'Aye, lord,' she admitted through lips swollen and tender from his assault, 'doubtless my body will triumph over my mind, for it recognises only the lust between us. 'Tis my mind that yearns to rediscover the knight I knew and thought I could come to love.'

Had come to love.

'Love?' Raoul laughed, an ugly sound to Katrine's ears until she realised it was the result of a broken voice. 'What could you know of love? You are too young, too ignorant of the ways of men. But your duty is clear. I demand your loyalty, your lust, too, if that is what you wish to term it. And I will brook no denial, no chilly reception of my passion. I gave you Lionel's life. That must suffice.'

CHAPTER FOURTEEN

SUPPER was almost over. Katrine had heard sounds of coming and going in distant parts of the camp as she toyed with her food, too busy wondering how best to bring Raoul and his family together to be hungry.

It was almost dusk when the summons came. A messenger from the Prince of Wales demanded the immediate presence in his pavilion of Messire Raoul de Chalais and his lady.

'So he has returned,' mused Raoul, pushing himself to his feet. 'It seems we must appear before His Grace in the apparel we wear, since he requires us to attend him without delay.' The air of insouciant arrogance had descended upon him like a mantle. 'No doubt he is displeased by reports of the combat. 'Tis no more than I expected. Come, my dove, his men and horses await us.'

Katrine smoothed down the blue sendal and grey cendryn of her skirts, glad that she had chosen to change from the soiled gown she had been wearing earlier and had had Dorcas dress her hair and cover it with a heart-shaped head-dress. It had been her small celebration in honour of Raoul's survival, and in consequence she felt at least respectable. Her husband, despite his disparaging reference to their apparel, wore his scarlet pourpoint over grey hose. As usual, he looked magnificent. Neither of them need feel ashamed to appear before Prince Henry in the clothes they wore. And Raoul was unlikely to feel guilt over his past actions.

Someone lifted her into the saddle of a strange horse while Louis assisted Raoul, who, wincing with pain, did not refuse the help.

'Do I come with you, *mon ami*?' demanded Louis, concerned.

The knight in charge of the escort intervened immediately. 'My instruction was to escort the Chevalier and his lady only. They will be safe enough.' He indicated the half-dozen men accompanying him.

'Nay, remain here and take command in my absence,' Raoul told Louis, as though the Prince's man had not spoken. 'We will not be long absent.'

'So I pray,' muttered Louis uneasily.

'My wife is commanded too. I do not think the summons presupposes any dire outcome,' said Raoul cheerfully. '*Au revoir*, Louis, my friend.'

Curious eyes watched as the escort led them through the camp to the Prince's pavilion, the largest and most lavish there, naturally, set in the midst of the pavilions of his immediate entourage and well-protected against intrusion. Upon entering his tent, Katrine was immediately struck by the austerity of the interior. This soldier-prince did not believe in indulging in unnecessary luxuries while on campaign, that was evident. And, of course, his accommodation lacked the touch of a feminine hand.

She did not waste much time on appraising her surroundings, however, being far more interested in the people already present. Besides the Prince himself, who waved them to waiting seats as they entered, she saw Lord and Lady Thame, Lionel d'Evreux, and his brother Ned, the latter looking distinctly uncomfortable at being drawn into the dispute. For, by the disposition of the parties and his own judgmental position on a dais, the Prince clearly meant to hear both sides. Two men Katrine did not know sat with him behind a table, one his scribe, the other a nobleman by his apparel, perhaps an adviser. He was not introduced.

Katrine sat where told, on a stool beside Raoul, facing the Prince. The others sat near by, similarly disposed. Philippa smiled across at her, a friendly, encouraging glance that slightly lifted Katrine's spirits. Raoul did not appear to be nervous and she envied him, for she could scarcely contain her own agitation.

Outside, the life of the camp went on. Sounds of laughter, singing, the strains of musical instruments as the evening's entertainment went on were a counterpoint to the clip of hooves, the jangle of harness, the sharp metallic clang of weapons, even the distant ring of hammer on anvil. Inside the pavilion the silence seemed the greater. No one had yet spoken. Katrine's nerves were stretched so far that she ached.

The Prince allowed the silence to linger awhile. Then he looked straight at her and spoke, his tones ringing around the enclosed space, surely clearly audible to the circle of sentries posted around outside—whether to contain them or to protect the Prince she was unsure. To protect Prince Henry, she hoped.

'You are the lady Katrine Lawtye, I understand,' he said. 'A ward of my father's, whom we feared dead.'

Katrine cleared her throat. 'Aye, Your Grace.'

'And yet you chose to wed without his permission. Is that correct?'

'Aye, lord.' Katrine could not drag her gaze away from those compelling eyes. Why had he picked on her?

'Why?'

The question was rapped out. Raoul made to answer but was imperiously waved to silence. 'Let your wife answer me, Chevalier. Your turn will come.'

It sounded more like a threat than a promise. Katrine gripped her fingers together, wondering how to reply. She did not wish to make matters worse for Raoul.

'Because,' she said at last, 'isolated at Dryslwyn, there seemed no way to communicate with him at speed and for my reputation's sake we wished to wed before undertaking the journey to join Your Grace here.'

'And,' guessed Harry, smiling sardonically, 'the Chevalier was persuasive?'

Katrine blushed. 'Yes, lord.'

'Did he force you?'

Again the question was rapped out. Beside her, Katrine felt Raoul tense. Afraid of what she would say?

'Nay, lord,' she said steadily, without hesitation. 'I wed of my own free choice. I wanted no other as husband.'

A glimmer of true humour flashed across Harry's face. 'And you had determined to choose your own mate?'

'Indeed, Your Grace.' Suddenly Katrine smiled, her face, had she realised it, radiant as she glanced at Raoul. 'I fear I allowed my strong desire to wed the

Chevalier to render me careless of the duty I owed my guardian.'

'But you were the Chevalier's hostage, were you not? In his power?'

'Aye, lord, but he was always most chivalrous towards me, unlike Rhun ab Brechfa, from whose clutches he rescued me. He would not have forced me. In any case,' she admitted, 'he had no need.' Katrine suddenly spoke with confidence. At the time she had wondered whether he would resort to compulsion, but now she was convinced that he would not have done so.

Raoul turned a brief glance upon her, his eyes holding an expression which made her blush anew. Her declaration of trust had brought a response she had little expected.

Harry's voice broke across her momentary confusion. 'My father will be thankful to hear of your safe return to our midst, my lady. He may be incensed by your undutiful conduct, but mayhap will feel that the circumstances excuse it. I doubt he will try to have the marriage annulled. What say you, Lord Chancellor?'

The greying nobleman at his side, whom Katrine now guessed to be Lancaster's chief official and therefore representing the duchy and acting in place of her guardian, glanced keenly from Katrine to Raoul. 'Since the marriage appears to be legal and binding, as well as felicitous to the parties, there is little one can do about such a *fait accompli*,' he pronounced, 'however unsuitable. As for the Huntershold fortune, I must consult further. Under the terms of the late Earl's will, without her guardian's agreement it cannot be released to his daughter—and therefore into her husband's control—until she reaches the age of five and twenty years.'

Katrine stared at him. 'I did not know that.'

'Few did,' remarked Henry. 'You did not, I dare say, Chevalier?'

His penetrating gaze turned upon Raoul, who smiled and inclined his head.

'No, Your Grace. But I did not wed Lady Katrine for her fortune. At least,' he added truthfully, 'not entirely.'

'No? Then why, Chevalier?'

'Among many other reasons, it suited my purpose at the time to put her beyond the reach of Lionel d'Evreux,' stated Raoul simply.

The Prince ignored Lionel's sudden shift of position, his grunt of anger, and seemed not to notice the flash of pain which crossed Katrine's face. 'Ah,' he remarked calmly. 'Now we come to the crux of this matter. You used the Lady Katrine in pursuit of your quest for vengeance against the d'Evreux family?'

'To my shame, I did, my lord.' Raoul, admitting shame? Katrine gazed at his impassive face, scarcely able to trust her ears. 'I realise now that I could have attained my end without causing the lady pain,' he explained.

'That at least does you credit, de Chalais, though perhaps the sentiment is a little tardy. But now I wish to hear the reasons for your—to me—incomprehensible accusations against a family held in the highest esteem by the Crown. A family to which, I understand, you claim kinship?'

'Indeed, Your Grace. My grandfather was full

brother to the Marquess of Thame's father, who is therefore my great-uncle.'

The Prince's gaze rested consideringly on Giles. 'You knew nothing of this?'

'No, my lord.' Giles's clear gaze passed briefly over Raoul's features, as though seeking some clue as to the truth of the other's claim. 'My father still has no idea that his brother was wed, let alone that he fathered a legitimate child. Although——' he smiled slightly '—it would cause no surprise to discover that Stephen had scattered his seed liberally across the continent during his time as a mercenary.'

'You see, my lord,' rasped Raoul, 'how my grandfather is maligned by his kin? No one asks why he was forced to earn his livelihood by joining the White Company. He was no soldier when he was hounded from these shores.'

Giles merely lifted his brows at this outburst, content to bide his time. Harry pursed his lips.

'Mayhap you should tell us your version of this story, Chevalier.'

'With pleasure.' Raoul climbed to his feet to address his Prince, unable to disguise completely the discomfort of this wound. 'It begins with William d'Evreux, Baron Wenfrith. He had three sons, Richard, his legitimate heir, and Stephen and Thomas, bastards borne him by a villein's daughter.' He went on to relate his story, just as he had told Katrine. 'Stephen,' he finished bitterly, 'was treated dishonourably by his half-brother Richard and killed by his full-brother Thomas. Do you wonder that I sought to avenge him?'

'Not if your information is correct,' admitted Harry judicially, 'but is it? Thank you, Chevalier.' As Harry turned to Giles, Raoul sank down to sit on his stool. 'I believe your father tells a different tale, Lord Thame,' the Prince observed. 'May we hear it?'

Giles nodded, and in his turn rose to make his statement.

'I have this account of events from both my father and mother, who witnessed them and are still living. De Chalais may hear it from their own lips an he so desires. Lionel, his father Dickon and I all had precisely the same story from Richard, William's legitimate heir and my sire's half-brother, and from Richard's wife Eleanor, both of whom are now unhappily deceased. Eleanor lived to a great age and died but two years since. After her marriage to Richard she suffered greatly at the hands of Stephen.' Giles paused and Raoul made an impatient movement.

'Go on,' said Harry.

'Eleanor was the intended bride of William, who believed Richard, his only legitimate heir, dead at Crécy and wished to beget another. She arrived to find Richard returned and her betrothed husband dead. It was agreed that she should wed Richard instead, for he too now needed an heir. Richard was in total ignorance of the existence of Stephen and Thomas until after his return, and on discovering his bastard brothers set himself to be generous to them. Thomas, who had been serving as a scullion in the kitchen, became page to Eleanor and later served your grandfather John of Gaunt, my lord, fighting with him at Najera. Stephen was raised to the position of steward of his brother's estates, a position of great responsibility and power. But Stephen desired to be the lord. . .

'Suffice it to say that he made two attempts upon Eleanor's life and at least two on Richard's. He was caught during the last such outrage and subsequently confessed to the murder of his sire William, whom everyone had thought dead of an apoplexy. But Stephen had used his young brother Thomas to feed their father poison.' Giles hesitated fractionally, as if he found the next words difficult to utter. 'It took my father many years to recover his trust in people after such a cruel betrayal by his half-brother.'

Raoul sprang to his feet. 'You lie!' he accused.

Giles eyed him sadly, shaking his golden head. 'I fear not, Chevalier. Your grandfather was imprisoned awaiting trial but escaped, this at the time of the Great Plague in 1348. The family thought him dead, until he reappeared subsequent to the battle of Najera. The White Company, like John of Gaunt, had joined Edward, then Prince of Wales, in his endeavour to regain the Castilian throne for its rightful occupant. Stephen had recognised his brother Thomas there. Lionel's father, too. Afterwards he came to England and attempted to abduct my mother, Marguerite, who was held as hostage by Prince Edward but in the custody of my father, and return her to *her* father, a *comte* in Limousin. He aimed not only to gain reward but to discredit his brother, who was so well thought of by John of Gaunt that John later persuaded King Richard to grant him an earldom. But my sire gave chase and prevented the abduction. The brothers fought, both over her and to settle old scores, while my mother watched. 'Twas a fair fight, she swears to that. Stephen was killed, my father wounded. He bears the scar to this day. Stephen's followers removed his body before it could be recovered. We have never known what became of it.'

'It lies in Aquitaine,' said Raoul. 'Brought back by loyal servants to his widow and daughter, my mother. He may have been a mercenary, but my grandmother told a very different story from yours, my lord, of a man wronged and cast out by his family.'

'No doubt fed her by her husband, a consummate liar,' interjected Giles.

Raoul looked his scorn at this remark and continued his defence of his grandfather. Katrine had to admire his loyalty in the face of such damning evidence.

'My grandmother was well-born—a prize of war, 'tis true, but my grandfather was good to her. He wed her when she became pregnant and set her up in some style in Aquitaine. My mother never heard her mother complain of his treatment. It was the mistreatment he had received at the hands of his brothers of which he spoke. On Stephen's death his wife discovered a chest filled with valuables, which kept her and their daughter Louise thereafter, and provided a sufficient dowry to enable Louise to wed Antoine de Chalais, a local seigneur. Unfortunately he, my father, rebelled against the English Crown and was dispossessed of his lands.' Raoul looked directly at Prince Henry, meeting his eyes with confident pride. 'As well as seeking vengeance for the wrongs done to my grandfather I also hoped, by proving my own loyalty to your cause, Your Grace, to recover the lands my father forfeited in Gascony.'

'I guessed that much,' said Henry, 'but you did your cause little good by indulging in mortal combat in my absence. Particularly in such a poor cause.'

'I did not consider it poor, my lord,' replied Raoul with dignity. 'Neither do I now. My grandfather has been consistently misrepresented——'

'Enough!' Henry sounded impatient. 'I have heard you out with patience, Chevalier, for I believe you to be an honest and courageous knight. And intelligent. So you must see that the weight of evidence is all against you. Lord Thame's statement has been attested many times over down the years by all those concerned, not only the principals but the minor characters in the drama too, I can assure you. Your account of events relies entirely upon what one man, Stephen, chose to say. He convinced his wife, of course, and she in turn convinced your mother, who convinced you. But you must admit that the balance of evidence lies with your kin here. Admit it, Chevalier, and relinquish your hatred, seek no further vengeance, rather hold out the hand of friendship to your family.'

Katrine could sense the struggle taking place within Raoul, though outwardly nothing showed. He had been persuaded despite himself, she guessed, and found it a struggle to relinquish views held for so long that they had become part of him. But when he did finally speak she thought he had never appeared more splendid, more courageous or proud in what he must regard as defeat.

'If what you say is truth, then I do not deserve to be accepted by my kin,' he said. 'I come of flawed stock and am not worthy of the bride I have wed.' He directly addressed the Chancellor. 'You must have the marriage annulled. I am certain some priest some-where will be able to discover a cause.'

Katrine leapt to her feet. 'No,' she cried, anguished. 'Of course you are worthy, my husband. I wed you, the man I know to be a true knight, not your ancestors!'

Philippa spoke for the first time, her gaze concentrated on Raoul's face. 'The lady Katrine is not only loyal, Chevalier, but speaks the truth. Were all men and women judged by their ancestry the world would be short indeed of worthy citizens.' She smiled suddenly, her dark eyes glowing. 'You, Chevalier, resemble my husband, did you not know? He is fair where you are dark, but it is so. And you and Ned, here, are much alike, too. You are a d'Evreux, of that I have not the slightest doubt. Do not, I beg of you, reject your kin now. If for no other cause then for your wife's sake, who for love of you will stand by you till death.'

Silence fell. Raoul stood, allowing the truth to seep into his consciousness, to be accepted and dealt with. His father Antoine had been wiser than he had allowed. 'My mother is retired to a nunnery,' he said at last. 'I pray she need never discover the truth. 'Twould be too painful for her.'

'As it must be for you, Chevalier.' Giles stepped forward, his hand outstretched in a gesture of friendship. 'I admire both your courage and honesty in accepting that you were misinformed. An you can overcome the shock of such a discovery, and sup with us in our pavilion on the morrow, we should be delighted to give you welcome, as we do all members of our family.'

Raoul accepted the hand held out to him and Giles nodded in approval. 'As for Lionel,' he went on,

turning to his cousin with a persuasive gesture, 'he is
not used to being bested in battle. But I am sure he
will find it in his heart to forgive your provoking him
into such a contest now he knows your reason. Is that
not so, Lionel?'

The big man stood up, still inclined to scowl.
''Twould have been better for my honour had he
killed me,' he growled.

'You have my wife to thank for your survival,'
Raoul told him, 'but that you know full well. Were it
not for her I should now feel myself a murderer. I was
possessed by such fury—but you faced death with the
courage of a true knight.' He thrust out his hand. 'I
would there were now peace between us.'

Lionel's hesitation was fractional. As the two men
clasped hands the very atmosphere in the pavilion
seemed to relax as held breaths were expelled.

'Excellent!' exclaimed Harry. 'We will forget the
entire incident.' He addressed Raoul again. 'I received
a representation from Rhun ab Brechfa earlier. He
says he has sworn fealty to the King through you,
Chevalier, and seeks to join our army here.' He gave
one of the sardonic smiles he seemed to excel in. 'You
apparently promised to speak for him, but, hearing of
your transgression, he thought it prudent to approach
me more directly. What say you to his suit?'

'He appears genuine in his desire, Your Grace.
Although he treated the lady Katrine shamefully while
in his hold, even to the extent of beating her, he did
her no real harm, and more recently has done her a
service. Did he mention his son, Dafydd?'

'Aye. My clerk, who parleyed with him, reports that

he seeks to place him in a noble household where the lad will learn all the knightly virtues.'

'I removed his nephew, Dai Prys, from his household because I did not like to see the boy ill-treated. Dafydd would thrive under a more benign regime.'

'You make this Rhun sound a monster. Do I really need him in my camp?'

'Mayhap not, lord, yet I would advise it. Otherwise he may well feel obliged to continue his rebellion and cause you trouble.'

'Very well. My clerk instructed him to await my decision. I will send for him on the morrow. Giles, have you room for another page in your household? It seems that Dafydd ab Brechfa shows promise.'

'We have several pages, my lord, whom the lady Philippa treats as sons.' Lord Thame grinned. 'The lad will be welcome. You intend to keep Dai with you, Raoul?'

Giles's use of his given name startled Raoul somewhat, but he recovered quickly. 'Aye—Giles. The lad has settled well and is useful.'

'Then all is settled,' declared Harry, rising. 'It pleases me to know that such an illustrious knight is at last fully gathered into the bosom of his family. Fear not for the Huntershold legacy. I am certain the Chancellor will recommend its immediate release. As for your lands in Gascony, Chevalier, those I cannot promise will be returned. But mayhap others, here in England, would atone for their loss, an my father agrees?'

Henry had left the dais and stood ready to speed the departure of his vassals. Impulsively, Raoul knelt at his feet and Henry took his extended hand between his own. 'My liege lord,' he murmured, 'I hereby vow my lifelong fealty.'

'Go you in peace, Chevalier. I will doubtless have need of your loyalty in the days to come.'

Everyone's relief was patent when Raoul and Katrine returned to their pavilion. Louis in particular had been extremely concerned by the peremptory summons, and perhaps he alone of those waiting to receive them could sense Raoul's subdued mood.

'What happened?' he wanted to know.

'I'll tell you in a moment. First—Dai, Dafydd, come here.'

Dafydd had been allowed to remain with his cousin and moved forward at Dai's urging. 'Yes, lord?' asked Dai anxiously.

Raoul smiled down reassuringly. 'You will remain with me, Dai, and, with his father's consent, which I am certain will be forthcoming, Dafydd will join the household of my cousin, the Marquess of Thame. Will that content you both?'

The incredulous, joyous looks on two young faces told everyone that it would.

'Thank you, Chevalier,' gasped Dai, a sentiment which was echoed by Dafydd, but with a gulp.

In the privacy of the pavilion, with Hugues the only other besides Louis present, Raoul related the events of the last hour.

Louis shook his head. 'I always suspected the story you had been told might not be the entire truth,' he confessed. 'I did attempt to warn you to take care.'

'I know, my friend.' Raoul clapped Louis on the shoulder and sighed. 'I find it difficult even now to

believe what I have learned, yet I must. I was blink-
ered, blinded by faith in what I was told. 'Tis as well
my kin have behaved with generosity. But I believe
they understand that I did but attempt to right what I
perceived to be a wrong, and that out of mistaken
loyalty to a man I had never met.'

'You must be happy to discover that you belong to
so fine a family, rather than the scurrilous one you
have imagined,' observed Louis.

'Aye, though as yet the idea is strange to me.' Raoul
yawned hugely, and Katrine suspected the cause to be
as much due to relaxation of strain and a desire to
avoid further discussion as to real tiredness. 'However,' he went on, 'all is now settled and I, for one,
am ready to retire. Send Dorcas in to tend my wife,
an you will.'

'Before I leave mayhap you should know that
Gruffydd Gethin received appropriate chastisement
for his crime.'

'Oh?' drawled Raoul.

Louis grinned. 'I knocked him out,' he said complacently, massaging a set of broken knuckles.

'I see,' said Raoul drily. 'Many thanks, my friend.'

'He and his lady Myfanwy have departed to rejoin
Rhun ab Brechfa. He would, apparently, rather face
his old lord's wrath than yours, Chevalier. Myfanwy
felt duty-bound to accompany him. She sends her
regrets, my lady, and hopes you will forgive her abrupt
departure.'

'I shall miss her,' admitted Katrine, 'but not as
much as I would once have done. When Rhun moves
his camp here I have no doubt we shall meet again,
but I have other ladies to converse with now, even if

they are not of this household. The lady Philippa has been most kind, as have the others with her. I shall not lack for company.'

It seemed to take an age for Dorcas and Hugues to prepare their mistress and master for the night. Katrine fretted under Dorcas's ministrations, wanting to be alone with Raoul and yet nervous of what might transpire.

She could not forget that he had tried to be rid of her. He had admitted that he had wed her partly for her fortune but mostly to prevent her marriage to Lionel. But she had known that. Why, then, did his reiteration of those facts hurt her so?

Because she had hoped he might love her a little, she supposed. But even without his love their marriage could now return to the passionate closeness they had previously enjoyed, for things were back to what they had been—nay, they were better, for the desire for vengeance had left her husband and the gulf of misunderstanding over his motives and activities had disappeared. She must make the best of what she had, for it was more than most women could hope for. Even if he did not love her she loved him, and she would make her love enough for two.

A grunt of pain escaped Raoul as Hugues removed his hose and Katrine immediately went outside the screen to make sure his wound required no new dressing. She could see no sign of blood penetrating the bandage, he showed no trace of fever, and he told her sharply not to fuss, so she returned to her own toilet. 'Twas a pity about his leg. 'Twas like to impede their passion, for the wound obviously pained him now more than it had the previous night.

At last Dorcas departed and Raoul came to her. She already lay in their bed and she smiled up at him, making her welcome plain. Raoul grunted as he joined her under the blankets but he made no move to take her into his arms.

'So I am back in favour, am I, wife? Now I have been proved wrong and you right you find your duty less onerous, eh?'

Katrine went cold. For his part, it seemed, the gulf had widened, not closed.

'Raoul, how can you think that?' she whispered. 'I could not readily lie with a man who bore such a fierce desire for vengeance in his heart, who was so determined to kill a man innocent of all wrong towards him, that is true.' She touched his arm. 'But now that curse has left you we can be as we were.'

His muscles flinched under her fingers. 'Can we?' He sounded almost weary. 'I think not, my dove. Everything has changed. You cannot imagine how it hurts to discover such damning truths about a forebear. I have changed. I am no longer the man you wed.'

'No,' admitted Katrine slowly, though her thoughts were racing. What ailed her husband now? 'But an you have changed 'tis for the better. Having an evil man for a forebear does not make you evil. And Stephen must have possessed some virtue, for he sired your mother, whom you love.'

'She never knew him,' pointed out Raoul. 'All the tales came from my grandam.'

'Who must have wished to justify her husband as he had justified himself.'

'And in doing so passed his venom on to me.'

'My love,' said Katrine softly, 'you could not help it.'

'I could have listened to my father,' admitted Raoul bitterly.

Katrine continued as though he had not spoken. She had to give him back his pride, his self-respect. 'I loved you even while you bore so much venom in your soul,' she told him, 'knowing it was not part of your true nature. Now that has gone, think you I could love you less?'

'Love, Katrine?' His whole body tensed beside her and he sounded scornful, but she could not see his features to discover whether it was truly scorn or mayhap incredulity that he expressed. 'Lady Thame said something about love. Is it true? Is it more than passion you feel for me, and not some misplaced adolescent infatuation for one who treated you more kindly than Rhun ab Brechfa?'

Katrine had not meant to declare her love, the words had slipped out, but now she could not deny them. 'Yes, my husband. I fell in love with the chivalrous, splendid Chevalier who had saved me from Rhun's clutches. It was never infatuation. Even although you did, at times, make me extremely angry,' she added, remembering the occasions when she had almost hated him. But that had just been the other face of love.

'How can you love me?' he groaned. But he turned towards her and she felt his fingers caressing her jaw, brushing the golden hair from her ear so that he could fondle the lobe, his touch arousing sensations which set her nerves shivering in anticipation. 'How, when I used you so cruelly? And I would have forced you to wed me, you know. I wanted you too badly to let you deny me, my love.'

No, he had not said 'dove' but 'love'. Katrine turned towards him. Their bodies touched; her breasts brushed against the roughness of his chest. It was like being struck by a thunderbolt. Katrine gave a cry as his arms closed about her.

He kissed her deeply, so that she forgot everything but the feel of his mouth on hers, the touch of his hands on her skin. When at last he moved it was to turn on his back, taking her with him so that she lay along the length of his body.

'You will have to do the work, my love,' he told her breathlessly. 'My cursed wound is too painful tonight. Give me your breasts.'

Katrine lifted her body above his, her hair a gleaming tent in the darkness, enveloping Raoul's face as his mouth found one of the peaks hovering above him. Katrine cried out again, her body moving instinctively over his. And then his hands were on her buttocks, guiding her towards his own thrusting body, and she sheathed him, gathering him into the depths of her being. She lay still for a long time, with him pulsing inside her, while he continued to adore her breasts. When she felt him stir urgently, again Katrine found herself moving by instinct, her hips rising and falling, the movement becoming ever faster as their sensuous excitement mounted.

Release came simultaneously. She lay crying softly into Raoul's neck. At length he eased her off to lie beside him and wiped the tears from her cheeks with his lips. He knew they were tears of happiness.

'Is that why you agreed to wed me?' he whispered at last. 'Because you loved me?'

'Of course. But, husband, you said you had several reasons for marrying me. What might they be?'

'The deplorable ones you already know. And I realise now that I made them an excuse, because I wanted you so badly. What I did not or would not admit at the time was that I loved you, my sweet dove. From the very first, I think. Had I admitted that, I would not have been able to use you, you see. So I hid my true feelings even from myself.'

Raoul did love her. Hate had left him and love entered in. She sighed happily and reminded him of something she had almost forgotten herself.

'Today is the anniversary of my birth,' she told him softly. 'I had scarce expected such a perfect gift as that of your love, my dearest lord.'

'Sweetheart! You are sixteen today?'

'Aye, my love.'

As he kissed her again Katrine thought her heart would burst with happiness. Particularly as she had become convinced over the last days that she was bearing his child.

'When the castle falls,' she said dreamily, 'we must go to Huntershold. I would like your son to be born there.'

Raoul's stroking hand stilled. 'My son?'

'Or daughter. I cannot guarantee the gender, husband, but, God willing, there will be others. We shall surely get a boy one day.' She sighed in content. 'A boy just like his illustrious father.'

Raoul said nothing, but she could feel his tears now as she kissed his eyes, his nose and then his rugged, wonderful mouth. A hard man crying, and for such a cause. Could there be anything more endearing to a woman? Katrine thought not as she settled contentedly into her husband's strong, tender arms.

LEGACY *of* LOVE

Coming next month

MISTRESS OF HER FATE
Julia Byrne
Stratford and Wells, 1464

Lady Eleanor fitzWarren had barely seen her father since he
gave her into the 'care' of her uncle's dissolute household.
Only by deceit and manipulation had Nell managed to hang
on to her virtue, so it ill became Lord Rafe Beaudene to think
her a whore, however things might have looked! Rafe might
have been delegated to bring her to her father, prior to any
marriage fitzWarren might arrange, but Rafe clearly had an
agenda of his own. Was Nell simply to be a pawn between
two powerful men bent on revenge?

AN UNSUITABLE MATCH
Alice Thornton
Bath 1826

Mary Drayton's improvident father had left her, on his death,
in quite degrading circumstances. So when Justin, Lord
Hawkridge, fell in love with her, and she with him, Mary was
heartbroken but not surprised when he apparently came to his
senses.

To find him again in Bath, years later, when she was on a
mission of mercy, was a shock—more so when he clearly
thought that *she* had abandoned *him*! But nothing had
changed; she was *still* an unsuitable match for him…

LEGACY *of* LOVE

Coming next month

PIRATE BRIDE
Elizabeth August
Carolina coast 1673

No man had ever stirred Kathleen—until now. As Jonathan Ashford stood, proud and defiant, awaiting 'justice' at the hands of his pirate captors, he touched something deep within her. He could not, *must not* die! With reckless courage born of desire, she acted to save them both.

A buccaneer beauty with blood on her hands—that had been Jonathan's first sight of Kathleen James. But all she had done to ensure his survival had proved the young woman was no ruthless pirate wench. Why, then, did she refuse to be his true-bound bride?

RAIN SHADOW
Cheryl St. John
Pennsylvania 1894

Raised among the Lakota Sioux, Rain Shadow was the picture of an Indian princess—exotic, ethereal. But away from the glamour of Buffalo Bill's Wild West Show she was a mother alone. An orphan in search of her past. And, armed with a six-shooter, easily the most perfect woman Anton Neubauer had ever seen.

Anton was as sure and steady as the land he worked. Here was a man who believed in family and tradition. A man with roots. A man who was everything Rain Shadow had ever dreamed of—and knew she could never have…

GET 4 BOOKS AND A MYSTERY GIFT

Return the coupon below and we'll send you 4 Legacy of Love novels and a mystery gift absolutely FREE! We'll even pay the postage and packing for you.

We're making you this offer to introduce you to the benefits of Reader Service: FREE home delivery of brand-new Legacy of Love novels, at least a month before they are available in the shops, FREE gifts and a monthly Newsletter packed with information.

Accepting these FREE books and gift places you under no obligation to buy, you may cancel at any time, even after receiving just your free shipment. Simply complete the coupon below and send it to:

HARLEQUIN MILLS & BOON, FREEPOST, PO BOX 70, CROYDON, CR9 9EL.

No stamp needed

Yes, please send me 4 free Legacy of Love novels and a mystery gift. I understand that unless you hear from me, I will receive 4 superb new titles every month for just £2.50* each postage and packing free. I am under no obligation to purchase any books and I may cancel or suspend my subscription at any time, but the free books and gifts will be mine to keep in any case. (I am over 18 years of age)

2EP5M

Ms/Mrs/Miss/Mr _____

Address _____

_____

_____ Postcode _____

mps MAILING PREFERENCE SERVICE